Ovidia Yu is one of Singapore's best-known and most acclaimed writers. She has had over thirty plays produced and is the author of a number of comic mysteries published in Singapore, India, Japan and America.

She received a Fulbright Scholarship to the University of Iowa's International Writers Program and has been a writing fellow at the National University of Singapore. *The Paper Bark Tree Mystery* was shortlisted for the CWA Historical Dagger award 2020.

T0276732

Also by Ovidia Yu

The Frangipani Tree Mystery
The Betel Nut Tree Mystery
The Paper Bark Tree Mystery
The Mimosa Tree Mystery

The Cannonball Tree Mystery

Ovidia Yu

CONSTABLE

CONSTABLE

First published in Great Britain in 2021 by Constable

1 3 5 7 9 10 8 6 4 2

A CIP catalogue record for this book
is available from the British Library.

ISBN: 978-1-47213-203-1

Typeset in Contenu by SX Composing DTP, Rayleigh, Essex
Printed and bound in Great Britain by Clays Ltd, Elcograf S.p.A.

Papers used by Constable are from well-managed forests
and other responsible sources.

Constable
An imprint of
Little, Brown Book Group
Carmelite House
50 Victoria Embankment
London EC4Y 0DZ

An Hachette UK Company
www.hachette.co.uk

www.littlebrown.co.uk

Dedicated with respect and gratitude to
the memory of real-life war hero,
Halford Lovell Boudewyn

The Flyers

———◆———

During the Japanese occupation, radios were banned in Syonan – as our Japanese lords and masters referred to Singapore – and our only news came through their official channels.

Until the flyers started appearing.

The first I saw read,

> US President Roosevelt & Brit PM Churchill & Chiang
> Kai-shek in Cairo talk combined forces against the Japs.
> The Allies are Coming. Hold on to Hope, brothers and
> sisters.

It was a poorly typed carbon copy and I didn't take it seriously till a rash of official Japanese announcements claimed the Cairo Conference (a) didn't take place, (b) was a complete failure, while (c) offering cash and extra rations as a reward to anyone who turned in the traitors producing the flyers.

In other words, what the flyers said was true or they wouldn't have bothered to deny it.

1

After that, I watched out for them.

British, Canadian and American troops take back Italy!
Hitler's pal Mussolini is out. The tide is turning. Hold
on, brothers and sisters.

I couldn't help feeling encouraged, though even if the tide was turning in the West, Japanese boots still crushed the back of the East.

Then the flyers showed hope moving closer to home:

USA Marines crush Jap stronghold in the Gilbert
islands. Japs Pacific blockade cracked! Don't give up.
Won't be long now, brothers and sisters.

The official Japanese news announcements were silent on these events. But they no longer celebrated the glorious victories of their brothers in the West, and the authorities increased the bounty offered for information on the criminals who distributed printed lies.

So, of course, we went on believing them.

But, day to day, it was hard to believe that anything would ever change. The Japanese were using Singapore much as the British had. Our island's natural deep-water port and strategic location made it the ideal hub from which to channel arms and supplies across the seas to Japanese-occupied territories all over the region.

But to hold their advantage, the Japanese forces had to consolidate their sea-to-land transition. India's location at the tip of the Indian Ocean made it their ideal entry point to the South Asia mainland.

It was becoming clear why the Japanese had funded the formation of the Indian National Army (or Free Indian Army) with Indian PoWs captured in Malaya and Singapore. Indians would be sent to fight their brothers, leaving the Japanese to move in after the worst of the carnage. They already occupied India's neighbour Burma, and would likely launch their attack from there. Even knowing that, the extensive border, along with the coast of the Bay of Bengal, made it impossible to prepare an adequate defence without more information.

And if British India fell to the Japanese, regardless of what Allied victories were won in the West, here in the East we would have Japanese bayonets at our necks for ever.

Eve of 1944, Syonan

———◆———

'You people can't even find out who's leaving those damn flyers all over the place – and you want to investigate the army and the INA?'

'The flyers are irritating, like mosquitoes. This is serious. You, girl,' this was to me, 'come back. Eat this. Don't just put it into your mouth. Swallow it!'

Major Dewa watched me swallow a spoonful of the soup I had just brought him. For one crazy moment I thought of clutching my throat and making gagging sounds, just to see how the new chief of the Syonan Police Investigation Bureau would react. Of course I didn't. That would have got me killed faster than any poison – and probably a lot more painfully.

'Well, girl?' Colonel Fujiwara was already halfway through his own soup.

'The soup is delicious. I hope you'll like it, sir,' I said.

'Ha! If he doesn't want it, give me his bowl!'

Major Dewa glared at me as though waiting for the poison

to take effect. Maybe he sensed how much I would have liked to poison him.

It was 5 p.m. on 31 December 1943, eve of 1944, in Syonan. Singapore Island, once the British Empire's 'Gibraltar of the East', was now a supply port to the Japanese Empire.

We were in the Shori headquarters, the office and official residence of Colonel Fujiwara. His ceremonial photograph hung next to that of the Japanese Emperor in all schools, factories and offices. In person, his face was red and sweaty, and his belly was bigger than his chest. Colonel Fujiwara was fonder of food than of work. If it hadn't been treasonous, I'd have said he would have been much better off – and happier – running a restaurant than an island.

However, Colonel Fujiwara was Syonan's highest-ranking Japanese military administrator, and Major Dewa probably wasn't the only one who didn't understand what a crippled local girl was doing there.

'The girl makes good soup,' Colonel Fujiwara said.

'You should have a cook and staff who have been vetted by the proper authorities. You know nothing of this girl—'

'Miss Chen is the daughter of my late cousin,' Hideki Tagawa said. 'If you have any objection to her, you may address it to me.'

He had been so quiet in his corner of the room that the others had forgotten he was there. Hideki Tagawa was a small, dark man, who had a way of hunching and dipping his head as though he was trying not to be noticed. He had no official post in Colonel Fujiwara's government, but those in the know feared him. Hideki Tagawa represented and reported directly to Prince

Yasuhito Chichibu, Emperor Hirohito's only brother. It was whispered that Hideki Tagawa had helped Prince Chichibu establish the military dictatorship in Japan. Also that he had instigated the assassination of the prime minister, Tsuyoshi Inukai, and steered Japan into the alliance with Nazi Germany, even though he had attended university in Great Britain. Now Hideki Tagawa was part of the Kin No Yuri or 'Golden Lily' organisation that collected 'donations' from Japan's colonies to finance the Japanese war effort.

'I'm surprised to see you here too, Tagawa,' Major Dewa said. 'It is only one of the many things that surprises me.'

Did the clumsily officious Major Dewa know he was casting suspicion on one of the best-connected (and probably most dangerous) men in the Japanese military empire?

Colonel Fujiwara and Joben and Ima Kobata stared at Hideki Tagawa. They reminded me of children half afraid a dog might bite and half hoping it would. Major Dewa's aide moved a hand to his pistol, as though preparing to defend his master.

Hideki Tagawa bowed slightly and Major Dewa looked triumphant.

We could hear the trucks of soldiers waiting outside. They were en route to their festive dinner, but it looked and sounded like a coup – maybe intentionally.

Perhaps it wasn't surprising that the Syonan Police Investigation Bureau was investigating the Shori headquarters. In the past year, some bizarre things had happened there. A senior officer had committed suicide, the editor of the *Syonan Weekly* had vanished and the entire household staff had been fired.

Colonel Fujiwara was not cooperative. The assassination attempt against him by one of his own officers had left him paranoid and suspicious. Now he trusted only me and Hideki Tagawa because we'd foiled the would-be killer. The colonel had even rejected the trained staff provided by the military. He had brought family from Japan to manage his household for him.

Joben Kobata, bored and half asleep in a chair next to Colonel Fujiwara, was broad-faced and chubby. He looked enough like the colonel to be his son, but was married to his daughter, Ima. The two men got along well, chiefly because they shared a love of comfort and a dislike of work. Ima was from the colonel's first marriage. His second wife had left no children, and the third was in Japan with his younger son and daughter.

Ima Kobata's complexion was fair and she had thick brown hair. She wore a lot of powder and had drawn-in eyebrows, giving the impression she was dressed up for a special occasion. She always looked like that. The powder was because she had spots. She had her father's chubby face and chunky build and wasn't much taller than me, though almost three times as broad.

'In fact this girl makes better soup than you will get anywhere else on this island!' Colonel Fujiwara said loudly. 'You're mad if you think Ebisu-chan wants to poison me. She saved my life – not one of your over-trained soldiers!'

Colonel Fujiwara called me 'Ebisu' because childhood polio had left me with a limp, like the god of good fortune. He trusted me because – well, because I'd saved his life. I hadn't intended to, but it's difficult to think straight under pressure.

I was twenty-four years old and didn't know if I would live

to see twenty-five. Or even next week. I had just discovered that my long-dead mother had not only been Japanese but a cousin of Hideki Tagawa. In fact, my presence in the Shori headquarters was a favour to Hideki Tagawa, who also had rooms there.

I was assistant editor of the English-language *Syonan Weekly*, and helped with the management of the household since Ima spoke little English and no local dialects.

'Her soup is irrelevant. She should not be here.'

Well, Major Dewa shouldn't still have been there either.

Even I knew that when Colonel Fujiwara said, 'I'm going to take a break to have some soup. Will you join me?' It was a dismissal, and the correct thing to say was 'Thank you, but I was just leaving,' and bow your way out.

After all, others were waiting for their audience with Colonel Fujiwara. The New Year's Eve meetings were a formality for the island's top brass to congratulate Colonel Fujiwara on a successful year and exchange good wishes for 1944.

The hall and grounds were filled with officials and administrators waiting their turn to bow and present the small gifts that would formally wipe out all errors of 1943. Ceremonially, at least, the new year would start with a clean slate.

But still Major Dewa stayed. He seemed determined not to leave until Colonel Fujiwara had signed the authorisation forms he'd brought. 'I tried to make appointments to meet you. Many, many times I tried. But your people always say you're too busy. I don't want this swept under the carpet because the year is over.'

Major Dewa had announced his intention of eradicating all corrupt officials from the Syonan administration. This meant that while all officials applauded him, none helped him. It was impossible to get on without back-door help and black-market goods.

'You're chief of local investigations. Go and investigate whatever you want!'

'The local administrators won't cooperate. But once you sign these forms, the police can force them to do so.'

'Leave the papers. I'll look at them tomorrow.'

'Sir, tomorrow you have the official photograph ceremony. I don't want to inconvenience you.'

'You are already inconveniencing me. I'll deal with them in the New Year. Give them to Kobata.'

Colonel Dewa looked at Joben Kobata. 'Sir, if you authorise these investigations now, we can start immediately. No more waste of time.'

'The worst part of this war is all the nobodies that crawl out of the mud and think themselves important just because somebody gave them a uniform,' Joben Kobata said. He held out a hand for the papers, not bothering to stand up. 'Come on, bring them over here.'

Major Dewa held on to his forms. 'I just want to get all this paperwork cleared up before the new year.'

'This is no time for work,' Colonel Fujiwara said. 'It's New Year's Eve, man!'

'Once you've signed, you can leave the work to me.'

'Father, a lot of people are still waiting to see you,' Ima said.

Major Dewa should have been in and out of the office in less than fifteen minutes but still he hung on. 'We cannot close the year's records without resolving the matter of the missing funds and the pineapple grenades.'

The two captured American grenades had supposedly been sent to the Shori headquarters for inspection – and vanished. 'If you're looking for missing things, see if you can find our missing photographer while you're at it,' Joben said. 'Ryu Takahashi. Dark-skinned, dirty, lazy, drinks too much and doesn't wash very often …'

Colonel Fujiwara laughed but Major Dewa ploughed on, 'We say "missing" or "lost", rather than stolen, because there may have been an administrative error. They were definitely brought here after being captured from American soldiers in the Philippines. They were signed for by your office. Two yellow pineapple grenades.'

'Are you accusing me of stealing them?' Colonel Fujiwara said. His voice was suddenly very calm, a frightening contrast to his earlier manner.

'Of course not, sir.' Major Dewa looked taken aback. 'But they are to be sent to Japan. The technicians are waiting to work on them. I must trace them—'

'Even if they were brought here, they are not here now. Unless you're saying I ate your pineapple grenades as a snack.' Colonel Fujiwara laughed at his joke.

Major Dewa did not. 'Sir, you are not the only one with access to your office.' His eyes went around the room.

'They're probably in the snake shrine,' Joben Kobata said.

The snake shrine had stood under the cannonball tree at the back of the building since before the British colonials had arrived. It housed either a snake spirit or the spirit of someone killed by a snake. Or it might have been a shrine to the tree itself. The cannonball flowers look like the hooded *nāga*, the snake, and the tree is sacred to several religions.

Anyway, people sometimes left protection offerings there. I did, too. I wasn't particularly superstitious, but when there's a war on it doesn't hurt to cover all your bases. And if monkeys or squirrels ate the spoonful of rice or slice of fruit I left, that suited me fine.

'The snake shrine?' Major Dewa looked suspicious,

'The servants leave offerings there. Whenever something goes missing here, they say the snake spirit must have taken it. Do you want to check it for your pineapples? It's beyond the kitchen garden, behind the bamboo and banana trees.'

'Do things often go missing here?'

'It's the servants,' Ima said. 'They'll say anything. They're the ones stealing things and lying about it. Please, Father, a lot more people are waiting to see you. Some of them have other stops to make.'

'Just sign these.' Major Dewa went up to Colonel Fujiwara's desk but suddenly stopped and sniffed. 'What's that smell?'

It was the strong, strange fragrance of cannonball flowers arranged on the table behind the colonel. Since I'd told Ima their scent kept snakes and mosquitoes away, she'd insisted on always having some in the house.

'Haru! Get rid of those ugly flowers. They smell poisonous!'

His aide, in defiance of protocol, walked behind Colonel Fujiwara and reached for the vase. Colonel Fujiwara placed a hand on it, stopping him. But the man, in an even greater defiance of protocol, grasped the colonel's wrist and removed it.

'It's for your protection, sir,' Major Dewa said. 'Security is important. You never know who can be trusted. Or who may be bribed.'

'Damn you, dog!' Colonel Fujiwara swore. 'You are a dead man!'

Joben took this literally. He took his gun and shot Major Dewa's aide in the chest. The man dropped the vase, collapsed against the wall and slid to the floor.

'Score!' Joben crowed, like a boy who had catapulted a bird.

'How dare you? You had no right! I will take this up with the highest authorities!' Major Dewa's rage made his voice squeak.

I stared at the man on the floor till Hideki Tagawa, suddenly next to me, said, 'Su Lin.'

'Sir?'

'If there's any more soup I would like some.'

'Yes, sir,' I answered automatically, but didn't move. Like the others, I was staring at the man on the floor, who was trying to say something through the blood bubbling out of his mouth.

'Now.' Hideki Tagawa took my arm and pulled me roughly to the door.

As he pushed me out, I heard Colonel Fujiwara say, 'Clean up the mess.'

I heard the second shot through the closed door.

The Servants' Domain

———◆———

I was still shaking when I reached the kitchen. It wasn't that I didn't know the Japanese killed people. They killed people for not bowing low enough, for not understanding Japanese or for having been born male. But I'd allowed myself to believe the worst was over. They'd said the war was over for us and we were safe as long as we served the great Japanese Empire.

At least, I'd come to believe the Shori headquarters was a bubble of safety.

The house-boys and the maids looked almost asleep on their feet. It was already three hours past the time they normally finished work, and they had spent days scrubbing down every part of the building, as well as setting up the tents on the grounds in front of the house for the expected visitors.

'You can go back to your quarters,' I told them.

I felt responsible for them because I was the one who had interviewed and hired these children. None looked over sixteen, and I suspected Tanis, the fastest on his feet and best at catching and killing chickens, was closer to twelve, though he claimed to be 'almost sixteen'. I knew he desperately needed the pay and the protection of working for the Shori headquarters because his father had been killed and he was responsible for his mother and younger siblings.

It was impossible to find experienced adult staff because the Japanese had made a point of killing or locking up people who seemed good at anything. I was lucky that childhood polio had left me with a crippled leg. As I was short and skinny as well as crippled, I didn't look like a threat.

'There are still people outside,' Xiao Yu, one of the maids, said.

'Go. Make sure you get some rest. There will be many more people coming tomorrow and you must clean up tonight's mess before they arrive. Wash first. I'll come and lock the doors in half an hour.'

In his paranoia about the people around him, Colonel Fujiwara insisted the house staff were locked into their quarters behind the main house every night till 5 a.m. when the day guards came on shift.

Once I had the kitchen to myself, I checked the soup stock. I doubted Hideki Tagawa really wanted soup, but if he or anyone else did, I had only to strain some into a bowl, then throw in bean sprouts, dried seaweed and buckwheat noodles to make *Toshikoshi-soba*, symbolising longevity. Having grown up in a traditional household, I always had a stockpot waiting for fish heads, chicken claws and necks, vegetable peelings and leftovers. Tomorrow I planned to make *ozouni*, a traditional New Year's Day soup dish. I would add *mochi* balls, because their stretchiness signified longevity. Was I really wishing longevity on our oppressors? Well, *I* was quite fond of *mochi*. Sometimes you just have to focus on the immediate.

14

The kitchen window slats and both doors stood open to let in the cooling night air. It wasn't as hot as usual in Singapore – sorry, Syonan – because the rains had just come and gone. The night outside was dark and calm, apart from the whirring of insects and the rustle of night hunters.

It seemed impossible that a man had just been shot upstairs.

Suddenly I wanted to go out into the night and disappear. I could just walk out of the back gate and into the jungle-lined slopes linking Mount Faber and Frangipani Hill and never come back. But where would I go? Back east to Chen Mansion, where my whole family might be punished for hiding me? Into the jungles to scavenge?

I'd thought myself safe here, with guards at the front gate and the high security over the whole district. Even the wilderness beyond the fencing acted as an additional layer of security around Colonel Fujiwara, who claimed he was here to protect us.

What was Major Dewa going to do now? This was a hundred times worse than not getting his authorisation forms signed. Would he arrest Joben? Would Joben shoot him too?

If only Major Dewa had accepted and praised Colonel Fujiwara's *sake* and presented his request more obsequiously, the colonel would probably have signed everything without looking. But confrontation made him cross and determined to dig in his heels, like a child intending to make as much trouble as he can. Having Joben around didn't help either.

And what about the poor man Joben had shot? But I wasn't going to think about him. The only way to survive is by not driving yourself mad over things you can't control. That's why I didn't let myself think about my family, Chief Inspector Le Froy and all my friends who were missing or in prison.

But I could never put Ah Ma, my grandmother Chen Tai, completely out of my mind. It was she, the controlling brain behind the Chen family's black-market empire, who'd kept me despite fortune-tellers telling her I was bad luck. Instead of putting me down a well, as they'd recommended, she'd sent me to learn English at the Mission Centre because 'Su Lin will have to earn a living. Nobody will marry her with a leg like that.'

Later, reading the early signs, my grandmother apprenticed me to a Japanese hairdresser to learn Japanese. I've always been able to pick up languages quickly – growing up listening to the mishmash of Hokkien, Cantonese, Malay and English that makes up the Singlish patois probably helped.

It was thanks to Ah Ma that I spoke and translated Japanese well enough to work at the Shori headquarters and write for the *Syonan Weekly*. I owed her for that – even though she'd finally admitted cutting off my father for refusing to leave his pregnant Japanese wife.

According to Hideki Tagawa, my late mother Ryoko came from noble samurai lineage. But because she was Japanese, Ah Ma had driven her and my father out of the family mansion and into the slums. That was where I had been infected with the polio that had crippled me. And where my parents were exposed to the cholera that had killed them. She had killed them. I'd always known how much I owed my grandmother. Now I knew what she had done to me.

I wasn't ready to see her. And I still wasn't used to the idea of being half Japanese and related to Hideki Tagawa.

Hideki Tagawa had arranged for me to stay at the Shori headquarters, because he was worried that locals would react badly on learning that he was my cousin, now I was the assistant editor of the *Syonan Weekly*. It was the Japanese government's English-language mouthpiece. It didn't carry real news. Mostly I translated articles from their propaganda machine, telling of how grateful locals in Syonan/the Philippines/Taiwan adored their Japanese overlords and how proud we were to be part of the great Japanese Empire. Thinking about it, I went to the press room to get my notes for the next issue. It stood behind the house, with convenient access to the kitchen and the back service gate. It had been the men's billiard room in British times and the smell of cigar smoke and drink still hung in the air. Joben Kobata was the official editor of the *Syonan Weekly* and occupied the paper's large office in the main building. But he could barely read English, so it was left to me to get the proofs to the former Cathay Building where the Japanese Propaganda Department took care of printing and distribution.

I slept in the storeroom next to the press room. There was just enough room for my mat on the floor and a box for my clothes. And though my door didn't lock from the inside, I could lock the door of the press room so the area was all mine and private at night.

'Where were you?' Ima startled me when I went back into the kitchen. 'Where's everybody? Don't worry about the soup. That horrible Major Dewa's finally gone.'

'Thanks.'

Ima climbed onto one of the high kitchen stools with an effort, though there was nothing wrong with her legs.

'What happened?' I hoped Joben hadn't shot him too.

'My father told the major that he took the grenades to study

17

them. He said they're safely buried under some bureaucratic paperwork and he'll return them when he's ready.'

'Is the body – I mean, is the dead man still there? He is dead, isn't he?' I wondered whether clearing bodies out of Colonel Fujiwara's office was a routine task for the servants. 'I sent the house-boys to bed, but ...'

'Oh, Major Dewa got his men to carry him out. He'll think twice before trying to bully my father again. And on New Year's Eve too! Did you set up that *kadomatsu* behind my father's desk?' Ima said. 'In Japan we don't usually put *kadomatsu* indoors, but the snake flowers smell wonderful. Where did you learn to do it?'

'From Mrs Maki.'

'Ah, yes. The wonderful Mrs Maki, cousin of the wonderful Hideki Tagawa.'

Was she being sarcastic? Ignorance was always my best defence. 'Yes. She taught me smell adds an extra element.'

'We must always have lots of those flowers in the house if Major Dewa doesn't like them. If they can keep him as well as mosquitoes away, I don't care how ugly they are. At home we would decorate *Kagami-mochi* on a *tokonoma* – an elevated alcove in a traditional Japanese room. *Kagami-mochi* is a pair of cakes stacked in order of size with a *daidai* on top, used as a New Year offering, then cut and eaten on January the eleventh. *Kagami-mochi* is placed in the middle of a *tokonoma* as an offering to the New Year's god. I had to learn all this for myself – my mother never bothered to teach me anything. You're very lucky. Everybody says that Hideki Tagawa is going to arrange a good marriage for you. Could be what he and Mrs Maki were preparing you for.'

'What? No! He can't – he's never said anything to me–'

'It will be difficult, of course. Even if your mother came from a good family, there's still your father.'

I wondered if Ima was trying to warn me of something she'd heard. As she talked, she picked up scraps off the counter, even out of the pig-swill bowl, and ate them or wrapped them in a cloth to eat in her room later. She hated throwing anything away, even if it was broken or spoiled.

Ima was nothing like any of the other wealthy women I'd met. She inspected her clothes after they were ironed and put them away herself in locked drawers. The servants cleaned her room and emptied her bins, but were not allowed to air any of her cupboards.

Ima had once caught Xiao Xi, one of the maids, trying to open the large cupboard by the servants' staircase. She screamed and ranted so loudly at the poor girl that the guards came running with their bayonets pointed. A good thing came out of that: no one ever forgot again that the clean linen was no longer stored there – where it had been before Ima and Joben moved in – but in baskets under the back stairs.

'It's very good of you to be helping your father here but your mother must miss you very much over New Year.'

'My mother's dead. She left me all alone in the world. Why else do you think my father would bother with me?'

For a moment her mask slipped. In that instant I saw raw pain and loss on her face. I reached out and touched her arm. 'I'm sorry.'

'My mother was very beautiful and very clever. But my father was never good to her because it was an arranged marriage.

He always wants to do things his own way. And my mother was the same. She told me many times that if she had agreed to everything he said, done everything he wanted, kept her mouth shut, she would have had a much better life. But it just wasn't in her nature.' Ima laughed. 'Anyway, you know you should try to make a good marriage. Let Hideki Tagawa arrange one for you, and quickly. There may not be very many men worth marrying soon. Especially if you want a man with all his parts intact and functional.'

We were speaking in Japanese and the term Ima used was a lot more vulgar than 'functional'. It made me feel closer to her, like we were just two girls gossiping together in the kitchen about men. I missed Parshanti Shankar so much. She and I had been best friends since our schooldays, but now her parents were in prison and she was somewhere in the jungles up-country. I only hoped she was still alive.

Ima was not Parshanti, but I felt for her as the daughter of Colonel Fujiwara's first wife. It couldn't be easy for her, growing up knowing another woman was in her mother's place. And she might have guessed she had been sent out to Singapore to replace her father's mistress and bring some respectability to his household.

'What are those?' she asked, pointing to some fruit the servant children had found.

'Yellow rambutans. Some aren't quite ripe so I'm leaving them a few days.'

'Sour,' Ima said, grimacing. 'But I'll take a few to my room. I just need some string to keep them together. Where is it?'

'In the tin behind you.'

20

I helped Ima tie together the leafy bunches of rambutans. The children would be disappointed, but if I could keep them safe, there would be more rambutan seasons.

'My mother always said that the death of my father's second wife was payback for how badly he had treated her. My mother could never remarry because all of her income and status depended on her being Colonel Fujiwara's first wife. She couldn't afford to lose that.'

'Oh! I didn't know his second wife had died. Did it just happen? Is that why the photograph of her and the children is no longer on his desk? What happened to their little boy and girl?'

'Don't be so stupid. That was his third wife. His second wife died years ago when my mother was still alive. He could have come back to her. That was what everyone expected him to do. But he didn't. She could have reached out to him, flattered him and said how much she needed him, but she wouldn't. They were both so hopeless.'

I put a dish of pickled limes on the counter in front of her. They calmed her down as I'd known they would.

'Hideki Tagawa may marry you off as a political move.'

'What?'

'Of course, it would be better for him if he got married and had his own daughters to bargain with because the old families like his are dying out. Has Tagawa talked about marrying? Tell me the truth!'

She stared at me intently. When I looked blank, she added, with a little laugh, 'He hasn't taken a vow of celibacy, like a monk, has he?'

21

'What? No. Not that I know of! Can you think of anyone less like a Zen monk than Hideki Tagawa?'

We laughed, but that was when it first struck me that Ima wouldn't object to being married to him.

'It's no fun being a girl. My mother always said that if only I'd been a boy, the colonel wouldn't have left her. Even if that's not true I'm sure he would have claimed me earlier.' Ima shook her head as though trying to dislodge all her heavy thoughts. She climbed off the stool and grabbed her rambutans. 'Try to have sweet dreams tonight,' she said. '*Hatsu-yume*, your first dream of the year to come true. Some say it should be the first dream after New Year, but once past midnight it will already be next year. When it comes to good luck and a good marriage, it's dangerous to get left behind!'

'Sweet dreams,' I wished her in return, and started to clear up the mess she had left on the counter.

When I heard someone come in behind me, I assumed Ima had come back.

'Do they want something else?' I asked in Japanese.

'For a bad-luck girl you really had some good luck ending up here!' a voice said in English.

Startled, I whirled round and bumped my hip painfully against the table. Luckily I managed to save the bowl of peelings I was draining to add to the pig-swill. I stared at the woman standing inside the back door. 'What are you doing here?'

'I should be the one asking you that!' said Mimi Hoshi.

Mimi Hoshi

———◆———

You may already be familiar with the name Mimi Hoshi. If not, *hoshi* means 'bright star' and it's the name Ho Shen Mi adopted when entertaining Japanese troops. She had started calling herself 'Mimi' back when she was flirting with British soldiers. Even if that name's not familiar, you might know her as 'Mimi Bright Star' or 'the Mata Hari of the East'.

Mimi Hoshi was the elder sister of Ho Shen Shen, my uncle Chen's wife. Yes, the Chen family is not the most respectable, but we tend to keep our black-market and money-lending activities quiet. Mimi loved being famous and flamboyant.

Well, we all have our own ways of dealing with oppression and occupation.

Mimi was probably less than forty then, though she seemed ancient to me. After all, she was part of my parents' generation, part of the world I'd been born into, like the Egyptian Pyramids and British rule.

I had my own reasons for disliking Mimi. As her younger sister was married to my father's younger brother, 'Don't-call-me-Aunty'

Mimi told everyone she should have married my father. I'd since learned that my grandmother had rushed to arrange Uncle Chen's marriage *after* she'd cut off my father, her precious elder son, for marrying a Japanese girl without her permission. There had never been any arrangement between Mimi and my father.

'Mimi Bright Star' was the name she used on her 'artistic' photographs. I don't mean the early snaps of her with British soldiers that you see in the colonial archives – Mimi looks young, happy and gay in those pictures. She's laughing and holding up a glass of bubbly or blowing kisses at the camera. You can see she's the kind of girl all the soldiers in the squadron were in love with until they went home to marry the women they would have families with. I mean the artistic photographs Ryu Takahashi took of her. Of course they aren't as shocking now as they were back in the 1940s. In fact they were the focus of a war-museum art retrospective a few years ago, though restricted to viewers over the age of eighteen because of Nudity and Explicit Acts.

Those artistically staged shots, with crudely painted back-drops and props, men wearing what look like traditional Japanese masks and costumes and carrying traditional weapons … and Mimi naked, with paper blossoms taped to her nipples and blooming from her nether regions. In those photos, you can see her life, energy and vitality. She's hamming it up for the camera. Given the situation we were living in then, it was either very brave or blindly reckless, and probably a bit of both. Looking back now, it's like a kind of lost innocence. But, for a while, Mimi Bright Star was wildly popular with troops across all of the Japanese colonies.

Mimi lifted her skirt and reached under it.

'Why are you here?'

A sarong was tied around her waist and hips, like a baby-carrying cloth. As I watched, she pulled out the creased brown envelope that was tucked into it.

'What are you doing?'

I saw she had photographs in the envelope. I caught a glimpse of soldiers in uniform, like the staged propaganda shots we sometimes ran in the paper. But the photograph she held up showed me standing with Sergeant Prakesh Pillay, Sergeant Ferdinand de Souza and Corporal Wong Kan Seng in front of the Hill Street detective unit. It had stood across the road from the Hill Street police station and we had called it the Detective Shack when we worked there under Chief Inspector Le Froy.

'Where did you get that?' I asked her. 'What do you want?'

Mimi smirked, pleased with my reaction. 'It's you, right? No denying it. Can see your crooked leg.'

I remembered the day the photograph had been taken. We'd just got back from Ferdie de Souza's birthday lunch. Chief Inspector Le Froy had sent the four of us out with a whole five dollars to treat ourselves to de Souza's favourite *sup kambing* – mutton soup. A travelling Japanese photographer had stopped us in front of the Detective Shack and tried to talk us into having romantic photos taken. 'Which one of these handsome men is your boyfriend, young lady? You want to hold hands and take photo?'

'Me, of course! Me!' Prakesh said. 'I'm the handsome, smart boyfriend. Not that old man. Help! Save me, girlfriend!'

Prakesh darted behind me as de Souza pretended to box him and Wong laughed.

'We're colleagues,' I said.

'Yes. We're all colleagues.' Corporal Wong, the most recent addition to the Detective Shack, grinned with pleasure at being included.

'Wonderful! Then I must take a colleague photo. All four of you together,' the man said.

'He wants to know which of us you like best,' Prakesh said. 'He's going to cut us two out of the picture and keep the photo of you! He'll send it back to Japan and tell them you're his Singapore wife!'

'No, sir! No, I never do any such thing, sir!' The photographer was so alarmed that both sergeants were laughing at him.

'We don't have money to pay for a photograph,' I said.

'Never mind money now. I have to finish this roll of film before I go and develop. When I bring back photo to show you, you decide whether you want. If you want you pay, okay? You all four are working here?'

We posed for that photograph.

We'd never seen that man again. I'd assumed the photo hadn't turned out. Or that he'd decided we didn't look as though we could pay.

Anyway, I hadn't thought anything of it. Now that day seemed a lifetime away. Back then, people thought Chief Inspector Le Froy crazy for accusing travelling Japanese photographers of being spies. He'd since been proved right, but I doubt that was much comfort to him in the Changi PoW camp.

I'd steeled my mind not to think of him and the old days, but the photograph had caught me by surprise and yanked me back. Suddenly I missed him and my old life so much. I hadn't seen or heard from Le Froy since the one visit I'd been granted as a reward for saving Colonel Fujiwara's life. I could only assume he was still alive because I hadn't heard he was dead.

'Scared, huh?' Mimi had misread my expression. 'You know, these days evidence that you were working for the British police can get you into big trouble.'

'What do you want?'

'This is the only one I found. But there may be more.'

Was she trying to warn me or to blackmail me? I pushed away all thoughts of Le Froy and the past. I needed to focus on not grabbing the stone pestle on the counter and hitting her on the head with it.

She laughed and ate a spoonful of *kaya* from the jar on the table, licking the spoon, then sticking it back into the jar. 'You think you can suck up to the Japanese like you sucked up to the British, eh? By being good? Hah! You make me sick. You never have any fun. You're so boring, you don't even know what fun is!'

I turned down the heat under the soup pot.

'You think you got a good thing going here? You don't know what good is! Do you know there's Western-style fine dining in the Raffles Hotel? The Japanese took over British supplies and now you can eat noodles with canned ox tongue and Worcestershire sauce, sushi with Colman's mustard, and drink bottles of Hennessy and Johnnie Walker! How does that compare to your lousy food here?'

'Very nice,' I said. My eyes went back to the photograph. We were so young and blissfully unaware of all that was coming towards us.

'But look here, girl, I can help you. I can try to find the negative for you. Do you know what a negative is? If you have the negative you can print as many photos as you want. But if you want me to find the negative it will cost you extra.'

Ah. Blackmail, then. 'I'm not going to pay you for this,' I said.

'You pay Ryu Takahashi to take photos for that weekly paper, right?' Mimi grabbed for the photo. She had to tug it out of my hand because my fingers didn't want to let it go. 'Get the money from there. If you want this picture you must pay me. Real money, not banana money. Or else.'

Banana money was Japanese-issued currency. Food shortages had led to gigantic price inflation. The Japanese had tackled this by printing more and more banknotes as their value dropped further and further. My grandmother, who ran the black market in her district, also refused to deal with Japanese banana money, saying, 'Burn it to boil water. Better than trying to buy charcoal with it.' It was strange to think of my grandmother having anything in common with Mimi Hoshi.

'Or else what?'

'You know what. I don't want to get you into trouble. We are family, after all. Even if your slut mother robbed me of my rightful husband. But if you refuse to help me, I will have to find somebody who will. I'm only thinking of you. Do you think they'll let you stay on here if they know you used to work for the British police? Think about it. And one more thing. I want to see Joben Kobata. Privately.'

I could hear the murmur of voices from the main house. Joben Kobata would still be greeting guests with Colonel Fujiwara, the dutiful son-in-law.

28

'He's busy,' I said, 'He's going to be busy for the rest of the night. How did you get in here?' A sudden thought struck me. 'Did Ryu Takahashi bring you? Is he inside with them? Did you get this from him?'

I didn't like Ryu Takahashi, but he was a good friend of Joben's and had been supposed to come earlier in the day to take casual pictures of the New Year visits before the official photographs the next day. He hadn't appeared.

'I'm here as a guest,' Mimi said. 'Where is Joben Kobata's room? I'll wait for him there. If you get me in I might let you have this photograph for free ...'

I looked at her more closely. Mimi was dressed more like a *baishun-pu*, or prostitute, than a guest, wearing lipstick, stockings and a party dress that might have been the height of fashion before the war. But her hair was messy, her dress was damp and her shoes were worn and muddy. She looked like she'd travelled in a lorry or jeep, a vehicle that let in all the monsoon winds and rain. I guessed one of the men in Major Dewa's entourage planned to party with her after the formal meeting. Mimi must have got bored of waiting in the transport when things dragged on.

I felt a mean pleasure, thinking of how uncomfortable those fancy wet shoes must feel. Should I offer her something to dry her feet with? No.

'You'd better leave before anybody sees you. You could be arrested for being here without a permit.' Or shot. I remembered Major Dewa's poor aide.

'I was only giving you a chance,' Mimi said. She lifted her dress again, without embarrassment, and returned the photograph to its hiding place. 'I don't need you. I've got men who will do anything I want.'

That might have been true once. But Mimi was getting older as soldier boys got younger. And, unlike British royalty, powerful Japanese officials liked their women young and fertile.

'Who is this woman? What is she doing here?' Ima was back.

'This is Mimi. Her sister is married to my uncle.' I bowed low to Ima. Usually we were more informal in the kitchen, but I wanted Mimi to see that Ima wasn't someone to be messed around with.

Ima acknowledged Mimi with a curt nod, which was good of her. She would probably tell me off later for allowing a family member to visit without warning.

For a moment, Mimi looked frightened. But once she'd registered Ima's appearance her sneer returned. 'I didn't come to see Su Lin. You're Joben Kobata's wife, right? Tell Joben I have something from Ryu Takahashi for him. Tell him if he doesn't see me, I will show it to you.'

First Sunrise

The traditional expression 'Mount Fuji for first, hawk is for second and aubergine for third' stipulates the luckiest things to dream of in Hatsu-yume. There were no mountains, hawks or aubergines in my dreams. Instead, after finally getting to sleep, I dreamed of Mimi chasing after me and threatening, then crying that she was lost and begging for help. Every time I tried to find and help her, she chased and threatened me again, shouting, 'I should have been your mother!'

I wondered what my dead mother had thought of Mimi. Growing up, I'd blanked out the whispers of her being a prostitute, possibly Japanese and definitely unworthy of my father. Now I was angry on her behalf as well as my own. Since learning how they'd treated my parents, I'd felt detached from my Chen relatives. I told myself I was responsible only for myself and my own survival. To be honest, it felt like a kind of freedom I could get used to. And I was entitled to it. After all, hadn't my grandmother and uncle lied to me all my life?

Even if my father had fallen in love with a prostitute instead of a woman who'd run away from from her equally powerful family, how had that justified cutting off my parents to die in the epidemic?

It felt only fair that I was cutting off my family now. And I resented Mimi turning up. I wouldn't let her drag me into her lousy scheme. She wasn't even very good at blackmail.

Last night I'd almost wanted to shake her and tell her that if she meant to blackmail Joben Kobata with a photograph of him and some pretty girl, the last person to mention it to was his wife. I find it hugely frustrating when people don't think through what they're trying to do. Though maybe when it comes to blackmail that's not necessarily a bad thing.

Ima hadn't seemed to get the message. 'Office hours are over. The Shori headquarters are closed for business from the afternoon of December the twenty-eighth. Come back next year after the third day.'

'It's not official. It's a private and personal matter.' Mimi spoke coarse gutter Japanese, like the soldiers she kept company with.

'Pree-vart and peri-shonal? Really?' Ima mimicked Mimi's accent.

Mimi's Japanese ear wasn't sophisticated enough for her to tell the difference. But she could tell she was being mocked. 'Oh, yah. And this is something he'll want to hear about, I promise you. Tell him I have an important message for him from Ryu Takahashi, and if he doesn't see me, he'll be sorry.'

'Ryu gave you a message for Joben? When?'

'Just now.'

'Today?'

'Yah, of course today. That's why it's urgent, yah?'

'Tell Ryu to send his messages during office hours. How did you get in here tonight?'

Mimi hesitated. 'I came with a friend.'

'Oh, yah?' mimicking her again. 'Who?' Ima looked prepared to take down the man's name and have him charged.

Mimi shook her head. I guessed she didn't want to say in case it got them both into more trouble.

'Go and get one of the guards to take her away,' Ima said to me.

Mimi gave her a dirty look and walked to the door, but she hadn't given up. 'You don't want to see it before it's printed in the flyers on the streets?'

We both looked round. Did Mimi know something about the flyers?

Ima's mouth twisted but, to my surprise, she didn't answer straight away. Instead she busied herself picking up a glass I had just wiped and wiping it again. Finally she faced Mimi. 'People like you always get what they deserve. You just have to wait. Now, get out.'

And Mimi did exactly that.

Ima had the right attitude. She had handled Mimi wonderfully. I wanted to be more like her.

I would have been glad never to see Mimi again. But I had a feeling things weren't going to stop there. 'Are you going to warn Joben someone's trying to blackmail him?' I asked Ima.

She looked confused for an instant. Then suspicious. Then her blank mask returned. 'Who said that woman was blackmailing him? What do you think she was blackmailing him for?'

'I won't say anything,' I said quickly. The last thing I wanted

33

was for her to think I was going to make trouble. 'I know Mimi used to work at the officers' clubs, that's all. But that was before you came to Singapore – I mean Syonan. She probably has a list of all the officers who went to those clubs.'

'Well, men have needs,' Ima said.

I could tell she was relieved.

I was grateful to Ima who, with class and pride, had sent Mimi away and protected me. At the same time I wondered what I had missed.

And I was worried as to what Mimi might try to do next.

Now, in the bright new morning of a new day and year, she seemed less a menace than a nuisance. If Ima wasn't upset, there wasn't much Mimi could do to Joben.

I loved the early morning when there were no people around. At such times I could almost believe things had gone back to the way they were in the old days. I smelt night jasmine and heard the sound of crickets. Life went on for them unchanged. The birds and bugs ignore human problems because their lives are too short. Just like the giant trees ignore us because their lives are too long.

The servants were already hard at work in the house. After using the outhouse and splashing my face in the rain barrel behind the kitchen, I went out into the garden with the shears and a kitchen stool. I would cut a couple more snake flowers from the cannonball tree since Ima liked them.

The grounds behind the Shori headquarters were extensive. This was the area where the wealthiest, most important people had had their mansions built during the British occupation. Yes, the British colonial rule that the Japanese claimed to have freed us from had been a foreign occupation too. Even I, educated by English missionaries, could see that.

In the old days this was where the top government and trade families lived. No matter how rich they were, the wealthiest Arabs and Chinese hadn't been allowed to build houses in this area. There were token fences around each property, but what really shut people out was the social order and, beyond the carefully tended lawns, the wilderness of the island's primary jungle.

Now there were no more gardeners, but workers still came to cut the grass every two weeks. The unnaturally smooth carpet-grass lawns of the old days were gone, but it was still possible to walk across the buffalo grass right up to the fence.

I'd lived in this area years ago, during my first job as a babysitter for Deborah Palin. At the time I'd thought it was my big chance to get away from the life I'd been born into as the Chen family's bad-luck girl. Back in those days, my biggest problem was not being allowed to study for a university degree as my teachers at the Mission Centre school had encouraged. That, and the risk of being married off: my family's idea of providing me with a livelihood.

I wondered where Deborah Palin was now. She'd returned to England when her father, Governor Palin, was recalled. Her brother Harry had remained and trained as a fighter pilot, but disappeared up-country to join the rebels just before the British surrender. Most British – and most of us locals too – had assumed the Japanese would follow international guidelines on the treatment of PoWs and non-combatants. Harry Palin had predicted the worst and he had been right.

I hoped he was safe, wherever he was. Beneath his standoffish exterior, Harry Palin had had his own struggles. He deserved better than to be hunted like an animal through the undergrowth. We all did.

I breathed deeply, enjoying the sweet morning air and the touch of dew-tipped grass blades on my ankles. Despite everything, I knew I was lucky to be alive and to be here. More and more I thought that any decision, wise or stupid, had little to do with your choice and everything to do with what Fortune decided to throw at you.

Today was Hatsuhinode, the first sunrise of the year. It was supposed to bring new hope and spiritual renewal for the year to come. Since our island was run on Japanese time, it was still dark when the call came over the loudspeakers for us to bow to the east, in the direction of the Emperor. Traditionally the whole family comes together to pray for spiritual blessings and good fortune. I bowed to the stone shrine under the cannonball tree and asked whichever gods might be listening to protect my family. I was concerned for them even if I wasn't talking to them.

Bracing myself against the trunk of the cannonball tree, I climbed onto the high wooden stool and cut down several flowers. It wasn't easy. They grew directly from the trunk on thick tangled stalks. Their thick, fleshy petals were pale yellow on the outside and bright pink within. If you tore one the tissue inside was white at first but turned blue. And they smelt glorious. If nothing else, I could try to make this day a little easier for Ima, who'd been nice to me.

I heard Ima in the kitchen now, shouting for something.

Probably the colonel wanted his breakfast. Well, I had flowers to surprise her. I climbed down and went to the kitchen.

'Where were you? What were you doing outside? Today is a very busy day,' Ima said, before I could catch my breath.

I had left the stool outside. It's not easy to lug things around with a limp. But I showed her the flowers. 'You like these, right? I thought we could arrange them for the photographs. For good luck.'

'They'll attract so many insects – no, don't throw them out. Since you brought them in we might as well use them. But don't arrange them now. My father wants his breakfast and these stupid servants haven't even started washing the rice!'

'No need. It's already cooked. I made *ozouni*.'

'*Ozouni?*'

One of the house-boys lifted the lid of the pot already reheating on the stove to show her.

'You found ingredients to make *ozouni* here?'

'Kansai-style *ozouni* soup. Apart from the white miso, I put in local ingredients, like tapioca, jackfruit seeds, water spinach and dried mushrooms and I just need to add the rice cakes and fry the *ikan bilis* to put on top.'

The good thing about *ozouni*, besides its association with the idea of 'starting the year with a clean slate'? It was a single-pot meal that could be served for a couple of days just by topping up ingredients and reheating. According to Mrs Maki, who had taught me to make it, it tasted best on the third day.

'There'll be *jubako* for later in the dining hall. Everyone can eat at their own time.'

The *jubako* was a four-layer bento box and would be filled

with small helpings of various dishes (leftovers nicely presented).
It was an easy meal to keep everyone going on a heavy day.

'Let me see.'

Though we complain that the Japanese think locals don't feel
pain or hunger, we're just as guilty of believing that the suffering
of animals we put into soup doesn't count. But, like animals, we
want to survive. We keep the most dangerous creatures well fed
so they don't turn around and attack us.

Ima already had her nose over the pot. I handed her a ladle
and she dipped it in and tasted. 'Not much flavour.'

'Sit down and have a bowl while I prepare your father's tray.
It will taste better once I add the fried anchovies and some soy
sauce.'

'Do you make this for Hideki Tagawa?' Ima waited, like an
expectant dog.

'It's for everyone in the house. Is he breakfasting with your
father?' I reached for another tray.

'No. He's gone out somewhere. He should really find you a
husband soon, you know. or you'll be stuck here for ever, cooking
for my father and doing Joben's work for him. I'm going to tell
him to take care of it. Even if you are half *gaijin*, he should be
able to make a good arrangement for you. But, first, get that to
my father. And can you make him something sweet for later?
He'll be in such a bad temper after going through all the official
photographs.'

Official Photograph Day

Colonel Fujiwara was in a bad temper even before the official photograph sessions started.

Actually, it began to seem that they never would because the official photographer didn't appear. People in fine clothes were getting sweaty and impatient in the front garden where they had been arranged in gradations of importance. The higher officials had seats in the shade, while their helpers, assistants and lower-ranked functionaries stood in the sun further down the driveway and stretching out into the road.

I stayed well away from the formal hall – the former colonial ballroom – but I could hear Colonel Fujiwara venting his temper on all around. I wasn't sorry Ryu Takahashi hadn't materialised. I was sure he had given Mimi those photographs, and if he got into trouble for this, all the better for me.

Since I'd had nothing to do with the arrangements, all I had to do was stay out of the way and watch what was going on. Of course I made sure I put a worried look on my face.

I'd thought Ima would be more upset, but I found her in the

39

kitchen eating rather than throwing away leftovers. 'No point wasting food. People are starving. I can't stand any kind of waste.'

'Still no sign of the photographer?'

'I'm not surprised,' Ima said. 'I never liked that Ryu Takahashi. Never trusted him. He'll turn up and say he was off on some secret government mission but I don't believe that. Do you? I think he's gone off with a woman, or on an extended drunken orgy. He's no secret agent.'

'Or maybe he's a very good agent, good at misleading people,' I said.

'Nah. I can't stand the man. You look at someone like your Hideki Tagawa. You can see he's good at undercover work. He's the strong, silent type. So different from men like Ryu and Joben. Has he ever talked to you about what he did before the war? Or what he's doing now?'

Though nobody knew exactly what Hideki Tagawa did, soldiers bowed to him wherever he went, and officials watched him warily. And men like Major Dewa looked for ways to expose him as corrupt. I'd even heard whispers that he was the illegitimate son of the Emperor or his brother, and once asked if any of those rumours was true.

'No. We're connected to royalty,' he said, 'but descended from a completely different line. Ours is an old samurai family.'

Another thing I wasn't yet used to was his saying 'we' and 'our' in conjunction with 'family'.

'Well?' Ima prompted.

'He doesn't like talking about what he does.'

'See? The exact opposite of men like Ryu. And Joben.'

I didn't know why Ima was so down on her husband that day.

Usually she was the first to stand up for him. Maybe because she was angry with Ryu Takahashi. Ryu and Joben were friends, so Joben had insisted that only Ryu's photos were to be used in the *Syonan Weekly* and that only Ryu could take the official photographs. Or maybe Ima had taken Mimi's late-night visit to heart after all ...

Joben Kobata had married into a very powerful position. And, in public at least, Ima was the perfect wife. You could tell she was well brought up from how she said all the right things if she spoke at all. Japanese etiquette rules are so rigorous that if you've been brought up with the right manners, you can be perfectly charming to someone you can't stand, just by following the rules.

'I'll go and see what's happening outside,' I said, forgetting my manners when I saw a familiar face at the door. 'Excuse me.'

It was Formosa Boy.

Formosa Boy, as my family called the new commanding officer of their district in the east, was Lieutenant Tsai Chih-wei. He had been conscripted in Japanese-occupied Taiwan and risen in the ranks since.

'Good to see you looking healthy,' he said to me, in Hokkien. 'Your family is all well. Your uncle is working too hard. Your grandmother also. I will tell them I saw you.'

'Thank you.' I knew it was easier for my family that I wasn't living at Chen Mansion with them.

'Some of your other friends are waiting outside too.'

'I'll go and see. Would you like some soup? I'll bring it out here.'

'Of course!' Formosa Boy was always hungry.

I'd already glimpsed my old colleagues Prakash Pillay and Ferdinand de Souza. Prakash, who had joined the INA, the

Indian National Army, winked and blew me a kiss, and de Souza, who had rejoined the police force under the Japanese, smiled awkwardly and mouthed, 'You okay?'

I knew I had no more right to judge either of them than they had to judge me, but I was uncomfortable around them. Especially after I'd heard about the atrocities that went on inside the Hill Street police station and barracks, which were now *kenpeitai*, or Japanese military police, offices under Major Dewa.

I'd thought of warning them they were in Mimi's blackmail photo but there was no chance to talk privately. They were both in uniform, Prakesh with the other INA representatives and de Souza with the police.

And still there was no sign of Ryu Takahashi.

Joben Kobata came towards us from the house, his eyes darting around the crowd.

'No sign of him,' I said, knowing whom he was looking for. 'And still no message.'

'Colonel Fujiwara wants you to send for Mr Takahashi.' A guard had hurried up to tell him.

'I've been sending messages – messages and men. They can't find him. I don't think he's on the island. Nobody's seen him.'

'Colonel Fujiwara says that–'

'Tell him I've sent word that if Takahashi isn't here within the hour he's dead. Go,' Joben Kobata said, to the man with him. 'Find him. Or at least get his bloody camera and work out how to use it. Let everyone know the photography sessions start in an hour with or without him.'

Inside the formal hall, which I had set up for the photograph, there was a wide ornamental teak bench for Colonel Fujiwara, flanked by Ima and Joben, and, in less fancy chairs at either side, top-ranking officials. Those whose rank didn't qualify them for seats would stand behind.

I followed, just to see what was happening. Hideki Tagawa was in a corner, keeping an eye on the room as well as the crowd outside the window.

Just then Ima came through the door leading from the storerooms. She was dragging a camera and tripod with her. When she saw Hideki Tagawa her face brightened and she moved towards him. 'I found this in a storeroom. Must have been left behind by someone. Do you know how to use these things?'

Hideki Tagawa took it from her and studied it. Ima seemed pleased. 'Your husband knows cameras better than I do,' he said. Joben Kobata was looking surprised, then angry. Since he was the one who'd insisted on having Ryu Takahashi and no one else to take the photographs, he should have been grateful for her solution.

I looked more closely at Joben and realised he wasn't angry but, rather, frightened of the camera. Why? He talked a lot about his interest in photographs and films. I'd expected him to be the first to grab it and show off how well he could operate it, but he stayed away from it.

From what I could see, it was the Hansa Canon, a Japanese-made Leica imitation. It was a good, fairly modern machine, probably made not long before the war. And the tripod was in pretty good shape too. Had the British left it behind? If not, where had it come from?

Someone else asked Ima the same question.

43

'Who knows?' Ima said. 'Maybe the gods sent it in answer to our prayers!'

Officially, black-market trading was frowned on, but none of the officials, not even Major Dewa, said anything. A camera was needed and one had appeared. They smoothed their shirt fronts, dabbed at their moustaches and straightened their shoulders.

The camera looked like the same model as Ryu Takahashi used. I wondered whether he had given or sold it to Joben. That might explain why Ima wouldn't say which storeroom it had come from. Had she found it among Joben's things?

'Did this come from Ryu Takahashi?' Hideki Tagawa asked Ima. 'Have you seen him?'

'No one's seen him. What difference does it make where it came from? If it works, just use it.'

'Yes, get on with it, Tagawa!' Colonel Fujiwara said. 'Well? Can you figure out how to work it?'

'I'll need an assistant.'

'I'll help you!' Ima said.

'You have to be in the photographs. Su Lin?' said Hideki Tagawa. 'You used to take photographs, right?'

How could he have known about that? 'Yes, but I used a small Brownie camera. With the Brownie, all you had to do was point and click the only button.'

This camera was huge, full of dials and knobs.

'Same principle,' Hideki Tagawa said. 'Here. Now.'

As I watched him set up the camera on the tripod, it was clear he was familiar with it. Very likely he had also travelled around Malaya as an itinerant photographer-spy long before the war officially started. As Ryu Takahashi was rumoured to have done.

Those photographers had travelled the region taking photographs of important people and locations and sending them to Japan. Which was why, when the invasion happened, the Japanese had an idea of where everything was and how it was run.

'Stand beside me so that you can see how it's done and you can handle it the next time,' Hideki Tagawa said to me.

'Show her how to work it, then come and be in the photograph,' Colonel Fujiwara said.

'It's not that easy. Besides, you can't have an inexperienced photographer today of all days. Anyway, I don't have an official position here so I shouldn't be in the official photographs.' Hideki Tagawa never had his photograph taken if he could help it.

Had he turned up for the session because he'd known the official photographer wouldn't be there?

'You should be in the photo! Come and stand beside me! Tell the girl which button to press and come here,' Ima said to him. 'Just set it up quickly and don't keep everybody waiting.'

'Do you want all the servants in the photographs too? I can call the gardeners and rat-catchers in as well, if that's what you want,' Hideki Tagawa said. 'Now, look over here and don't move!' After the first flash he announced, 'I'll take three photographs of each group. The first one formal, for the annual report, the second smiling, for the company room, and the third relaxed. When you tell your grandchildren and great-grandchildren what you did in Syonan, you'll show them the third photograph, so try not to look too fierce.'

I didn't see any difference in most of their expressions. The officials stared at the camera, wearing the same corporate military face for all three photos.

But that, more than anything else, showed Hideki Tagawa had worked as a jobbing photographer before. Any hobbyist can learn how to work a camera, even the most new-fangled sophisticated machine, but only someone who has been photographing people for a living knows how to manage his subjects.

In a lower voice, he explained to me, as the next group, of slightly lower-ranked officials, arranged themselves, 'You can't keep everything in focus all the time. Always put the most important people in the centre and most clearly in focus. But you don't know who is going to be important in five or ten years' time. So, if you can, you should always take additional shots, with the people at the sides and at the back more clearly in focus.'

Hideki Tagawa was swift. Once he had adjusted the settings to his liking for the first photograph, the rest followed quickly.

The next batch of officials was ushered into place around Colonel Fujiwara and his family. No one saw Hideki Tagawa as anything other than the photographer. Like the photographer who took that old photograph of me and my colleagues had managed us. Surely he couldn't have been ...

But this was no time to worry about that. I tried to pay attention and learn from Hideki Tagawa as he took the photographs.

It seemed impossibly unlikely now, but if I ever got my dream job of becoming a real journalist, knowing how to work a camera would be a very useful skill. I'd always believed in making the most of every opportunity. Besides, what was the alternative? To watch Hideki Tagawa's face instead of his fingers, as Ima was doing?

The Hairpin

———◆———

The official photograph sessions had been scheduled to end by lunchtime, but thanks to the delay caused by Ryu Takahashi's non-appearance, it was past five o'clock by the time we had finished. I was exhausted. At times it felt like the tide of important people would never stop coming and we were trapped on one of the eighteen levels of Chinese Hell, where we had to smile and bow to bad-tempered important people for all eternity.

Colonel Fujiwara was the most used to it. Once the actual photo-taking started, he sat stoic in his medals, radiating authoritative splendour as people sat or stood around him, between shuffling in and out.

The *kadomatsu* decorations I'd made, reproducing the classic 'gate pine' decorations with local bamboo and cannonball flowers for New Year, looked good in the background, but the humans were wilting and withering.

Ima was tired and fretful. I saw her looking around for someone to find fault with and made sure to keep away from her. Several officials had earnestly offered her clumsy congratulations on her 'happy occasion', and she was scowling. Ima was not fat, but she had a way of standing awkwardly, her hands folded over her belly, that drew attention to the part of her body with which she was most uncomfortable.

Her husband clearly enjoyed having his picture taken. Joben responded to Hideki Tagawa's instructions with enthusiasm, looking fierce in the first formal photograph, grinning in the second, and in the third turning casually (but making sure his profile was perfectly posed) to talk to someone behind him or reaching across Ima to say something to his father-in-law.

Joben Kobata was an actor. He remained charming throughout, making polite conversation with each new group of visitors who filed in, sat for three flashes of the camera and filed out. The officials standing nearest him left better-tempered than those closest to Ima or Colonel Fujiwara. Watching him, I saw for the first time that cheerfulness was a useful gift – or possibly a skill worth cultivating.

When the last officials had gone, I went to the kitchen to arrange for dinner trays to be carried to their rooms, with extra warmed *sake* for Colonel Fujiwara. There's something comforting about a well-arranged bento box. Even when you feel too tired to eat, it's easy to sample the contents of one compartment, then another, rather than facing a steak and kidney pie or a platter of fried noodles. And I enjoyed arranging them.

Even with all the privileges of the colonel's household, the bentos contained a poor selection compared to the traditional *osechi* I'd helped Mrs Maki create in the old days, when each dish was chosen as much for its taste as its symbolic blessings to the eater. I had sweet stewed black beans (representing hard work rewarded), thinly sliced pickled lotus roots (for good foresight), sweet rolled-up omelette with anchovies, and, of course, rice and seaweed. There would be enough for all of the household, as well as Hideki Tagawa and myself.

The servants had been given the option of fish porridge, which they seemed to prefer, and allowed to take the bento leftovers back to their quarters.

'He's not acting.' Hideki Tagawa startled me into dropping the pot I was holding and splashing myself with dirty, soapy water.

'What are you talking about? Didn't you get your dinner? I told the house-boy to leave it in your room if you weren't there.'

He held up his bento box to show me, then put it on the kitchen table next to mine and lifted a wooden stool from the stack. 'Sit. You're tired.'

Normally I enjoyed scrubbing out the rice pot. It's rewarding to rest your mind cleaning something that has fed you and will feed you again. But not that day. I was exhausted.

'You should leave it for the servants to wash tomorrow.'

'I'm a servant. I might as well do it now.'

'Anyway, as I was saying, Joben Kobata isn't acting. I saw you studying him. You think he's good at putting on a happy face for people.'

I, on the other hand, clearly needed to learn to hide my own feelings better. 'Nobody can be so happy staring at a camera for hours.'

'Joben Kobata is happiest when he's surrounded by people looking up to him. When he's alone, with no one to bow to him, he's miserable. Colonel Fujiwara is very pleased with his dinner bento, by the way. You may find yourself permanently in the kitchen rather than behind the editor's desk.'

'Assistant editor's desk,' I said. 'Joben Kobata is the editor.'

'Of course.' He handed me a small cloth-wrapped bundle. 'I want you to look at something.'

'What is it?'

Not wasting words, he gestured to me to open it.

I dried my hands on the good-morning towel around my neck and unwrapped the bundle. It was a piece of jewellery. A delicately worked medallion set into a long double-skewered hairpin. It looked a bit like the *chuchok sanggul*, or 'bun-catcher', hairpins my grandmother wore in her tightly coiled *sanggul*. It was beautiful. 'What is it?' I asked again.

'A *kanzashi* hairpin. Not many are left. The motif on the head is the crest of our samurai family. These wavy lines here,' he turned my wrist and pointed at the centre of the intricate pattern, 'show the chrysanthemum surrounded by growing leaves.'

I'd never believed in women being won over by jewellery, but that pin made me forget my tiredness.

'It was crafted in Kyoto more than a hundred years ago by professional artisans who served our family for generations.'

'I can't believe something so beautiful was made in Japan. Sorry, I mean—'

'You have a very limited understanding of Japanese culture.'

'My understanding of Japanese culture comes from living under Japanese boots and bayonets.'

I wouldn't have dared say that to him three months ago. Maybe not even yesterday. But the hours of working side by side had created a kind of camaraderie. I felt as if we were exhausted fellow survivors of a long trek.

'You have a point.'

I watched him fill a porcelain *tokkuri* with *sake* and put it into a pan of hot water to warm. He took two small ceramic cups out of their cloth-lined box.

Priming a camera, then recording names and designations might not sound much like work, but by the end of the session I could barely focus on the paper as I scratched down names, ranks and whether the officials were from the military, the navy, the INA, the police or some administrative department in charge of importing dried fruit.

Hideki Tagawa, who'd been hefting and bending over the heavy camera, should have been even more tired but, then, he was probably trained to withstand torture and he had two straight legs.

I should have offered to warm and serve the *sake*. But now I was finally sitting down, I didn't want to stand up again unless ordered to. Maybe not even then.

As though he had read my thoughts, Hideki Tagawa lifted the *tokkuri* out of the warm water and filled our cups.

'To the future.' I held mine up in a mock toast.

'The future,' he agreed, responding.

The *sake* tasted smooth and flowery. It warmed and soothed me, and when I picked up the hairpin again I was able to appreciate its beauty even more. It was like a delicate blossom realised in fine metal.

'Every country exports its best and worst people. Don't judge Japan until you get a chance to see our people in our homeland. People are not really that much different. If you're stable in your homeland, you stay put. It's those on the edges who travel, the high-ups who want even more, and the low-downs who have to travel to survive.'

I looked at the delicate pin, so light on my fingers. I didn't know anything about jewellery but remembered my grandmother saying, 'Always buy gold, never silver. Gold is easier to resell.' For her, jewellery had nothing to do with sentimentality. It was currency.

'It should have been Ryoko's,' he said.

I didn't want to like this man but he was the only connection I'd ever had to the mother I couldn't remember. Looking at him, I hoped to see something – anything – he might have had in common with her. I suspect he was doing the same with me. Whenever he spoke her name – Ryoko – there was as much longing in his voice as there was in my mind.

'A poem is engraved in miniature characters on the reverse. You need a magnifying glass to read it–'

'What's that? Where did she get that? Did you give it to her? Why?'

Neither of us noticed Ima till she took the hairpin out of my hand.

'It looks so real, doesn't it?' she went on. 'Is it real? Is it one of your old samurai family traditions to dress up in costumes for the New Year?'

Though her tone mocked 'samurai' and 'traditions', she examined the ornament with yearning hunger.

'Traditions don't stand still,' Hideki Tagawa said, 'tradition adapts to its environment. Same for the samurai.'

Ima glanced at him, held the hairpin close to her eyes and squinted at it. Then she stuck it into the side of her mouth and bit down hard on it. It was an old way of telling if a jewel was real. Twenty-four-carat gold is soft enough for your teeth to leave slight marks on the surface.

Hideki Tagawa snatched it from her. 'How dare you? This is a priceless family heirloom!'

I thought he was going to hit her and Ima thought so too. She cried out and shielded her face. 'Forgive me! I only wanted to see if it was real.'

Hideki Tagawa ignored her. He wiped the hair ornament on his tunic and examined it. Then he handed it back to me. 'Take good care of it,' he said.

'You're not giving it to me?' I said.

At the same time Ima said, 'You can't give that to her!'

'It's yours now. Take care of it.'

'No.'

'You people should not forget your place!' Ima glared at me. 'This is a valuable treasure. It should not have been taken out of Japan in the first place!'

'Isn't this part of Greater Japan now?' I shouldn't have answered back. But it had been a long day and my mental muzzle had worn thin.

Ima turned on Hideki Tagawa. 'I'm only speaking for your own good. What if you decide to get married one day? What are you going to give your wife if you hand over all your family jewellery to strangers now? You won't get it back from her, you know. Her kind doesn't understand the value of things. She'll sell it to someone and they'll melt it down – your precious heirloom! Look at her! She doesn't even have enough hair to wear something like that!'

When the Japanese first came, my grandmother chopped short the hair of all the females under her roof and smeared our faces and thighs with bougainvillaea sap, causing massive rashes

53

to break out. It was horribly uncomfortable, but none of us was raped by soldiers.

Because I would not take it from him, Hideki Tagawa put the pin on the kitchen counter and turned to walk back to the house.

'It's not mine,' I said. I left the kitchen too, by the back door that led to the toilets and servants' quarters.

I was fuming. Even if it should have been my mother's, he had had no right to force the pin on me. Especially not in front of Ima. If she became jealous of me, Ima could make my life hell.

But I couldn't leave it on the counter.

I returned to the kitchen and saw him at the other door. The hairpin was gone. Before he could try to persuade me to take it, I said, 'Please don't mention it again.'

He nodded.

In my room I looked into my hand mirror and saw my hair would be long enough to coil into a bun soon. I could already plait and pin it. And my skin had cleared up. If you didn't see me walk, I looked like a regular girl. At least to Ima. There had definitely been jealousy in her eyes. I would have to do something to deflect that.

But I was too tired to think about it now. I had to be at work tomorrow, which meant I should get some sleep.

I felt a twinge of longing for the beautiful *kanzashi* hairpin. But what Ima had said was true. If desperate, I would have sold it to feed my family, I couldn't be trusted with such a precious heirloom. Thinking of my family brought up the confused feelings I didn't want to deal with.

I was glad he had taken it back. But also a little disappointed.

The *Syonan Weekly*

———◆———

The next morning I was back at work in my little press room.
I'd discovered an unexpected connection with the *Syonan
Weekly*.

It wasn't Colonel Fujiwara's English mistress, Emily
Bennington-Smith, who'd originally set up the paper but Miss
Joan Briggs, who'd been one of my favourite teachers years ago
in the Mission Centre school.

'Your Miss Briggs volunteered,' Colonel Fujiwara told me. 'Smart
woman. She saw at once it was better to make herself useful to us
than to be put in prison. If you're smart, you'll learn from her.'

I didn't believe him. The Miss Briggs I remembered would
have stood up for what she thought right. She had taught us
domestic science and arithmetic, often at the same time. In her
domestic-science classes we'd calculated investments (always
plant a portion of the vegetables you buy) and asset management
(assigning each group of girls three laying hens at the start of
term). Several of her students went on to manage their family
businesses with great success.

Miss Briggs believed in basic principles that worked across different societies. She said once you understood the 'codes' of any society – its beliefs, taboos and etiquette – you could fit into it.

'Languages are codes.' She'd tried to learn Malay and Hokkien from us, an anomaly when the British in Singapore assumed anyone speaking a language other than English (and perhaps French or German but not Dutch or Spanish) was ignorant and uneducated. Miss Briggs told us that, as girls, she and her cousin Ruth had spent their summer holidays creating codes and secret languages. 'We just transposed every letter a few places up or down the alphabet. Once we knew the key for the day – like up five or down one, we could share messages that looked like gobbledygook to the grown-ups. We had such fun.'

It was because of her cousin that Miss Briggs had lost her job with the *Syonan Weekly*. Emily Bennington Smith had gone through Miss Briggs's personal mail and learned her cousin Ruth was a member of the team decrypting the Germans' Enigma machine. Once she had informed the Japanese of this, Miss Briggs was detained as a dangerous enemy alien. Miss Emily, of course, had taken her place at the *Syonan Weekly*.

As far as I knew, Miss Briggs was still alive somewhere in the women's PoW detention centre. Miss Emily, who had tried to help her lover kill Colonel Fujiwara, had disappeared and died of either malaria or snakebite, depending on which official report you read. She might still have been alive, too, not that I cared. Neither the British nor the Japanese wanted to discuss her. It was almost impressive how one woman had managed to alienate so many disparate groups.

I turned my attention to the next issue of the *Syonan Weekly*. I would put in the New Year photographs once they were developed. Keen to show off modern Japanese technology, Joben insisted there must be photographs in every issue, taken, of course, by his friend Ryu Takahashi.

For once I already had the photographs, along with my notes on the names and ranks of the officials. Not having to hound Ryu Takahashi for his photographs – he was so slow and always late – meant that, for once, I could get ahead on the issue.

I started to go through the personal advertisements. There was that strange message again, from 木造住宅, Mokuzō Jūtaku: 'Take two steps forward from each new beginning and if you ever need HELP, just give Noriko ribbons.' It ran as a pre-paid advertisement, appearing monthly or once every four issues. Miss Briggs had done the layout and it had remained unchanged since her day.

When I asked Joben about it, he said, 'Probably some artistic-poet type made a romantic promise to a dead lover.' Joben didn't think much of romance or poetry. But as long as the advertise-ments were paid for, they ran. According to the records, the account had started at the same time as the paper.

The reason I found it interesting was that '*mokuzō jūtaku*' meant 'wooden house' and made me think of Peveril Wodehouse, who'd liked to sign off as 'Mù Zhú' meaning 'wooden building' in Chinese.

Peveril Wodehouse was a nondescript Englishman with a glass eye who'd worked with the Hong Kong police before the war. I'd met him when he came to Singapore to 'have a little chat' with the staff of the Detective Shack before a foreign dignitary's visit.

'Vetting us before the event,' Le Froy had said later. 'Lucky you all passed.'

'How do you know we did?'

'You're still here, aren't you?'

Some said Wodehouse was really with the Secret Intelligence Service, the section specialising in foreign intelligence. Could Peveril 'Mù Zhū' Wodehouse still be around?

But I'd also heard his younger brother was broadcasting propaganda for the Nazis, so maybe the whole family had gone over to the other side.

There was a knock on the door. I barely had time to dread Mimi turning up again when the door opened and Prakesh Pillay stuck his head around it. 'Su Lin? Hope it's not a bad time.'

It took me a second to recognise him in the unfamiliar INA uniform. Prakesh was the last person I'd expected to see, but a hundred times more welcome than Mimi. I wasn't surprised he had joined the INA. It was made up of roughly forty-five thousand ethnic Indians, locals and PoWs, and run by Subhas Chandra Bose. Bose had been Prakesh's hero since before the Japanese invasion.

'Prakesh! What are you doing here?' It was so good to see him. 'I was just thinking about you. You and de Souza. I have to talk to you. I didn't get a chance yesterday.'

'Talk about what?' Prakesh said. His eyes darted around the small crowded room. My desk, covered with papers. The shelves, with overflowing files, the bottle of water and single cup.

'Would you like some water?'

'No, thank you. Luxurious surroundings you've got here.'

'I've got to warn you—'

'Warn me? About what?'

'Someone came to see me with a photograph.'

'Photograph?'

'Of you, me and de Souza with Corporal Wong in front of the old Detective Shack. She wanted money in exchange for it.'

'Where did she get it?'

'She wouldn't say, but she seemed to think it would make trouble for us. Do you think so?'

'Depends. How good do I look in it? Will she make extra copies?'

'Come on Prakesh, this is serious!'

'Don't worry.' Prakesh moved a box file and a ruler, then sat down opposite me. 'Times have changed. An old photograph isn't going to make trouble for you unless someone's looking for an excuse. And in that case you'll have more than a photograph to worry about. Anyway, you wouldn't be working here unless they'd already decided to trust you. Major Dewa's approved de Souza, so he's all right for now. And nobody can do anything to Wong.'

Sweet, earnest Corporal Wong had been taken away in the early days of the Japanese occupation.

'And you – you're all right?' I asked him. 'What are you doing here?'

'Official visit. There's something I have to talk to Colonel Fujiwara about.' Prakesh looked uncomfortable. 'Or someone who has his ear. I've got an appointment with Joben Kobata, but that's just to get me into the building.'

'I don't handle Colonel Fujiwara's appointments. Ima does that.'

'The thing is, everyone says the colonel likes you. I thought, if you get the chance, you might mention something.'

'Why don't you submit a written request? Do you want me to translate it into Japanese for you?'

'Is that what you do here? Translate stuff into Japanese?'

'The other way around. Most of the articles come directly from Japan, calls to appreciate the honour of being part of the great Japanese Empire. I translate them into English and make sure Joben gets the credit.'

It wasn't so different from my old job in which I'd spent a lot of time translating police orders, instructions and queries into Malay and Chinese for the locals. My grandmother and Miss Briggs had been right about the importance of learning different languages.

'I don't know how you stand it. I can't even read it.'

'It's better than working in a factory crushing coconuts or, worse, in a comfort house.'

'Granted. And I guess you get first chance at the ads and offers.'

The most popular section in the *Syonan Weekly*, and the only reason most people picked up the paper, was the personal column. Here, for a small sum, people could buy, sell and barter goods and services. Though, of course, the bulk was composed of missing-person notices, with offers to pay for any news of family members.

'If it's INA business, why not just go through the army business channels?'

'I am. That's why I've got a meeting with Joben Kobata in an hour's time. I came early, hoping to have a word with you. Kobata oversees the INA funding. But talking to him can be ...' Prakesh shook his head and glanced at the closed door. 'You don't know what it's like. The man wants total control so he has to approve everything. But he gives money to people he likes and ignores everything else. And we can't do anything without his agreement.'

It sounded like the same problem Major Dewa was having. 'He's in charge of everything here too,' I gestured around the room, 'so I do know what it's like. Not easy.'

'Is he giving you trouble?' I saw a flash of anger. For all his joking and teasing, Prakesh had always protected me like a brother. 'Is he bothering you?'

'Oh, no. I'm too skinny, ugly and crooked. He doesn't bother me.'

'Don't put yourself down. More likely Tagawa's warned him off. Or Joben's wife. She's the dangerous one. You'd better watch out for her.'

'Ima?' I laughed, 'She's very good to me. Anyway, if you've got a meeting with Joben Kobata, ask him to speak to Colonel Fujiwara for you. What's it about anyway?'

I watched Prakesh deciding what to tell me. Finally he said, 'We're not traitors, you know, the men who joined the INA. We're Indian patriots. The British have been exploiting India for the past hundred years. We're fighting for Indian independence and self-government. Colonel Fujiwara is a great supporter of this plan. He says we're not fighting for Japan but for India. For ourselves.'

'Oh,' I said cautiously. Colonel Fujiwara might have made the announcements, but I knew Hideki Tagawa had come up with the strategy: 'Appealing to Indian patriotism will work better than threats,' he'd said, 'If you threaten them, they'll fight you to the death, so get them to fight the English instead.' It seemed to have worked. But Prakesh still looked unhappy.

'Did someone call you a traitor?' I asked.

'Not directly. But almost all the higher-ranking officials and the entire Gurkha contingent chose to remain PoWs. They don't understand. I tell them the Japanese will treat us better than the British ever did, but they don't want to hear it. Not one single man. Those chaps are more British than the British.'

'They chose a different path. That doesn't mean you're wrong. Remember, your first duty is just to stay alive for one more day.'

'Yah, I know. It's not that. It's—' Prakesh waved his hands, dismissing my platitudes.

'If it's about the missing grenades the INA captured, someone's already brought it up with Colonel Fujiwara. I think that's been settled.'

'That's no big deal. They got two precious samples of the Americans' yellow pineapple grenades that burst into fragments when detonated. Apparently they can produce casualties up to fifty yards. But that's more a territorial thing. Everybody wants to be the first to get their hands on them and take them apart. Probably some department's already working on it but won't admit it until they're successful. Or until they blow themselves up.'

'Then what is it?' I glanced at the alarm clock on my desk. It wasn't just the timing of his meeting with Joben, I had my own work to get through.

Prakesh took a deep breath and came to a decision. 'It's about some PoWs who've gone missing.'

'Escaped?' For one wild, heady moment I thought of Le Froy. Could he have got out? But even if he had, how far could he get, with a foot amputated?

'Mostly Indians and Eurasians. Men we were working on to come over to the INA. They were taken out for exercise and never came back. All the paperwork on them has just disappeared. It's like they never existed.'

'You know they're probably all dead in a hole somewhere—'

'No! No, it's not like that. The men they took, they weren't the kind they'd just get rid of. I mean they were in good shape. They could have been put to work even if they refused to sign on. And why are the records gone? Also, a lot of money's missing that was supposed to come to the INA. But there aren't any records of that either. And we're supposed to have paid for medical supplies, but we haven't ordered or received anything.'

Prakesh was starting to sound like Major Dewa.

'Maybe you should work with Major Dewa. He's eager to clean up everything.'

'Major Dewa thinks all Indians are liars, cheats and thieves. He's got no choice other than to work with us, but if he could shut down the INA and shoot us all, he would.'

'Prakesh, you don't regret signing on with them, do you?'

'Of course not. Why would I? What gave you that idea? How can you say things like that?'

'"The lady doth protest too much,"' I said. 'Or the laddie, in this case.' Say what you like about the British, no one puts things better than their Shakespeare.

'Okay. Well, I've got nothing to complain about. But seeing

how they're treating Indian PoWs who won't sign on, I don't know
what the INA is planning to do to other Indians in India.'

'Please be careful.' I said. 'You know what happens to people
they notice.'

We both knew only too well. Corporal Wong Kan Seng had
dutifully reported to them when they called in people who had
been working in the civil service or the police force. He'd never
been seen again.

'I saw Wong Kan Seng's mother the other day outside the
Changi PoW prison.' Prakesh's thoughts had gone the same way.
'She and his grandmother are still looking for him. I tried to tell
them to go home and wait. Why put themselves in danger? But
they said they have nothing else to hope for, nothing else to
live for.'

'What are they living on?'

'They're selling vegetables, and *kueh* and *achar* they make at
home. I'm trying to get the prison kitchens to buy from them.'

'Do they really have enough to sell?' For most, finding enough
food for themselves was difficult. It was especially so for people
living in town, without land for vegetables or chickens.

'I don't know where they're getting them all from. Whatever
they produce themselves or buy from families around them,
I guess. But they said if I got them a pass to the prison kitchen
they'd find the vegetables somehow.'

'You're giving them an excuse to go to the prison and ask if
anyone's seen their boy so they won't be just hanging around
outside trying to spot him. If they're delivering vegetables,
nobody will bother them. That's very good of you.'

I meant it. Prakesh had a sweet, practical side I loved. He

might have a prickly way with words and flare up at the least provocation, but he would also do all he could for someone he considered a friend. 'Some of those missing PoWs were your friends, weren't they?'

'They would never have run off without letting me know.'

'I'm sorry.'

Just then the door opened, and before we could wonder who it might be, Joben Kobata and Hideki Tagawa came in.

'Entertaining, are you?' Joben said.

'Sir.' Prakesh stood at attention and saluted. 'I was early for a meeting and didn't want to bother you.'

'You're working hard on the paper,' Hideki Tagawa said, picking up the sheet I had been annotating. 'Make sure you get all the names and ranks in correctly.'

'Things like that are important,' Joben Kobata said, as though it had been his idea and his work being praised.

Actually, I was the one who'd thought of printing the men's names and ranks. So many mid-level officials had begged extra copies of previous issues to send home because they didn't have money for photographs. And since the *Syonan Weekly* was an official paper, the censors allowed copies through.

'Anyway, since you're here, there are some things I need to talk over with you.' Joben put a hand on Prakesh's shoulder. 'The INA hasn't been responding to my mail so you'd better tell me what they're doing over there.'

I suspected the INA had been sending Joben a lot more mail than he read. He was notorious for letting communications and transmissions pile up on his desk until Ima got fed up with the chaos and ordered the lot burned.

As Joben was the husband of the colonel's daughter, there was very little anyone could do to touch him.

'Still no word from Ryu Takahashi?' Hideki Tagawa asked me.

Joben stopped in the doorway at the mention of the name.

'No. And we'll need more photos from him once we've printed all these. Unless you can take some more for us.'

'Takahashi will come back. He's probably gone drinking,' Joben Kobata said. 'He knows he's the official photographer. If he wants to keep the position he'll come back.'

I was sorry to see Prakesh go. But at least I could get on with my work, or so I thought.

'Colonel Fujiwara wants to see you,' Hideki Tagawa said to me.

Colonel Fujiwara

———◆———

Colonel Fujiwara's office was large and airy, with polished wood floors and teak shelving. A ceremonial portrait of the Emperor hung next to one of Colonel Fujiwara in ceremonial uniform. It had clearly been taken some years back as it showed him with considerably more hair and less belly.

Another photograph of Colonel Fujiwara with his wife and children used to stand on his desk. In it he appeared happier than I'd ever seen him in person. Maybe he missed his family too much to look at them.

I entered the room as I'd been taught by Mrs Maki, taking off my shoes before stepping in with 'Excuse me' and a low bow.

'Ebisu-chan, you're a good girl,' Colonel Fujiwara said. 'You're clearly half Japanese. I would believe you were completely Japanese if not for your crooked leg, ha!'

I was used to him blaming the childhood polio on my Chinese genes just as my Chinese relatives had blamed it on my bad-luck curse.

'I've picked the photographs for the official cards. What do you think?'

I'd sent him portrait shots I'd developed in the press room's cupboard after cropping him head and shoulders out of some of Hideki Tagawa's New Year photographs. He had been waiting for Ryu Takahashi to deliver them for so long.

'You look very good in them, sir.'

My friend Parshanti's father used to develop camera film in the dark room behind his pharmacy and had stressed how important it was not to expose undeveloped film to sunlight. I knew I had to keep the room totally dark and undisturbed while the film developed. That was why the pictures I developed in the tiny windowless cupboard came out better than those developed *en masse* after they'd been examined and passed by multiple departments.

'These are good, you know. They will be my new official photographs. I should pay that no-good layabout's fee to you.'

I bowed gratefully, knowing I wouldn't see any bonus. Even if the colonel remembered to tell Joben Kobata to pay Ryu Takahashi's fee to me, Joben would likely either forget or pocket it himself.

'Now I need you to get these put up as soon as possible. The New Year portraits should have been up on the first day of the New Year – you people are useless!'

He swept the photographs onto the floor and, my moment in favour over, I knelt to collect them. Hideki Tagawa picked one up and looked surprised.

'Where is that *deku* Joben?' Colonel Fujiwara asked him.

Deku meant a useless person or someone who couldn't do

anything well. So, something had come between Colonel Fujiwara and his son-in-law.

'He has a visitor,' Hideki Tagawa said. 'A representative from the INA.'

'Who is hoping to see you,' I put in. If I could get Prakesh in, why not?

Not that I thought talking to Colonel Fujiwara would do Prakesh any more good than talking to his *deku* son-in-law. But if Prakesh could tell his superiors that he'd seen the colonel about the matter, his investigations might go further.

'I'm not seeing anybody else today.' Colonel Fujiwara shook his head. 'All full of nonsense, these people coming and asking me for things. Nothing I can do about it. I don't want to see anybody who's talking to Joben. That man gives me a headache. And his wife, worse, all the time nagging, nagging. At least her mother was too stupid to talk much. Never thought that would be a blessing. If you want to have a peaceful marriage, cut out your wife's tongue!'

I stood silent, with my eyes on my toes. I knew when to be deaf. Hideki Tagawa didn't respond either.

'All the people here, all they ever do is demand more, more, more from me. But do they work? If they're working I'm not seeing results. So what do I do? Replace them? The replacements are even worse.' He leaned back in his seat and sighed. 'What's for dinner?'

That was the real reason he'd asked for me. Colonel Fujiwara's main interests after *sake* were food and teas. In any other era, he would have been a fascinating gourmet master. But in this time and place, all he could do was lament the miserable quality of everything around him.

Until I had come into the household.

Since moving in, I'd taken over supervising the kitchen as well as much of the household management. When I'd translated Ima's orders to the staff, I'd adjusted them to suit an establishment of the size of the Shori headquarters. Thanks to growing up in Chen Mansion and watching my grandmother manage her tenant farmers and businesses, in addition to the kitchen garden, I knew better what needed to be done.

Besides, I like things done right and systems running well. I'd realised very early on that it was easier to take on extra work than try to patch up somebody else's mistakes.

Ima's heart wasn't in housekeeping. She was a feminist: she believed she could do anything that a man could do. On the other hand, she didn't think much of other women. To be fair, Ima didn't think much of men either.

'You are the only one around here who knows how to cook.'

That wasn't true. But, thanks to Mrs Maki, I was familiar with the idea of *katei-ryori* or family cooking. That's the basic home-cooked comfort meal every Japanese child grows up on. It includes a main course, rice, miso soup, and a small side dish. As long as I served Colonel Fujiwara some variation on this, his temper was soothed enough that he didn't throw plates.

Anyone who grew up in old Singapore feels comforted by hot rice and a clear soup, with something green, salty or savoury on the side, something as simple as long beans fried with salt fish.

I wasn't even cooking fancy food. There was little enough to eat on the island, but there was always tapioca. Tapioca is the perfect food. It grows without too much trouble. It's filling, sustaining, and not delicious enough to tempt you to overeat.

But in the past, perhaps because tapioca was eaten in the poorest homes by people who would otherwise starve, food snobbery made people avoid it.

In the old days, people coming to my grandmother to borrow money were always asked to stay for a meal. And they were always surprised to find that the most powerful woman running the black market ate tapioca rice porridge with soy-pickled lettuce stalks like they did.

I'd tried these poor man's pickles on Colonel Fujiwara too, and he'd liked them.

'Dinner,' Colonel Fujiwara said. 'What's for dinner? Gah! You women are useless. Can't even answer a simple question.'

'There is some fish,' I said, 'very fresh *ikan kembong*. I can grill it. There's spinach from the garden for soup. And the soybean sprouts are ready to harvest.'

'Pickle them.' Colonel Fujiwara licked his lips. 'Are there any more snails?'

'I can send the house-boys out to collect some, sir.'

There were always plump, juicy snails to be found behind the outdoor latrines and on top of the papaya trees.

'Do that. I want them cooked with that dried chilli-soy sauce the way you did it last time.'

'Yes, sir.'

'And hurry up. Meals around here are getting later and later!'

There was talk and raised voices outside the door. I distinctly heard Joben yelling at the security guard, then the sound of a slap. I winced for the guard.

'I told them not to let him in.' Colonel Fujiwara looked pleased with himself.

'He's not going to like that.' I couldn't help smiling at the colonel's childish look of glee. 'He'll be angry with you and he'll tell Ima.'

'I'll say that the security got the orders wrong. Don't worry, I'll slip the boy at the door something for doing his job well.'

It was all very well for Colonel Fujiwara to use his men to keep Joben Kobata out of his rooms. As soon I left him, and before I had walked two steps away from the security guard stationed at his door, Joben Kobata grabbed me and slammed me against the wall.

'I knew it was you. You were in there with him. You gave the order to have me shut out. How dare you?'

I was used to Joben's bullying, but being slammed into the wall without warning was still a shock. I saw the guard outside Colonel Fujiwara's door look round and quickly return to standing at attention. 'I'm sorry,' I said.

You never argued with the Japanese. The only thing to do was apologise and go on apologising. If it turned out that they were wrong and you were right, you apologised for not explaining yourself better. Like I said, you had to know the rules of the game to survive.

I had learned the rules. I just had to figure out if this was worth surviving.

'I know you're spying for Hideki Tagawa. What's he doing in there? What's he telling that big-bellied Colonel Kusoyarō about me? You two are turning him against me, aren't you?' He slapped me again, hard enough to knock me to the floor, and was standing over me about to kick me when Ima appeared in the corridor. Had she heard her husband call her father an arsehole?

Ima was sweating and breathing fast. She looked furious. Her normally immaculate powdered white face was flushed red with dark smudges around her carefully drawn eyebrows. 'Fool! What are you doing?'

'Sorry,' I said, just to be on the safe side.

'None of your business, woman! This traitorous little slut has been spying on us. I have to find out what she told your father about me. Your father is refusing to see me. I know someone has been telling him lies about me.'

'I'm the one who told him to keep you out of his room when you've been drinking. It's on my orders. I don't want my father to see you like that. You're always barging into his office while he's having meetings and demanding that he authorise things for your friends. Do you know they suspect you of taking those papers that are missing from the official boxes?'

'So you're turning on me too! What kind of wife are you?' Joben snarled. But I could tell he was acting. He was more apprehensive than angry. Like all bullies, he only bullied the weak, and Ima was definitely stronger than he was. 'People are using me. Taking advantage of me. Those INA people come here demanding things of me. All they want is for me to get them favours from your big-shot father. They don't know I can't get in to see him myself. Or maybe they do know. Today I offered to buy a man a drink and he couldn't get out of here fast enough.'

Prakesh, I thought. At least he'd got out.

'That's because he saw you're already drunk. Don't you get it? Things have been going missing from the top-secret security boxes. I don't want you to come under suspicion. Can't you get

73

that into your stupid head? They're going to be investigating, no matter what my father says. This is bigger than he is.'

'Everyone knows the old man is going senile.'

I seized the opportunity to change the subject. 'I still have the camera you found for us to use. I can return it to you anytime, but it is safe in the press office storeroom at the moment. We have still not heard from Mr Takahashi. We will need more photographs soon, for the next issue. Mr Kobata says there must be photographs in every issue.'

'Mr Kobata' was standing right there but I hoped to remind him of his official position on the *Syonan Weekly* at least.

Ima took the hint. 'Consider the camera the property of the *Syonan Weekly* and learn to use it. You might as well make yourself useful. What photos were you expecting from that drunkard? Go and find some soldiers looking happy, find some locals eating and playing and that will do.'

'Scheming again, are you?' Joben turned on his wife. 'The old man already agreed that the only photos appearing in the paper – my paper – must be taken by the official photographer. Ryu Takahashi is the only official photographer. I am the only editor. Not this ugly, crooked slut.'

But Ima stood up to him. 'You don't know what you're talking about. You have a brain like a *tatami* mat!'

'Take the camera and get the photographs,' Ima ordered me, her eyes on her husband.

'What if Ryu comes and finds out she's taking pictures? He'll be furious! Where did you get that camera? Ryu will take it out on me!'

'Why are you so worried about what that man says?'

'I'm not! Only we have an agreement. We have a contract. I have to keep my word!'

'Rubbish. Your word is not worth the breath you waste on it. I should know that better than anyone else!'

I backed away, bowing. I managed to leave without either of them noticing me. I had snails to collect. But, first, I went by Joben's office to make sure he hadn't left Prakesh lying there with bullet holes in him.

Chinese New Year

———◆———

Life went on in this fashion till Chinese New Year.

Chinese New Year in 1944 was Tuesday, 25 January, three weeks after New Year on the Gregorian calendar. The Japanese celebrated it as Koshōgatsu, the first full moon of the new year. I had prepared the traditional *azukigayu*, rice porridge with sweet red azuki beans, and Colonel Fujiwara was in a good mood.

'When you finish eating you can go and visit your family,' Ima told me. 'If there are any leftovers you can take them with you. This day should be spent with family.'

'What about the decorations?'

Koshōgatsu was also the day when the New Year decorations were taken down and burned. The burning of the *kadomatsu* was supposed to release and appease the spirits and bring good luck to those taking part in the ritual.

'That's a family matter. I'll take care of it.' Despite her pragmatic nature, Ima was very superstitious when it came to some things.

'I've got some errands to run. I'll drive you to your grand-mother's house,' Hideki Tagawa said.

'Oh, but, Hideki-san, I'm counting on you to help to build the special bonfire!' Ima cried.

'I can take the tram,' I said quickly.

There was no point in reminding Ima that Hideki Tagawa was not part of the Fujiwara family any more than I was – or that I had no intention of going back to Chen Mansion to visit my grandmother.

I wondered if Ima was going to burn offerings at the stone shrine under the cannonball tree. I'd seen her looking at it with some interest after the servants had placed their offerings there.

'You can take any leftover food for your family,' Ima said again. 'No need to hurry back.'

'Thank you very much,' I said.

Growing up, I'd hated Chinese New Year at Chen Mansion. It was when all the most remote relatives and connections crawled out of their corners to visit. I saw them looking at my withered leg and whispering about the bad luck I'd brought to the family. Or, at least, I thought they did. Now I knew they'd been spreading even worse rumours about me – that I was the daughter my father had had with a Japanese whore.

It was ironic. I had once been shunned because people thought I was part Japanese. Now people looked askance at me because I was half Chinese. You just can't win.

Of course, given that we were in the middle of a war and I was alive with my fingers, toes and virtue intact, I had nothing to complain about. But I knew how precarious my position was, and I was sure Mimi hadn't finished making trouble.

Had she already been to Chen Mansion to try to blackmail them? I was afraid to ask. There had been something desperate about her that night. Maybe Ryu Takahashi had dumped her for someone else. I'd never liked Mimi and wouldn't lose any sleep over her, but desperate people do desperate things.

I washed a couple of banana leaves and cut them into rectangles to wrap the food in. Later, on the tram, with the cloth-wrapped banana-leaf packets on my lap, I was grateful to Ima. I wasn't going back to Chen Mansion, but wherever you went, these days, food was welcome.

And if I wasn't welcome, well, I would leave it at a temple where it would be distributed. Times were hard for everyone.

I didn't feel guilty for not taking the food to my grandmother because I knew things were not as bad at Chen Mansion as they were in some other places.

Salt, that most essential ingredient, was abundant in the sea that came right up to the breakwater at the end of the garden. For sweetening there was palm sugar made from the sap of coconut-flower buds. There were coconut trees everywhere, even though the Japanese considered coconuts a controlled commodity. Coconut milk made anything taste better, and coconut pulp could be ground to thicken gravy. And, though it was hard to find soy sauce for sale, fish sauce was easily made by fermenting fish too small to eat in barrels of sea water. Fishermen from coastal villages brought round their catch, with the dried shrimps, *ikan bilis* or split dried white anchovies, and *belacan*, shrimp paste, their wives made. Chen Mansion stood on enough land to produce a small but steady supply of vegetables, fruit, eggs, chickens, ducks and occasionally pork.

In the kitchen plots Shen Shen grew ginger, blue ginger, lemongrass, limes, kaffir limes, turmeric and chillies. I wondered what she and my grandmother were preparing for Chinese New Year, but I wasn't ready to see them yet. I didn't know if I ever would be.

Instead I was going to visit Corporal Wong Kan Seng's mother and grandmother in Pasir Panjang on the south coast. After that photograph I hadn't been able to get him out of my mind.

I had brought generous quantities of adzuki bean porridge and chicken stew with me. Even if they didn't want to see me, I hoped they would accept the food. Then I thought maybe the food alone would be enough of a surprise. Walking from the tram stop down the winding slope to their house, my spirit failed me. What could I say? 'I'm sorry your son is still missing'?

Maybe I could leave the food on their doorstep and sneak off. But I didn't want to go back to the Shori headquarters too early and interrupt the family ceremony. And I didn't want to be picked up by a patrol for loitering. I especially didn't want to be picked up with a seditious flyer on me.

I'd found one up at the tram stop. Like the others, it was so badly typed, with scrawled-on corrections, that it didn't inspire confidence. Inability to spell doesn't mean you can't be trusted, but carelessness shows you didn't bother to put in the effort.

By the time I reached the house I'd decided to leave the food and say I couldn't come in. But I found I wasn't the only one who'd thought of Corporal Wong's family.

'Oh, it's you. Hello there.' Ferdinand de Souza looked hugely glad to see me when Mrs Wong opened the door to me.

He was squeezed between the wall and one of the kitchen tables that took up most of the small front room. This was clearly where the two old women prepared and packed their *achar* for the market. Today, though, it was filled with little jars and dishes of New Year snacks. I needn't have worried about them being short of food.

'You two know each other, of course,' Mrs Wong said.

'Of course,' de Souza said.

'Of course,' I said.

I wished I'd come at any other time. For Wong Kan Seng's family, seeing two of his former colleagues at the same time must have been twice as bad as seeing only one.

I started to say, 'I can't stay. I have to get back to the Shori headquarters ...'

What was de Souza doing there at Chinese New Year anyway? He wasn't even Chinese!

'Please sit down,' Madam Ngoh, Corporal Wong's grandmother, said. She was sitting on a cane chair facing us. 'We so seldom have visitors, these days. Our boy's friends used to come over all the time in the old days. It's so good to have young people here again. When our boy gets back I'll tell him you came to see us.'

'Aunty, you were telling me about Kan Seng being scared of firecrackers when he was young,' de Souza prompted.

'Oh, no.' The old woman laughed fondly. 'He wasn't scared, even though he was only four years old. But he wouldn't let us or any of the neighbours set off fireworks because the dog was scared.'

I pulled out a chair and sat next to de Souza, facing her. It would be cruel to leave before she had talked about her Kan Seng.

'We've made all his favourite snacks – not the same, of course. So hard to get sugar, these days, but I use sugarcane water and my daughter says it tastes quite good. I can't wait for the British to come back so that we can get proper sugar again.'

'Careful,' de Souza warned. 'You can be arrested for such talk.' He was joking, but we all jumped when the door slammed open.

We weren't used to doors being shut. In the old days, front doors stood open to welcome fresh air, friends and neighbours.

'Oh, you two are here.' It was Prakesh Pillay. His arms were full of packages, which was why he'd shouldered the door open with a bang.

'Prakesh. So good to see you too. All our poor Kan Seng's best friends. He would be so happy that all of you arranged to come and see his ma and grandma today.'

Except, of course, we hadn't arranged anything. It was pure coincidence that we'd all turned up with food for our missing colleague's mother and grandmother.

So it was really sweet, shy Corporal Wong who'd brought us together again.

'So, how's it going, your building of the Greater Japanese Empire?' Prakesh sat down across from us.

I winced at the Prakesh-Pillay-style humour.

'How's the Indian National Army doing?' de Souza countered. 'How much of India have you freed from the British so far?'

They stared at each other. I hoped they weren't going to fight in the Wongs' front room.

'Try this bean rice.' Mrs Wong came in from the kitchen with a tray. 'Su Lin brought it with her. *Wah*, so long since I've seen such beautiful white rice.'

There was no white rice to be had on the market, of course. Even in Colonel Fujiwara's kitchen it was scarce. This white rice had been sent from Japan specially for the New Year.

'You pinched that from Colonel Fujiwara's table?' Prakesh asked.

'If it's good enough for the colonel it's good enough for me,' de Souza said.

'Might be poisoned.' Prakesh watched de Souza take a mouthful. 'They're very good at poisons. You'll feel very thirsty first. Then your throat will swell so you can't breathe, and your eyes pop out of your skull. I think they're starting to bulge already.'

'My eyes are always bulging. This stuff is good. Did they bring some special cook in from Japan to cook it for the big man?'

'I cooked it,' I said. 'And I didn't pinch it. They said I could have some to bring to my family.'

'Well, your family appreciates it,' Prakesh said. He took a big mouthful and chewed thoughtfully, then said, with his mouth full, 'Good stuff. Whoever is poisoning Colonel Big-shot is welcome to poison me too.'

We all ate. The adzuki bean rice tasted much better in the dingy room, which smelt of drying fish, than it had in the grand dining hall at the Shori headquarters.

'Have you seen the reports?' Mrs Wong joined us at the table after putting a small bowl on the altar with photographs of her late husband and father. 'It sounds hopeful, right?'

'The reports?'

'You haven't seen the flyers? The ones taped to lampposts and stuck between seats on the trams?'

'It's dangerous to be caught with them,' Prakesh said. 'You can be arrested just for picking one up.'

'I know. I try to be very careful. I bring them home to read to my mother, then take them back and leave them for somebody else to find. The Japanese don't want us to know what is happening in the outside world, but that just shows there's still hope.'

I wondered if Mrs Wong had left the flyer I'd just found at the tram stop. I shouldn't have brought it back into her house.

Memories and Revelations

———◆———

We all ended up staying longer than we'd meant to.

I saw Prakesh give Mrs Wong a delivery permit. 'It's authorisation to deliver vegetables to the Changi prison kitchen. If anyone stops you, show them this and say you collect rotten vegetables for the camp. Don't bribe them even if they ask. They can't stop you because of the INA chop.'

'How did you manage that?' I asked.

'I'm coordinating food supplies for the PoWs,' Prakesh said, 'and I see Mrs Wong and her mother outside the prison several times a week. Right, Aunty?'

'We just go to see whether anyone there has any news of our boy,' Mrs Wong said. 'It's not like we have anything else to do. But I don't know. If your suppliers have vegetables, why don't they just bring them over themselves? Why pay us to do it?'

'They can't spare the time,' Prakesh said. 'Not for such small amounts.'

'With this paper, nobody can stop you going around to ask about Kan Seng,' I told her.

Prakesh knew as well as I did – probably better – that there was little chance they would find Corporal Wong. But neither of us could make them stop hoping. The best we could do was try to keep them safe while they searched.

'Security patrols and checkpoints allow approved food providers to pass. If anybody stops you and asks what you're doing there, just show it to them,' I said.

'You're a good boy, Sergeant Pillay. Thank you very much. When my boy comes back he'll thank you himself for looking after his old mother. But we don't want you to get into trouble.'

'Then don't get yourselves into trouble,' Prakesh said. He was never comfortable with being thanked.

'You're going to pay them yourself, aren't you?' De Souza thumped Prakesh on the shoulder when Mrs Wong left us alone again. We could hear her in the back kitchen, explaining to her mother, who was preparing some complicated sweet soup for us, what Prakesh had proposed. 'Can I contribute?'

'Nah. I got a food budget. Not that it's anywhere near enough. I don't know, the way the Indian National Army treats Indians who didn't sign up – they're worse than the Japanese!'

'Because it's personal,' de Souza said. 'Like when the Japanese first moved in, they were particularly vicious to the people who looked most like them.' He jerked his chin towards me. 'The Chinese got the worst of it. Not just because they supported China against Japan. Hey, we all supported China against Japan. But because you look so much like them it messes with their minds. They think they're descended from the gods. So either you're descended from the gods too or maybe they're shaped from mud like you.'

'Half of Su Lin is descended from their gods, don't forget,'
Prakesh put in. 'I won't say which half.'

It was a half-hearted tease but enough of the old Prakesh that
I dared ask, 'What's wrong? What's bothering you?'

'You mean besides the occupation, starvation and genocide?'

'Yes,' I said.

Prakesh warned de Souza in a loud mock-whisper, 'Don't talk
to Su Lin about the invasion plans if it concerns India. She is
orang China. Her loyalty will always lie with China.'

'Like your loyalty will always lie with India, that country
you've never set foot in,' I said.

'Hey, I'm joking. That's just what everybody says. You should
know that.'

'"Everybody"?'

'"Everybody" also says not to trust you because you're that
Japanese big shot's mistress,' de Souza said.

'Don't you start, Ferdie. You know very well that that Japanese
big shot is my dead mother's cousin. Prakesh, what's worrying
you?'

Prakesh knew me well enough to see that I wasn't going to
let it go. 'It's the missing PoWs,' he said. 'I told you the other day.
There's still no sign of them. And now records show they were
transferred up-country. But I would have known if they were.
And I checked with Muar where they're supposed to have ended
up and nobody up there knows anything. INA says it's a civil
matter now.' He looked at de Souza.

'Outside my jurisdiction. I'm not just making excuses.
Everything beyond wiping my own backside is out of my jurisdiction. They only call me in when they need something translated.'

'You're a translator?' I couldn't help saying. 'You?'

'Hey, even I can understand what people are saying better than the Japanese. My Chinese dialects are shaky but my Malay is good enough to talk to most people. Sometimes I just tell them to nod and bow and say, "*Hai, arigatōgozaimasu*," first – always say "sorry" and "thank you" – so the Japanese officers know they're respectful and cooperative, and that I'll figure out what the officers want them to do and let them know later. At least it's better than the Japanese police getting angry and cracking their skulls because they don't understand.'

It was true. Anything was better than that. I remembered Joben's flare-up, Major Dewa's dead aide, and felt my bowels shiver.

'Did you hear about anything happening to one of Major Dewa's assistants?' I asked de Souza.

'Like what? There are so many of them. I think he wears them out.'

Nothing, then. If Major Dewa hadn't mentioned the shooting to his own people, I wasn't going to tell de Souza anything that might get him into trouble. Joben Kobata would get away with shooting a man.

'But why are you so worried?' de Souza asked Prakesh again. 'People are missing all over the place, not that it makes it any better. Like Corporal Wong. We're not going to find out what's happened to him by selling vegetables. I doubt we ever will.'

'I just have a bad feeling about it. I don't know why, but I do. And I don't understand why nobody else is bothered. Like everybody knows something I don't.'

'Not knowing is a big thing.' De Souza glanced in the

direction of the kitchen. Neither of the women had reappeared, but we could hear low chatter and food-preparation sounds.

'I hate that they're going to so much trouble for us,' I said. 'I should be in the kitchen with them. Preparing food and serving you men.'

'They see us as friends of his. They're doing it for Wong, not for us . . .'

'Hey, did you warn de Souza about your blackmailer?' Prakesh asked.

'What blackmailer?'

'I haven't had a chance yet.'

Mrs Wong had just appeared in the low doorway.

'Some woman's trying to blackmail Su Lin with evidence that she used to work at the Detective Shack,' Prakesh said.

'I must help my mother to the WC,' Mrs Wong said, and disappeared again. She had been a policeman's wife as well as a mother.

'What's he talking about?' de Souza asked.

'This woman turned up at the Shori headquarters with a photograph of the four of us in front of the Detective Shack,' I said. 'I think it was taken that day we went to Kallang for your birthday.'

'I remember. Oh, that *sup kambing*.' Prakesh rolled his eyes skywards. 'That soup was magic. It's from a secret recipe. No ordinary human knows what goes into it!'

'Coriander, fennel, cumin, star anise, cinnamon and mutton,' I said. 'Look, this is serious. We're standing together in front of the Detective Shack and she knows we were working there. She's got connections with important people. She might make trouble for us.'

'I'm being totally serious. That old *kambing* soup is gone for ever. Like our old lives.'

He was being melodramatic, but I knew what he meant. It wasn't just the soup that was gone. It was everything we'd taken for granted back then.

'Even if we didn't know where Uncle Razak's pushcart was that day, we could find it just by following the smell,' de Souza said. 'He used the toughest cuts. That's why his soup tasted so good. And by the time it was ready, the meat was melting soft.'

I could memory taste that spicy yellow-green soup, which had been boiled for hours. It was ladled hot from the vat into our bowls as we sat on low wooden stools by the drain and helped ourselves from tubs of torn coriander leaves and crispy fried shallots.

'Yes, I remember – but that's not the point. She's threatening to show it to people unless I pay her.'

Prakesh in the INA and de Souza in the Japanese-run police force were as vulnerable as I was to someone wanting to make trouble.

'We ate it with rice that day,' Prakesh said dreamily. 'Usually I have it with toasted bread but that day we had it with rice and it was so good. I think he gave us extra meat. I could hardly walk back to the office after that. I just wanted to lie down and sleep. She's probably making threats because she's desperate. Give her food if you can. Not money. It'll never stop.'

'He's right. She can't do anything to you without getting herself into trouble for having such a photograph. You gave me your brain that day,' de Souza said to me. 'There was brain and intestines in the soup as well as ribs and meat cubes. You said if I ate it on my birthday I'd be cleverer for a whole year.'

'Clever as a goat maybe!' Prakesh shrieked – just as he had that day. But he sobered instantly. 'It's never going to be the same again, is it?'

I suspected they weren't taking it seriously because Mimi was a woman. That attitude is one reason why I think women can do more damage than men.

But I could also totally understand them wanting to escape into the past.

'Look. We'll go back and have *sup kambing* again one day,' I said. 'When the war is over there will still be mutton. But we can't just remember the past. We've got to make sure we survive to have a future.'

'Wong Kan Seng was with us that day,' de Souza said. 'Even if the British come back, he won't.'

'The British won't be back,' Prakesh said. 'They have their own problems, and as far as they're concerned, we're part of the Japanese Empire now.'

'That's not true.'

Prakesh and I looked at de Souza in surprise.

'How do you know?'

'We've been ordered to confiscate wirelesses,' he said. He lowered his voice even though there was no one to hear. 'They wouldn't be so worried about us getting news if there wasn't something they don't want us to hear. America's come in on our side. Eisenhower's taken over operations in Europe. They're committed.'

'You've been reading those flyers,' I said. But I couldn't deny the thrill of hope his words gave me.

'Dreaming of the Americans saving us won't do any good,' Prakesh said. 'You don't know what you're talking about. What can the Americans do? If there's any sign they'll fight for us here, the Japanese will wipe us all out as a lesson rather than surrender. They won't lose face.'

'I kept one of the wirelesses I confiscated.' De Souza's voice dropped even lower. 'News from Australia, from the Allies. The tide is turning. The war is far from over, despite what the Japanese are telling us. I just want people to know. Especially those who need it most. Like the PoWs.'

'Propaganda,' Prakesh said. He looked at me. 'She makes up stuff like that every day, don't you? Just for the other side. Why do you want to give people false hope? Whatever happens in the West, they'll sort it out. They won't care what the Japanese are doing in the East.'

'They'll care about the Japanese here because of our harbour, even if not for us,' de Souza said. 'Without something to believe in, we might as well all die now. But even if we die, I would rather die with hope than in despair.'

That was true. De Souza's words had sparked a flare of wild hope in me. And something else that made me feel cold inside.

I pulled out the flyer I'd found at the tram stop outside. 'You made this, didn't you?' De Souza had always been hopeless at typing.

Prakesh actually shut his eyes, as though not seeing the flyer could make it disappear.

De Souza glanced at him, then nodded. 'Stupid, I know. But

I want people to have hope. It's worth hanging on.'

'I'm trying to make them move on with their lives and you're encouraging them to go on hoping long after there's no possible hope?' Prakesh turned on me. 'You shouldn't have picked it up. And you're crazy to bring it in here. Are you trying to give his police colleagues an excuse to arrest two helpless old women?'

De Souza looked at me. 'What did you think of it?'

'You were always a rotten typist.'

'I know. My fingers are too big. It's a hell of a job getting them done and it takes me ages. And I've got to do it in secret, but typing's so noisy. I do them when I stay back late to type up my own reports. With all those carbons it's no joke getting the keys down and I can't correct mistakes. I wish you could help me.'

'No!' Prakesh said. 'You're not going to get Su Lin involved in your suicide mission.'

'Su Lin? People need to know.'

'If you drag her into this I'll report you,' Prakesh said. 'I swear. Cross my heart.'

As they glared at each other, Corporal Wong's mother and grandmother came in, carrying more food.

'You are like a second family to our Kan Seng,' Mrs Wong said. 'So good of you to come and visit old women like us.'

'Cannot say no good things come out of the war,' Madam Ngoh said softly, in her Hakka dialect. 'Having you all here is a good thing. Otherwise we would never know what good friends our boy has.'

Now it was too late, I regretted I had spent so little time with Corporal Wong. He was not confirmed dead and possibly never would be. I didn't want to lose the few friends I had left.

The situation called for a polite response, praising their food and hospitality, and offering assurances that their boy would be home soon. Prakesh, the expert at flowery speeches, sat silent. So did de Souza, who would have said, done, given anything to make them feel better.

'It's not a good thing,' I said. 'This war is not a good thing. Corporal Wong disappearing is not a good thing. We all miss him.'

'I don't care if he comes back with no arms, no legs, no tongue. I just want him back alive!' Mrs Wong's voice was thick with tears.

'Now you've done it,' Prakesh said. He tried to sound sarcastic, but there were tears in his voice too.

Chinese New Year is supposed to be a time when you don't talk of bad things. But all those two women wanted to talk about was their precious lost boy. We spent the rest of our visit listening to their stories about Wong Kan Seng. How he'd been as a child: how bright, how promising, popular, and most of all how good to his mother and grandmother. Especially after the death of his father. He had always wanted to be a policeman like his father. He had been so thrilled to be promoted to the detective unit that he had brought home a soft-shell crab and three king prawns to celebrate.

'Happy memories are the worst. They remind you of how much you've lost,' Mrs Wong said.

'But we want to keep the memories,' Madam Ngoh said.

'Yes, Ma. Yes, of course I do.'

They needed to say these things and have them heard. I felt like we were attending the wake they would never be able to give Corporal Wong.

'This year will be a better year,' Madam Ngoh said. 'It cannot be worse.'

'Please don't say that, Aunty,' de Souza said. 'Mustn't challenge Fate. Quick! Eat some sweet cake to cancel it!'

The old woman smiled and opened her mouth for the forkful of *sugee* cake de Souza held up to her. 'Nice. Did your mother make it?'

'My mother?' De Souza pretended to be offended. 'I made it myself! My mother says I bake better than any of my sisters.'

'Very rare to find a man who can cook,' Mrs Wong said. We saw her struggle to shake off the pain of another happy memory. 'Your cake is very good. I would marry you if only you were thirty years older or I was thirty years younger.'

'What difference does age make when any of us can die tomorrow?' her old mother said. 'I'll marry him if you don't want him!'

We all laughed at de Souza's embarrassment, even de Souza.

Negatives and Developments

———◆———

'You know that business of de Souza's that I don't know about, that you're not getting involved in? Don't. It's not worth the risk. Good to see you both again. Take care. Goodbye.'

Prakesh Pillay left us, walking fast away from us up the steep trail to the main road. In the old days he would have walked me to the tram stop, making the wait seem shorter with his jokes and quips. In fact, in the old days, they would both have ridden with me back to my stop before going their separate ways, just so we could talk longer.

I didn't care. Anyway, I was still angry that the two of them weren't taking the Mimi threat more seriously.

We'd all left the Wongs at the same time, walking towards the tram stop. I had a permission slip to visit my family in the east and I assumed de Souza and Prakesh had their own passes. But, still, it was best that a passing patrol didn't see you dawdling on the roadside.

Things might have eased up, but all you needed was one soldier having a bad day.

'Are you going back to Chen Mansion?'

I didn't want to tell de Souza I hadn't been to Chen Mansion since I'd moved into the Shori headquarters. Chinese New Year would have been a good time to make up differences, but I wasn't ready.

I kept my eyes on Prakesh's retreating figure as though I hadn't heard the question. 'He's changed, hasn't he? He doesn't flirt any more.' The old Prakesh would have flirted with Corporal Wong's mother and grandmother and they would have loved it.

I remembered Le Froy saying, 'Pillay flirts like other men smoke or drink. It's comfortable and familiar and makes him feel good, and it gives him something to do with his mouth and hands. You mustn't take him seriously.'

Had Le Froy been worried I might take Sergeant (at the time) Pillay too seriously? Just thinking of Le Froy triggered a physical spasm of fear and pain in my guts. Where was Le Froy now? How was he? I bent over and clutched my belly.

'What's wrong?' de Souza asked.

'Nothing.' He looked unconvinced, so I added, 'Just a cramp. Sitting too long. I miss the old Prakesh. Why is he so negative?'

'He's trying to be positive. He thinks the British are gone for good and he's trying to work within the new system. He's afraid everything's falling apart before it's had a chance to get started. Did he tell you about the INA's missing money? He's afraid if he doesn't find out what happened to it, the Japanese will blame it on the Indians in the team. And he's even more upset by how the Indians who've signed up with the INA are treating the PoWs who refuse to.'

'I can't believe the British are gone for ever.' I thought, again, of Le Froy in prison, then of Dr Leask somewhere in the jungle up-country and the sweet-natured, foul-mouthed Scotswoman, Mrs Shankar, the doctor's wife and Parshanti's mother, in prison as an enemy alien. 'They've still got people here. They wouldn't abandon all of them. All of us.'

'The old Prakesh is still there underneath. Where are you going now? What time do they expect you?'

'I don't know. It's later than I thought. I should be getting back.'

But I didn't want to go to the Shori headquarters. I could still remember the shock on the face of Major Dewa's aide when Joben shot him. Had that young man made plans for the New Year? Did he have family in Japan? I could still hear Colonel Fujiwara say, 'Clean up the mess,' followed by the second shot. None of us was safe, no matter how much we seemed part of the Japanese system.

Prakesh had probably seen even worse things that he hadn't told us about.

'Please help me with the flyers.'

If it had been anyone other than Ferdinand de Souza I would have shown him the same finger that Diogenes the philosopher showed Demosthenes the orator in the fourth century.

Yes, a Mission School education can come in useful in real life.

I knew de Souza meant well. I even believed his flyers were doing good. I didn't want to put myself at greater risk. 'No. I just want to keep my head down and stay away from that woman and her photograph!'

'So, if she never bothers you with it again, you might help me?'

'How? It's hopeless. If you try to confiscate the photograph it'll just make things worse for you as well as me.'

All I wanted was never to see Mimi Hoshi again.

I walked away from him without looking back. So, despite our closeness, the Chinese New Year reunion/wake ended badly.

Though Prakesh had stormed off earlier, I thought I saw him get onto the tram after me. There was such a crush of people that I couldn't be sure, but it would be like Prakesh Pillay to apply his stalking skills to make sure I was safe. Even if he wasn't talking to me.

I didn't like him knowing I wasn't going back to Chen Mansion. But at least he couldn't ask me about it.

And there was comfort in knowing someone was watching out for me. For now, at least.

I wondered if we three would ever again sit down together to a meal. Would de Souza ever forgive me? I knew he was disappointed in me. But I couldn't go on living up to other people's expectations of me.

When I finally got back up the hill to Shori headquarters, the grass was still damp from the light shower I'd been caught in.

The air was already warming and I could see mist rising above the trees as the water evaporated, but it was still pleasantly cool.

The security guards at the gate called New Year greetings instead of checking my papers as I walked past. I didn't go through the front gate but walked around the side of the house and let myself in at the back gate as usual. The guard stationed there was supposed to check every person coming in, but he was having a smoke with a couple of the house-boys and waved me through.

I could hear voices in the kitchen. The servants were back from their family visits too. They should have been preparing dinner but their energy was high from their outing and I could hear them exchanging stories and laughing.

They were all so young.

Soon Ima would come down from the house and shout at them. I was surprised she wasn't already in there, yelling. Now, in the hour before dinner time, was when Colonel Fujiwara and Joben smoked and drank with visitors, and Ima took her daily exercise finding fault with the staff.

Wanting to postpone going back in, I decided to cut some bamboo sprays for the house. Whether you are Chinese or Japanese, a giant panda or a giant rat, bamboo is good luck. Or, at least, good eating. If I had gone straight through the covered walkway from the outside to the inside kitchen, that would have been the end of things as far as I was concerned. But I wanted to think over what de Souza had told me. I'd told him I wouldn't help, but we both knew that wasn't the end of it.

An arrangement of bamboo and cannonball flowers would make Ima happy and buy me some time. And maybe if I put a flower in the stone shrine it would give me some idea of what to do.

On the grass beyond the bamboo patch I saw what looked like a long black snake on the grass. No, it was too flat to be a snake. A long trail of shiny black liquid? Moving towards it, I saw a crowd of birds on the grass beneath the cannonball tree. They made me think of Mr Meganck, the ardent naturalist who'd been tutor to the former British governor's young sons.

Mr Meganck had been a keen birdwatcher and naturalist.

Though an *ang moh*, he'd taught me, and anyone else who would listen, more than I'd ever needed to know about local birds, bugs and other wildlife. This evening gathering of birds on the grass instead of up in the trees would have intrigued him. It was Mr Meganck who'd told me the collective noun for crows was 'murder'.

There was a murder under the cannonball tree, then. A murder of crows.

Mind your own business. Just go into the house and don't say anything, the smart part of my brain said. It's nothing to do with you.

I went closer to look, of course. I've always been more curious than smart. It looked as if the birds were feeding on something. I noticed a slight bad smell even from where I was standing, but the ripe fruit of the cannonball tree always stinks when it falls and cracks. At least, it smells bad to us humans. Birds, bats and rats love the mushy red pulp inside the hard shell. And if the cannonball tree was growing close enough to a river or canal, even otters and crocodiles came for their share.

It was the smell of fresh meat just going off. Not yet rotten but on the edge of it, like the area around the butchers' stalls when the blood is turning black and the rats have already carried off the best of the gristle. If a stray dog or cat had wandered in to die, I would have to clear it away. If it was just a couple of cannonball fruits or a dead squirrel I could chuck it over the fence into the jungle where they could feast in peace.

I headed towards the birds under the tree.

There was more of the dark, translucent strip I'd seen. Camera film? A long strip of camera film, unrolled from its cartridge. Any photographs on it would be ruined. But what was it doing there?

I picked up the end and started rolling it up on my fingers. Maybe something could be saved. Had Ryu Takahashi finally turned up and got into a fight with Colonel Fujiwara or Joben Kobata? Had someone thrown the film at someone else?

The other end of the strip was caught on the heel of a woman's shoe.

I knew at once it was a woman's shoe because the pale thing sticking out of it was a woman's foot.

Holding my breath, I limped closer to look. There was a foot and an ankle in a saggy ripped stocking beneath flies that ignored me and feasted on. And attached to it was the rest of a dead woman.

She was lying on her back with a leaf across part of her face. I reached out to pull it off, feeling ridiculously that it might bother her. The back of my fingers touched cold, bloated skin. For a moment I was afraid I was going to vomit but I forced myself to keep breathing. This was no time to faint. Especially now I saw it was Mimi that the crows had been feeding on.

It looked like the crows weren't the only murder there.

Dead Mimi

———◆———

It was clearly too late to do anything for her. The cold bloat of liquid under swollen skin was final. There was no more Mimi, only dead meat.

I should call for help, I thought. I should shout or something. But I just stood there staring at the two horrible holes in her face that would have been looking at the sky if the eyes and eyelids hadn't been eaten clean down to the smooth skull bone.

Animals always go for the soft tissue first.

Standing looking at her, I felt cold. As if death and decay had passed from her through my fingertips to the rest of me. The good food I had enjoyed so recently rose sour into my throat as my stomach threatened to expel it.

There was a large, cracked cannonball fruit about a foot from her head. It must have dropped and hit her. Not murder, then. Everybody knows the dangers of standing under a cannonball tree. That was stupid of her. But what was she doing here? How had she even got into the Shori headquarters gardens?

Had she been waiting for me? Who had let her in?

And why here? I was the only person who came to this corner of the garden to get cannonball flowers for the house, but how could she have known that? The servants occasionally came to burn something in the shrine bin, but otherwise this area was deserted. It was why I liked coming here. It was hidden from the driveway guards by the garage and from the house by the bamboo grove.

Mimi could not have got past the guards at the front gate, and only approved delivery personnel with passes were allowed through the back entrance. There was barbed wire on top of the fencing, but could she have cut her way through it? From what I could see, the fencing that separated us from the jungle beyond looked undisturbed. Beyond it, the primary rainforest stretched all the way across Bukit Timah up north to the Strait of Johor. It would be almost impossible for someone like Mimi to get through the tangle of vines and undergrowth, especially in those shoes and stockings.

I looked at the large cracked cannonball fruit. It was evidence, wasn't it? Like the other fruits at my eye level still growing on long stalks springing directly from the trunk, it looked as if it weighed eight or nine pounds. And falling from any height would add force to the impact ...

My brain started calculating. Thanks to my time and training at the Detective Shack, putting observations together was automatic. Otherwise it's all too easy to bend what you see to fit in with what you think happened.

Something didn't fit. Something was wrong.

This was the only large cannonball tree on the property. The others, growing closer to the fencing, were not yet tall enough to be dangerous. It takes about a year for each cannonball fruit to mature before it crashes to the ground, with an ear-splitting thud, and bursts.

Looking upwards from the huge cannonballs at my eye level, I saw that the fruits growing higher up on the trunk were much smaller. Those high enough to drop with any impact were still tiny. I could barely see them among the flowers growing around them. There were at least two feet of the cannonball flowers that Ima liked having in the house for the fragrance. That was why this cannonball tree was not considered dangerous. Weren't the only fruits large enough to do harm growing too far down to cause damage?

But I was only delaying what I knew I ought to do. Mimi was dead and I couldn't do anything to help her now. What I could do was help myself. I had found her before anyone else, so—

'Just go and look,' I ordered myself.

If the photo was still on her, I could burn it in the prayer bin by the stone shrine. I would make it up to the tree spirits later with incense sticks or sugar cakes or whatever. Or I could tear it up and push it through the fence into the bright dense primary jungle beyond. The bugs and damp would soon take care of it. But first I had to lift her skirt and find the folder.

Any fruit large and heavy enough to kill her must have had help from someone ...

I should grab this chance to see if the photograph she had used to try to blackmail me was still on her.

I ought to be grateful that I had found her and look for the envelope under her skirt ...

But I didn't move. I've never been very good at obeying orders.

How long had she been there, anyway?

I knew it wasn't possible to establish time of death precisely. Especially not after all the wildlife had feasted on her. But I knew how rigor mortis affects animals and I had learned from Dr Shankar that humans are affected in much the same way. A dog or cat takes longer than a chicken or duck, but not as long as a wild hog, to go stiff. Human beings come somewhere between pigs and dogs. Muscles lock into place, beginning with the small muscles in the head, the eyelids and the jaw, moving on to fingertips, neck, and then larger muscles. And rigor mortis sets in for eighteen to thirty-six hours before dissipating. But she couldn't have been there for as long as that. Surely someone would have noticed her.

I held my breath and took a step forward – but I had left it too long. Before I could touch her—

'Hey!'

I pulled back quickly and tried to look shocked. It wasn't difficult.

'Who's that?' It was Joben, coming from the direction of the house. 'What happened?'

What was Joben Kobata doing out here? He went right up to the body and stared with a hungry fascination.

'She's dead.' I gestured at the cracked fruit. 'Maybe the cannonball...'

'Well, don't just stand there like a fool. Go and get someone – get help. Go right away! Go!' He didn't take his eyes off the body.

I was grateful to go, but wished I had moved faster and searched her.

A new idea occurred to me. What if Mimi hadn't come alone? What if whoever had brought her in was still somewhere in the compound?

I stopped and looked back. I wanted to warn Joben not to move the body until the police – or the *kenpeitai*, or whoever was in charge of such things now – came to examine the scene.

And I saw Joben had lowered his trousers and was urinating on the body. His back was to me and my eyes fixed on what looked like a large blue-grey bruise, the shape of Australia, spread across his buttocks.

Talking on Tape

———◆———

As soon as I entered the kitchen I ran into Ima and grabbed her, forgetting all protocol and manners. 'She's dead! I just found her body! She's dead under the cannonball tree – she shouldn't be here. I don't know how she got in! Joben's there – he said to get help–'

Ima was wonderful in an emergency. She immediately understood and cut through to the most important point: 'Does my father know yet? Is anyone with him?'

'No. I don't know. I only just saw–'

Without waiting to hear more, Ima rushed off, heading for Colonel Fujiwara's office. I heard her shouting to the security guards to call for back-up and come with her.

Of course that was the right thing to do. Colonel Fujiwara was the most important person on the island and his safety was paramount.

I felt pretty much useless. If the Shori headquarters had a protocol for finding dead bodies in the garden, I hadn't been briefed.

'Go on preparing the vegetables,' I told the servant girls, who were staring wide-eyed. I didn't want them to get involved in case the *kenpeitai* came to drag me away. 'You know what to do.'

I went outside to wash my hands, scooping water out of the rain barrel and scrubbing hard. My fingers were trembling and there was a heavy throbbing in the back of my head. I sank into a crouch on the stack of charcoal, tucking my head into my arms. The abrupt swing from happiness to horror left me too drained to care about the ash stains on my clothes.

Crazed thoughts pounded at my brain: they would suspect me, wouldn't they? Ima would remember seeing Mimi in the kitchen with me. Worse, I could still smell the cold bloated meat that had once been Mimi on my fingers. It was as if the odour had seeped into my skin. And I'd hated her and wished she would disappear from this planet or at least this island so I'd never have to see her again. But I hadn't meant her to die like this.

'Is Miss Chen here?'

'Out at the back. Washing.'

'Still?'

'She hasn't moved for almost two hours.'

I hadn't realised how long I'd been hunched out there, but when I looked up to see Hideki Tagawa standing next to the earthenware jars of pickles and salt fish, every part of me ached, especially my neck. My legs had gone to sleep and wouldn't support me when I tried to stand.

'Su Lin?' Hideki Tagawa caught my arm to steady me, 'Are you all right?' His voice was professional but his eyes were kind and concerned. 'You found that dead woman?'

'I didn't kill her.'

'Don't answer questions you haven't been asked. Major Dewa is in Colonel Fujiwara's office. He wants to see you.'

Hideki Tagawa knocked and announced us. When Colonel Fujiwara told us to enter, I saw three other men in the office with him, Major Dewa and Joben Kobata. The third was Ferdinand de Souza, in his auxiliary police uniform.

'I believe you already know Corporal de Souza,' Hideki Tagawa said.

'Ferdie!' I said, my mouth moving faster than my brain. 'I'm so glad you're here! It's so terrible. How did you know?'

'Miss Chen,' de Souza said, 'I believe you are the one who first found the body. Major Dewa is heading the investigation and would like to ask you some questions.'

He didn't have to say any more. He wasn't there as my friend, but as Major Dewa's new aide. And he wasn't pleased that Hideki Tagawa knew we were friends. I wanted to tell him that Hideki Tagawa knew a lot more than he thought, but that probably wouldn't have helped.

But I was still very glad to see him. I hadn't expected to see him again so soon. I only hoped Joben wouldn't shoot him too.

The last man stood in the corner and spoke to no one. He had a large recording machine on a table in front of him, with two rolls of tape turning slowly. He also had a notepad in front of him. He looked at us when we came in and made several marks on his pad. They looked like rapid scribbles but were probably some kind of shorthand.

I learned that he, rather than de Souza, was Major Dewa's new aide.

Every time I saw the man, he never talked and always had his huge tape-recording machine running. Major Dewa didn't introduce him, but Joben called him Magnetophon Man and that was how I came to think of him too.

I looked at his scribbles but they made no sense to me. It must have been some kind of shorthand he'd worked out for himself. He wore very thick spectacles and I suspected his eyesight was poor. Once his bag was open, I saw he had a row of magnifying glasses inside.

He never spoke, but nodded when I put a cup of tea beside him. I didn't see him drink it but later the cup was empty. After that I always put a cup of tea and a rice cake or a *mochi* by him when I served the others.

They always disappeared, along with him and his Magnetophon machine.

'I think the major cut out his tongue to make him the perfect assistant.' Joben had seen me looking at Magnetophon Man. 'Major Dewa came to investigate the death himself – apparently the chief of the Police Investigation Bureau has nothing more important to do than investigate accidental deaths. What are you going to do? Arrest the tree?'

'We must give full attention to every incident in the Shori headquarters,' Major Dewa said. 'After all, it is the seat of government.'

'Of course,' Colonel Fujiwara said, won over. Or he might have been putting Joben down. Since the shooting in the office, there had been a coolness between the two of them.

'I've examined the scene,' Major Dewa said. 'The woman's death was clearly an accident she brought upon herself by standing under the dangerous tree. I have ordered the body removed.'

I suspected he was superstitious enough to fear disturbing any tree spirits if he did it himself.

'Anyway, what is more important is finding out who she is and how she got into the grounds.'

'Did you know the dead woman?' Colonel Fujiwara demanded, before I had finished my belated bow to him.

I started to answer, but before I could say anything, he continued, 'Do you know how she got in? Did she come here to meet you? Did you let her in? What did she pay you?'

'No, sir. I was out all day. I just got back—'

'I've told you a hundred times already,' Joben Kobata said. 'We found her together. That dead bitch is a stranger here. Nobody knows her.'

Major Dewa ignored him. 'Was it a fight over a man? Did you tell that woman to come here and kill her?'

'No, sir.' I noticed a low whirring. Both tape-recorders were on and Magnetophon Man was scribbling in his notebook.

'Don't be ridiculous!' Ima Kobata bustled in, pushing past the policeman, who put out a hand to stop her, and went to stand behind Colonel Fujiwara's chair. 'How could Su Lin have killed her? She was in the house with me. Dinner was being prepared. Besides, you know how dangerous those trees are. People are getting killed by them all the time.'

'Mrs Kobata, we agreed that we will speak to you one at a time.' Major Dewa had obviously already had trouble with Ima.

'We need to question everybody in the household who was here at the time.'

'You obviously don't realise we have much work to do. We don't have time to sit around all day talking. It was clearly an accident. Stop trying to make yourselves look important.'

Major Dewa seemed suddenly uncertain. I glanced at Ferdinand de Souza. His face was impassive and he made a point of not looking at me.

'We believe the dead woman was a relation by marriage of Miss Chen's,' Major Dewa said. 'We have to know why she came here in search of Miss Chen.'

I wondered if de Souza had told him Mimi was my aunt-in-law's sister. Otherwise how had they managed to dig up that fact so quickly?

'That dead woman was your relative?' Ima said to me. She looked shocked. I was right: she hadn't remembered meeting Mimi in the kitchen that night. Ima was rude to so many people in a day she must have found it impossible to keep track of them all.

'The dead woman was also a close and intimate acquaintance of one Ryu Takahashi. Who is one of the contributors to your paper, Miss Chen. When was the last time you spoke to him?'

'I haven't seen him for some time,' I said. 'I've been waiting to get pictures from him. He was supposed to come here for two events over New Year but he didn't turn up.'

'Do you use Ryu Takahashi's photographs in the *Syonan Weekly* because you have a special relationship with him also?'

'No!'

'Su Lin is only the assistant editor of the *Syonan Weekly*,' Ima said. 'My husband is the editor. It is the editor who decides whose photographs to use.'

'That's right,' Joben Kobata said. 'That's how it's always been. Any objection?'

'Who told you that woman was a relative of Miss Chen and working with Ryu Takahashi?' Ima asked.

'That's confiden—' Major Dewa started to say.

'Spit it out,' Colonel Fujiwara told him.

'Miss Mimi Hoshi offered to provide us with information on certain members of this household that she had connections with.'

Joben swore loudly.

'What information?' Colonel Fujiwara asked.

'Unfortunately my predecessors didn't think it worth paying for.'

'This is wasting our time,' Colonel Fujiwara said. 'The girl doesn't know anything. None of us knows anything. This woman got in somehow. That's what you should be trying to find out.'

'And that tree is dangerous and should be cut down,' Joben said.

It struck me that no one had mentioned what I'd seen Joben doing to Mimi's body.

'That tree has religious significance for the locals,' Ima said. 'There's a shrine underneath it. And you could say that by killing the woman the tree was protecting the Shori. It did a better job than the police!'

'The fencing around the Shori headquarters is old. It was put in place by the British,' Major Dewa said. 'It is rotting in parts. The jungle perimeter is not our responsibility. It is impossible to patrol the jungle. We have patrols and checkpoints on all the roads.'

'The fencing can't even keep out the monkeys!' Ima said. 'How do you think it's going to stop rebels and assassins?'

'She can't have come through the jungle,' I said. I knew the jungle trails around Chen Mansion well enough to find fruit in season. Some people were at home in the primary rainforest. But from what little I knew of Mimi I felt sure she was not among them. 'She can't have come through the front gate because there people are admitted by appointment only, and identity papers are checked and recorded. She must have come through the back gate.'

This was the service gate that led to the kitchens. It was where the rubbish bins were taken out and deliveries were brought in. A sentry stood there too, but it was commonly known that this was the more relaxed entrance. Even without an appointment, someone who had had a particularly fine catch of fish, crabs or eels or who had come across contraband liquor might try their luck there. Even if the inhabitants of the big house weren't interested, the house-boys might be willing to point them towards someone who would be.

'What are you talking about?' Colonel Fujiwara asked.

'Is there a record of deliveries?' Hideki Tagawa asked, startling everyone who had forgotten he was there. Even Magnetophon Man looked up, studied him, and made a couple of quick notes. 'Ima, you sign off on all the deliveries, right? Who is responsible for recording delivery times?'

'The servants are supposed to, but—'

'You have the delivery book for today?' Major Dewa said. 'Bring it to me now. That's how she must have got in. No one can just walk in. One of the delivery people must have smuggled her through. We'll check all the deliveries that came today.'

114

'I don't see how we're going to check with all the delivery people,' Ima said. 'All right, if you think it's important enough, I'll go and look at the book.'

But the book wasn't in its usual place on top of the rice bin.

Don't Sit Under the
Cannonball Tree

———◆———

'Su Lin, you know I wouldn't tell on you if you did kill her – but I want to know.'

'What?'

'She's the one who tried to blackmail you with the photograph, right?'

'Ferdie, are you crazy?'

'Just checking you're not, that's all. So you didn't take that photo from her?'

I shook my head. 'You didn't find it on her?'

'No.'

I was lucky the Japanese hadn't taken Mimi seriously when she'd tried to sell them information. They still weren't taking her seriously. It wasn't her death that concerned them so much as how she'd got into the grounds. Somehow their security had failed them. Still, she hadn't managed to penetrate the house.

'Whoever killed her probably has it.'

De Souza had been given permission to walk me around the death scene after Mimi's body was taken away. 'Just to make sure there are no more dangerous fruits about to fall.'

It was really quite safe. The cannonball fruits grow directly off the tree trunk, so it's a lot less dangerous than sitting under a durian or a cempedak tree.

'She must have been really desperate,' I said. 'I didn't know she'd already tried to report my family and been ignored. You don't really think I killed her, do you?'

'No. The gate guards saw you come in. And I know where you were all afternoon. You wouldn't have had the time. I'd barely got back to quarters when I saw the boss calling for a driver to take him to Shori headquarters. The regulars were off, so I said I'd do it. You sure you're all right?'

'The major thinks it was an accident, doesn't he?'

De Souza looked at the huge stinking cannonball fruits growing on stalks off the trunk. The fragrant flowers above were not enough to counteract the smell that lingered down here.

'Maybe it really was just an accident.' He looked at the stone shrine under the tree. 'Or the spirits here are trying to to protect you.'

'You don't believe that. You're supposed to be Catholic.'

'And you're supposed to be what? Christian-Taoist-Buddhist-Zen with a bit of Shinto ... Besides, "There are more things in heaven and earth, Horatio, Than are dreamed of in your philosophy."'

'Please don't joke about it.'

It didn't feel right to joke about this tree. Hindus, Buddhists and Taoists all credited the tree with religious significance while locals prayed to its snake spirit for protection and used juice from its leaves to treat stomach upsets, skin diseases and malaria.

At times like this it was easy to believe the superstitions hadn't come from nowhere.

'Look, Little Sister,' de Souza put an arm around my shoulders and squeezed, 'anything evil here didn't come out of the tree. It came out of that woman. And she's dead now. They'll find out how she got in and that will be an end of it.'

'No, it won't. What if the photograph is still on her? She had it in a package tied around her middle the last time I saw her. If they find it, they'll know she came to see me. They'll see you and Prakesh in the photo too.'

They would pick me if they needed a convenient scapegoat.

'Even if they hadn't found it yet, they will once they examine her in the morgue.'

'The photograph isn't on her.'

'How do you know?'

'Because I do. Someone pissed all over her, though.'

'Oh, my goodness – I didn't tell you what Joben did when he saw the body ...'

'Maybe it's some weird Japanese ritual. Or maybe he just wets his pants when he's scared. I used to, when I was a kid and had nightmares. But if you tell anybody I'll deny it. Look, they'll find that delivery book, find whoever she bribed to get her in, and that will be that. Don't look for more trouble.'

'Unlike you,' I managed to say.

'I won't pressure you. But if you ever change your mind about helping me, let me know.'

I was so relieved Mimi hadn't had the photograph on her when she died. After de Souza left, I went back to my room. That's one good thing about sleeping in a storeroom off your office space. Close the door behind you and you're in your bedroom. I curled up on my mattress and closed my eyes.

'When was the last time you saw Ryu Takahashi?'

The disadvantage of sleeping in a storeroom off your office space is that the door only locks from the outside.

Hideki Tagawa stuck his head in and looked around the tiny space as though there might room to hide something in there. 'Why are you still sleeping here? I told Ima to get you a bedroom in the main house.'

'I like it. It's close to my work. Anyway, what's happening? Have they found out how she got in?'

'The delivery book is missing.'

'It's probably fallen behind the rice bin, or been left with the dried mushrooms again.'

'No, it's not.'

He stood against the door frame and nodded to me to sit down. I'd stood up automatically when he came in, but he knew it hurt my back to stand for too long.

'Ima says it's probably been misplaced and it'll turn up. Do you know what's happened to it?' he asked.

'I think someone's hidden it because they're afraid they'll get into trouble for not recording all the deliveries.'

'How well did you know the dead woman?'

It was a stupid thing, but I couldn't help wondering whether Hideki Tagawa would kill to protect me. 'Not well at all. Her sister married my uncle, but they didn't have much to do with each other. Neither did I, with either of them. I know she was close to Ryu Takahashi and she said he sent her—'

'What's that? When?'

'Didn't Ima say? Mimi came here on New Year's Eve. She said she had a message from Ryu Takahashi for Joben. But Joben was busy with all the meetings.'

'You may like to know that Joben Kobata told Major Dewa you insist on using only Takahashi's photographs in the *Syonan Weekly*. He says Ryu is a ladies' man and has won you over.'

I didn't bother to answer that.

'I know that Mimi being married to your uncle doesn't make you best friends. But did you know that she was living with Takahashi? He called her his assistant. But they haven't been seen together for a while.'

'Ryu Takahashi hasn't sent in photographs for a while either. And he didn't appear for the official shoot.'

'Takahashi is the artistic sort. Unpredictable. Unreliable. He's going to be in big trouble after this,' Hideki Tagawa observed.

'He conveniently disappeared before Mimi came to try to blackmail Joben and me. No doubt so he could say he knew nothing about it. I'm sure he was behind Mimi's blackmail scheme. Where else could she have got those photographs if not from him?'

'What photographs?'

Oh.

He waited. I waited.

'Ask Ima,' I said. 'I didn't really see it. Mimi had a photograph she wanted to show Joben. But wait – what if they had a fight and broke up? Then Mimi might have stolen a bunch of photographs from Ryu. What if he found out and got angry with her? What if he followed her here and wanted to stop her showing the photos to Joben? Did the police talk to him? What does he say?'

'They're still looking for him. That man has a history of disappearing whenever there are bills to be paid. Anyway, it's officially an accident. The investigation is over. The fencing will be inspected and reinforced if necessary. It ends here. Ryu has friends in powerful positions who don't want his name connected with this. But you must be careful.'

'Me? Why?'

'Because whoever killed Mimi might have been waiting for you. If she was standing outside in semi-darkness it would have been easy to mistake her for you. And we all know you're the one who gets flowers from that tree and tends the shrine. Has anyone threatened you recently? Has anyone said anything or sent anything to the paper that might be seen as a threat?'

I couldn't tell whether he was trying to comfort or frighten me. 'So you don't think it was an accident.'

'I didn't say it was an accident. I said it's officially an accident. You don't agree?'

A good Chinese girl would have kept her mouth shut. 'The cannonball fruit that killed Mimi was a big one. It had to be. The tree is only about twenty years old. The only really big fruits are growing too low down on the trunk to have that much impact when they drop. I know that because when I go out to collect the cannonball flowers I have to climb up the stepladder to where the flower stalks are, higher up. Highest are the leaves and new buds, then the flowers, and any of the fruits forming up there are still too small to do any damage. Even if they had fallen before ripening they could not have cracked her head open like that.'

Hideki Tagawa studied me and didn't answer. I couldn't even tell if he agreed with me.

'Look, when I saw Mimi last week she was scared of something.' I'd only realised this on looking back. Maybe I'd known it then but not wanted to admit it because I didn't want to help her. I didn't want to get involved or have anything to do with her. Had my dislike of Mimi got her killed? I felt guilty for not acknowledging she had been frightened and desperate.

'What if she ran away from Takahashi and he came after her, found her and killed her here?'

'Unlikely.' Hideki Tagawa shook his head.

''Why? Mimi might have tried to blackmail him too. Maybe that's why he's been hiding. He didn't know who she'd already talked to. Then he followed her here and killed her before she got a chance to tell his secret to Joben.'

Hideki Tagawa shook his head. 'You've worked with the man. Do you think he's capable of it?'

'He's Japanese. The Japanese are very good at killing.'

'What happens in war is different. We've moved on from that now.'

'Look at Joben. That night when he just shot—'

Hideki Tagawa lifted one finger to remind me that that was not to be spoken of. 'Joben Kobata is a different case.'

'Because he's the colonel's son-in-law?'

'Because he's a different case.'

'It's more likely than someone killing her in mistake for me. She was much taller, much more fashionably dressed, and she had two straight legs.'

'Everyone knows it's dangerous to stand under a cannonball

tree.' Hideki Tagawa turned to leave. 'Not everybody knows it's dangerous to talk too much.'

'Somebody killed her,' I said. 'She wasn't killed by the cannonball tree. If you really believed that, you wouldn't be afraid that somebody wanted to kill me and got her instead. That's why you came to check on me, isn't it?'

'I'd just like to be sure that that wasn't the case.'

'But how do you think she got into the garden?' I asked. 'Did she come through the jungle and cut through the fence?' I remembered what had been left of Mimi. Those shoes and stockings had suffered less damage than the rest of her. 'She didn't come through the jungle in those shoes.'

'That's not your problem. They'll make sure nobody else gets in.'

Of course the servants said that the cannonball tree had killed her. And if it had, she must have deserved it because of her immoral lifestyle. I thought that hugely unfair. A whole lot of gods were tied to the cannonball tree – some Buddhists believe the Buddha was born under it and some Hindus see its hooded flowers as a symbol of the *naga*.

But I couldn't imagine any gods judging soldiers who slaughtered innocents more lightly than a woman who had drinks with them.

Ryu Takahashi

◆————

If you didn't know who Ryu Takahashi was, you might have mistaken him for a Byronic poet, a vampire or the wild man of the woods. He was tall for a Japanese man, much too thin, and too pale to be healthy. He had long, unkempt hair that he tied in a knot on top of his head when working, hated being out in the sunlight, and thumbed his nose at authority.

Ryu's family disowned him after he exhibited bathhouse photographs of naked old women, including his grandmother, at the 1937 Paris Exposition Internationale des Arts et Techniques dans la Vie Moderne (International Exposition of Art and Technology in Modern Life).

But I could see why Joben Kobata was so taken with him. Ryu Takahashi was an artist who didn't care for the rules and conventions that bound Joben.

'You say the man hasn't been seen for weeks?' Colonel Fujiwara directed this at Hideki Tagawa.

'Not since before the official New Year ceremony. Remember he didn't turn up?'

'Insolence. Insubordination. He got drunk somewhere and now he's scared and hiding. I want him found and questioned.'

'Sir, he's the official photographer,' Joben said.

'So charge him with treason for not coming to take the official photographs! Why are you such good friends with this no-good Ryu Takahashi? Anyone with any sense would just find another photographer. This fellow,' he pointed rudely at Hideki Tagawa, 'knows how to use a camera. Make him take your photographs. Give him some real work to do for once. Stop him walking around spying on people!'

I remembered the interest with which Hideki Tagawa had examined the camera and tripod when Ima had first produced it. Was that what he had been thinking?

Had Ima found a source of black-market imports? Had Joben really been part of it? Along with Ryu Takahashi? Was the fancy camera and tripod from some black-market source she'd discovered?

It was as though Mimi's death made me reckless. Or maybe that was a result of the sleepless night that followed. I woke the next morning more certain than ever that Ryu Takahashi had killed her.

'What deliveries came over Chinese New Year?' I asked Ima.

'Deliveries? Why? What are you waiting for? If it's the fish I sent it back. It was in a terrible state.'

'The last time Mimi came here, on New Year's Eve, she must have persuaded an officer friend to smuggle her in. This time there were no officers so she must have caught a ride on a delivery truck. They come in through the back gate behind the kitchens and they don't always check them so strictly. She couldn't get into the main house from there but she could have got into the garden.'

'I don't know where you get such mad ideas from.' Ima looked troubled. 'I will ask. But surely no one would dare . . .'

Even if someone had given Mimi a ride in they were unlikely to admit it now. And they might have had nothing to do with it, beyond falling for her charms.

If the police under Major Dewa were reluctant to call it a murder and investigate Ryu Takahashi, it had to be because of Takahashi's friendship with Joben Kobata.

Joben Kobata was a petty man, and when pettiness is close to power it can be dangerous. I knew I had to approach this in the right way.

'Why would you want to do a piece on the dead woman for the *Syonan Weekly*?' Joben asked. 'Nobody's interested in her.'

'Exactly,' I said, 'That's why Major Dewa and the police won't put much effort into the case. But readers of the *Syonan Weekly* will see that you're concerned about the death of a local woman who didn't have connections in high places.'

I felt certain Ryu Takahashi had killed Mimi, but I was careful not to say that to Joben. From what I knew of him, he wouldn't want to get Takahashi into real trouble that might reflect on him. But he wouldn't mind making his friend sweat a little.

'At the very least, we can talk about how dangerous the trees here are.'

'It's a totally ridiculous idea!' Ima said. She was always popping up in meetings that didn't concern her. I think her intention was to eavesdrop, but she found it impossible to keep quiet. 'You don't realise how lucky you are to be doing this job. Don't make trouble! Just stick to translating what they send you and don't come up with any more stupid ideas.'

She didn't know it but she was helping my case.

'I'm the one who decides what goes in the *Syonan Weekly*,' Joben said. 'I think putting in a bit of local colour is a good idea.' He was only saying yes to my idea because Ima didn't like it. 'Find out what you can. Get a nice photograph of her and one of the tree. Write something about a *kodama* in the tree. That should get people interested.'

'Don't make jokes about *kodama*,' Ima said. She was very superstitious about such things.

'Why? They speak occasionally, don't they? Especially when a person dies. Maybe you can interview the *kodama* in the tree and ask it what it saw!' Joben laughed loudly as Ima dragged me out of his office.

'Whoever killed that woman did you a favour,' Ima said outside. 'She tried to blackmail you. Why does her death matter so much to you?'

'It doesn't,' I said. I had already decided what approach to take with Ima. 'I was only thinking . . . if she had other copies of the photograph hidden among her things, who would find them?'

'You shouldn't get involved,' Ima said. But she didn't deny knowing what I was talking about. I saw she was thinking. 'What about your work on the paper? Do you have time to write about that woman?'

'The next few issues will be mostly photographs of the

administrators and their messages for the coming year. I've already done the translations.'

In fact, the messages were so similar I could probably have run the same translations week after week without anyone noticing. The Japanese administrators didn't read enough English to check, and the local English readers didn't care enough to read, despite how starved everyone was for news – real news.

Ima, lost in thought, seemed to have forgotten I was there. I decided to risk pushing a little further. 'Mimi said she had something from Ryu Takahashi to show Joben,' I said. 'Could she have come back to try to see him again?'

Ima looked at me. 'Do you want to see what that woman brought from Ryu for Joben?'

'You mean – you got them. Yes, I do want to see them.'

The two photographs she showed me depicted sex scenes. The faces were of real people but it was clear from the massively exaggerated genitals on males and females that some adjustments had been made. They couldn't have belonged to any real people.

'Ryu Takahashi is famous in Japan for his photographic *shunga* based on the original *ukiyo-e* block prints.'

Their facial expressions of ecstasy, delirium and satisfaction were as hugely exaggerated as their private parts and made me feel even more uncomfortable.

But they were not the photographs Mimi had been carrying in the envelope. I'd only caught a quick glimpse of the others but I was almost sure . . . I closed my eyes to try to revisit what I'd seen that night. Yes, I was sure those photographs had been of real people, standing around and holding weapons.

'So you're shocked, are you?' Ima looked pleased. 'You can open your eyes now. I've covered them up.'

I didn't correct her.

'I've heard of *ukiyo-e* block printing,' I said. Hideki Tagawa had been trying to educate me. Or, at least, show me that the Japanese made art as well as weapons. 'Artists like Hokusai and Utamaro design the prints. A carver traces and cuts the designs onto woodblocks and a printer inks the blocks and presses them onto paper or cloth.'

'You're always so technical. You're missing the point completely,' Ima said.

'What point?' Had Mimi also sold Ima the photograph of me and the others outside the Detective Shack? Was *she* hinting at blackmail?

'That it's art, stupid. People like you don't know how to appreciate art. The point is, *shunga* is not something civilised people talk about in public. But it's nothing to be ashamed of. Nothing for anybody to be blackmailed over.'

'Like a clean WC,' I said. 'Nobody talks about it in public but everybody needs it.'

'Yes ... but in an artistic way, not in a dirty way. Your English missionaries wouldn't approve, but for a long time, prints like this have been used to provide marital education for young couples in Japan. Hand scrolls and illustrated texts are among the dowry gifts a high-society Japanese bride brings to her new home. It makes a lot of sense, if you think about it. The original *shunga* were made with the *ukiyo-e* block printing method and are valuable artistic artefacts now – some are worth a lot of money. Ryu Takahashi made a reputation for himself by reproducing them. Joben must have bought some prints from him and didn't want me to know. He can be so ignorant. Being shocked by them is as absurd as a Westerner being shocked by statues of their gods naked. I know they have them.'

'Like Michelangelo's statue of David,' I said. 'Or the Venus de Milo.'

'Exactly. But Mimi found them as shocking as you. She found the order form and thought she could blackmail Joben.'

'So those are the photographs Mimi brought from Ryu?'

Ima nodded. I could see she thought she had successfully confused and convinced me and I was happy to let her believe that.

'But why is Joben so good to Ryu Takahashi? You've said yourself that Takahashi is irresponsible, rude and unreliable. Why does Joben insist he has to be the only official photographer?'

'You want Joben to make Hideki Tagawa the official photographer of the Shori headquarters?' Ima scoffed. 'Maybe that's a good idea. Then he wouldn't be able to disappear without telling anybody where he's going. Joben's just trying to help Takahashi, that's all. He appreciates his artistic efforts. It's difficult for artists when there's a war on. People only want to buy food and guns and nobody has time for poetry and photography.'

That might be true. But it was also true that she was lying to me and I didn't know why.

But I had an idea of who might help me find out.

Tracking Ryu

———◆———

'**W**hy is it so hard to understand? I'll help you if you help me,' I said.

To my surprise, de Souza was less than enthusiastic when I went to see him at the Hill Street police station, now run by the *kenpeitai*.

'I don't know,' he answered. 'Like Prakesh says, the risk is huge. After that day, I don't even know if I can trust *him* not to say anything. And if my typing is so bad people don't trust the info—'

'After everything you said the other day? I thought you were serious about making a difference. What happened?'

'When I first heard about them finding a dead local woman in the Shori headquarters, I thought it was you. I was sure something had happened to you. Maybe because of what we talked about. That was why I jumped in and said I would drive Major Dewa there. I would have come even he'd said he didn't need me. Pillay is right. I can't drag you into something so pointless and dangerous.'

'You didn't think it was pointless the other day.'

'Look, I can't stand to lose someone else I care about.'

'It's not your decision to make. It's mine. Anyway, how do you know Prakesh isn't going to report both of us for discussing it?'

De Souza grinned. 'Prakesh turned up at the Shori headquarters that day too. I don't know how he heard, but he was outside the gate when I left. He tried to pretend he just happened to be passing by. When I told him the dead girl wasn't you, I swear there were tears in his eyes. He's not going to report us.'

'He'll kill you for telling me that.'

'I know. That's why I'll be telling you again the next time we're all together. Remember to act surprised, all right?'

I only hoped we'd all be together again some day, but I pressed on, 'I'm going ahead with this whether you help me or not. And I know you're going ahead too. It'll be safer if we work together. Help me and I'll help you. I just want to find out what they have on Mimi. You can help me with that, can't you?'

'I don't think there's much to find out about that woman,' de Souza said. 'There are so many other things going on, it certainly won't get priority, especially now the major's decided it was an accident. But I'll see what I can find out and let you know. I still don't understand why you're so concerned about her. She tried to blackmail you. Maybe she tried to blackmail someone else and they finished her off.'

'Mimi came to me for help,' I said. 'She could have put it better, and she might not even have known it herself, but I saw she was in trouble and scared, and all I wanted was to get rid of her as quickly as possible and have nothing more to do with her. I got her killed as much as anybody else.'

De Souza looked at the ceiling. 'Sometimes you remind me of Le Froy. The man could never leave someone else's itch alone. What are you trying to do?'

'Find out where Ryu Takahashi is, for a start.'

He shook his head. 'Nobody's been able to find him. They think he left the island at least two weeks ago.'

'To give himself an alibi,' I said. 'It shows he planned this. Ryu Takahashi was a travelling photographer spy in the region before the war. He knows his way around. Can you get me in to see where Mimi was living with him? You can say I'm a relative wanting to claim and clear up her things.'

That was true, even if I couldn't remember the last time I'd seen Mimi at Chen Mansion. But I doubted Shen Shen and their mother had seen anything of her either, and the rest of their family was gone.

'You've got a good thing going where you are,' de Souza said, 'Look, if you're really committed to creating a new normal for Syonan as part of the Greater Japanese Empire, why not stick with that? I'll let you know if I find out anything.'

'In other words, lie low and stay safe?'

'In other words, stay safe and alive.'

'Isn't that what I've fought my whole life against? With my family, with the British missionaries? Not wanting to be stuck for ever in the kitchen feeding men? But that's what I'm doing now. Translating propaganda and feeding the biggest male Japanese boss on the island.'

That finally convinced him. 'Tell you what. Come in and file an official plea for help over Mimi's death. After all, she was a relation of yours by marriage. Say you're acting on your uncle's wife's behalf. It makes sense they would come to you since you speak Japanese. And it makes sense that you would come to me, an old friend now working with the Japanese police.

'If you want to see where she was staying with Ryu Takahashi, I'll get you a family-member pass. Officially it'll be to collect her things and settle any debts she left. Once you mention paying off debts, they usually let you in. But don't worry about the other matter. I'm sorry I asked you to get involved.'

'No,' I said. 'I meant it. We'll help each other. Besides, you really are a lousy typist.'

'And you want to risk losing your fingers so you never type again?'

'I've got an idea that won't involve typing,' I said.

New Normal

———◆———

I wasn't really surprised when days, then weeks passed without anything further being discovered about Mimi's killer. She didn't even have family worried about her, not that that would have helped much. I felt closer to her dead than I ever had to her alive.

Life went on at the Shori headquarters. I was fully aware of how lucky I was, yet at the same time it was frustrating. I had seen Joben Kobata shoot a man in cold blood in front of witnesses. Yet he wasn't considered a murderer. That was how little human life had come to be worth. Even if I found Ryu Takahashi and proved he had murdered Mimi, what difference would it make?

Ferdie de Souza came to see me a couple of times, interviewing me formally on what had happened to Mimi. He talked to me about other things, too. And even though I had not yet persuaded him to risk letting me help with the flyers, I was feeling better about the overall situation. Maybe there was hope, after all, though not on the small scale: I didn't think anyone could help us now without making things worse first. But on a big scale, maybe the war wasn't over yet.

Ima didn't seem to mind de Souza's visits. In fact, she seemed to flirt with him while calling him my boyfriend. Unsure if she was trying to make me jealous – it was better if she thought I was – I put on what de Souza called my *goondu* hero-worshipping face. I'd developed it for listening to British administrators who came out to deliver long drunken lectures, and now giggled at all her jokes.

De Souza was awkward. If only the old Prakesh had been around, he would have carried it off much better. After I whispered to Ima that de Souza might be afraid of getting into trouble if her husband caught a man in the kitchen with her, Ima found his awkwardness delightful.

'Don't worry about my husband. He can say what he likes but no one will listen to him. Joben Kobata did not take the Fujiwara family name, but he might as well have, you know. He's got no family to speak of. No connections, no brains, no looks. I am the one with the family brains and connections, and I can see you're an officer worth cultivating. Don't worry about that!'

Ima was spending more and more time hanging around in the kitchen and the press room. It was hard to get anything done, with her talking, but I felt sorry for her. The poor woman was clearly lonely and homesick. I wasn't an ideal friend but I was the only alternative to the wives of top officials.

Ima hated those women because their introductory gifts and good wishes had all been directed to Colonel Fujiwara's third (and current) wife and Ima's half-siblings. Ima preferred to believe those usurpers didn't exist, so she acted as though the officials' wives didn't exist either.

'Is there any more *zenzai*? If there is, my father wants some. And you'd better get a bowl for Joben too – he'll want some once he sees it.'

'Sure. Warmed up?'

'My father treats you more like a daughter than he treats me,' Ima said. She sat down heavily, fanning herself. 'I don't know how you can stand it here. It's so hot! My father wants to be posted back to Japan where the climate is better. He doesn't seem to realise there's a war on – he wants to retire to the mountains to drink tea. Now, when there's a war on!'

'He said after the war,' I said, stirring the red bean soup, then ladling it into the waiting bowls.

Since learning my late mother had been the cousin of Hideki Tagawa, Colonel Fujiwara had treated me not so much as a daughter but as an extension of Hideki Tagawa. One who could be trusted not to repeat anything I saw or heard within the walls of the Shori headquarters. This was not always a good thing. There were papers on his desk that might contain official secrets. I didn't want to see something accidentally that might get me accused of espionage.

And, as Ima had just demonstrated, he took for granted that I would drop everything to serve his every whim.

When Colonel Fujiwara wanted something from Japan that was slow to arrive, he told Hideki Tagawa to take care of it. And when he wanted to eat or drink something the kitchen couldn't produce, he asked me. He'd enjoyed the *zenzai* I'd made for the first time that day.

Zenzai was a thick, sweet red-bean dessert soup not unlike the Chinese red-bean soup I'd grown up on. Except *zenzai* was served with *mochi*.

I laid a couple of *mochi* cakes on the grill to heat as I put on the soup to warm: they would go into the soup just before serving. I also prepared two little saucers of pickled plums. Their sourness would go nicely with the sweetness of the soup.

Ima picked up one of the plums with her fingers and popped it into her mouth. 'Good. Where did you even get these?'

'They came two weeks ago. You signed for them.'

'Did I? I must have.' She ate another.

When I topped up the plums from their jar, I added a third bowl for Ima. Of course Ima signed for all the food. She didn't trust me to handle money and payments. But Ima didn't trust anyone with money so I wasn't offended.

But that meant she should have missed the delivery record book before anyone else.

'He's tired, of course. He says the war effort keeps demanding more contributions from him. But at the same time they want him to build up the island and get factories going again. And they refuse to understand that there's barely enough to keep the men paid and fed.'

I nodded. I wasn't expected to speak.

'Men must try to find work that suits them. But they also have to develop skills so that they can do their jobs better. My father isn't even trying any more. He seems to think that now he's got this job he's entitled to hold it for ever.'

'At least men have a chance to find jobs they're good at.' I tried to divert her. If Ima went on talking about her father she'd make herself angrier and angrier – and later she'd be angry with me for having heard her. 'Women don't get that chance.'

'Women can do a lot to help their men achieve what they can,' Ima said. 'Of course, a lot depends on the man's abilities and willingness to improve himself. You must be careful whom you marry.'

'I'm not going to marry,' I said.

'That's what all we women say before we get married. Afterwards, we say, "I shouldn't have got married." You'll change your mind when the time comes. You'll see.'

My view of Colonel Fujiwara and the rest of the Japanese administration had certainly changed over the past six months since I'd moved in. Previously, like the rest of the local population, I'd hated them. Hated, feared and despised them. The Japanese had come in killing, raping, looting, and all in the name of 'freeing' us from the rule of the Western devils.

No, the British had not been the most enlightened of governors. In fact, after hearing from Prakesh of what the British had done in India, I knew now that they could be seen as bullies and exploiters. Sometimes it's easier to see truths through an outsider's eyes. We tend to think that what we grow up with is the norm. Like a little boy who believes all men beat their wives because that was what he saw when he was growing up.

But the British had also built roads and schools, had set up and equipped the hospitals that the Japanese tore through with guns and bayonets, stabbing patients in their beds and making doctors and nurses strip themselves of anything useful before shooting and burning them. And most people in Singapore were descended from those who had fled homelands where conditions were even worse, whether due to the weather or their countrymen. Maybe that was why we viewed the British colonial rulers slightly differently. If you'd any kind of position or connections in India or China or Indonesia, you wouldn't have taken to the seas and ended up in Singapore. Singapore was the refuge of those who had nothing but their willingness to work and the drive to survive. The British, when they came, were just one more set of immigrants trying to keep things going.

And now the Japanese were the same – or were they?

That was the problem. They weren't even the same as each other. I couldn't hate them *en masse* as I had previously.

Ima was a strong woman. She might have been short and small in size, but her presence was much larger. And her pride was almost as great as her jealousy.

Pride in what? The father who had deserted her and her mother when she was a child?

There's a look women have when they feel they're married to men they consider beneath them in some way. Ima had that look.

Ima made it clear she looked down on the other Japanese officers and administrators. She was proud of being a certain class of Japanese, above the others. She found fault with her husband and her father when their manners didn't meet her exacting standards. But she was nice to me, someone who had no class and no right to be there. In fact, she was very protective of me – most of the time. Ima liked to tell people that it had been her idea to bring the cousin of Hideki Tagawa into the Shori headquarters and had taken it upon herself to educate me.

I say 'most of the time' because when no one else was around for her to impress she turned on me. It was as if she had so much jealousy swirling inside her that it needed an outlet. I knew I was just a convenient target, that it was not personal. But I never forgot Major Dewa's aide. That hadn't been personal either. But the poor man – I'd never found out his name – was dead. All he had done was follow his boss's orders.

Hideki Tagawa had his pride in being Japanese, even more his pride in being descended from one of the last great samurai families.

I was coming to believe that Ima had a crush on Hideki Tagawa and was being nice to me to get close to him. That was fine with me. I wondered if I ought to warn him. But he was supposed to be a smart man. He could figure it out for himself.

'Mrs Kobata's not here, is she?'

Luckily for de Souza, he turned up after the bowls of *mochi* and red-bean soup had been taken to the main house. They would keep Ima and her father occupied for some time. He pretended to hide his huge bulk behind the door, making the maids giggle.

'Can I talk to you? Business talk.'

'My office,' I said. I could tell he was excited about something.

I brought in a bowl of *zenzai* for him. I was quite proud of how well it had turned out. Maybe if I couldn't be a journalist I could be a cook. 'You found out something?'

'Mimi Hoshi. The investigation is over, so if nobody claims her body, it goes into the mass grave.'

Not a great thought, but so what?

'According to her identity papers, Mimi's last address was an apartment registered to Ryu Takahashi.'

'I told you there was a connection! Have you questioned him?'

'There's still no sign of Takahashi. But the family member claiming her body can ask permission to collect her belongings from the apartment.'

'Yes!' I was sure something among Mimi's things would tell me what had happened to her. 'But what do I do with her body?'

'Nothing. You just cover the expenses. I've got the form for you to fill in. I'll tell them you're making a fuss over what happened to her things and won't pay till I take you to see her place.'

'Yes, please.' I would feel better knowing Mimi was properly buried.

'Does she have any other relations who might claim her body?'

'I think Shen Shen is the only family Mimi had left. I'll let her know that I'll deal with it. Thanks, Ferdie.' I saw from the way his eyes were shining that there was something else. If it was something he'd heard on his shortwave radio it wasn't safe to ask—

'What is it?'

'The Americans are coming in.' De Souza lowered his voice. 'The US Sixth Army Corps is heading to the Pacific. They're going to take back the Philippines. And once they do, we'll be next. We've got to let people know, Su Lin, let the PoWs know we haven't been forgotten. Tell them not to give up for just a bit longer.'

Mimi's Room

———◆———

'What are you thinking of, Little Sister?' de Souza asked, as he drove us towards Ryu Takahashi's rented rooms in town.

'I haven't been in this part of town for so long. And I'm glad.'

It had been surprisingly easy to get permission to search Ryu Takahashi's apartment.

'Quite a few people have been looking for him. He's missed appointments and deadlines and hasn't responded at all, not even to the big shots at Shori headquarters.'

'That man is hopeless,' Ima said, when I'd told her where I was going that morning. She said she'd filed one of those reports herself, for her father. She also told me the friendship between her husband and Ryu Takahashi had come about as a result of Joben's love of gambling.

'Joben loves gambling on cards, on dice, on dogs. But he's not very good at it. That's because he trusts his own instincts over logic and he has lousy instincts. A man like Ryu is good at influencing him, giving him small wins along the way until Joben believes he is some kind of magician who can do no wrong. And then, of course, Ryu cleans him out. Or some associate of his. Of course he's too clever to do it himself, or even Joben wouldn't trust him the next time.'

When she saw de Souza had come to collect me, Ima teased, 'That handsome Eurasian policeman might be interested in you. I know someone who won't be happy.'

'It's nothing like that. We're friends.'

'Hideki Tagawa had better watch out. Haven't you heard him say that a union with a policeman is not the kind of marriage he has in mind for you?'

But at least Ima didn't object to my going out with de Souza.

'You think he's only doing his job, trying to find out who killed that woman behind the tree shrine. So, what has he discovered so far?'

'Nothing,' I had to admit.

'So unless he suspects you of killing her, he's not spending his time very usefully, is he? Don't worry. I won't tell on you. I can remember what it was like to be young and hopeful. Not that I had a very good time of it when I was young!'

I had worried a little about what Hideki Tagawa might say, but there was no sign of him. He had left the Shori headquarters the previous evening without saying where he was going, and nothing had been heard of him since.

Hideki Tagawa and Ryu Takahashi definitely had a lot in common.

'Do you think Takahashi kept all his photographs and negatives in his apartment?'

'If he did, they'd have been found,' de Souza said. 'Major Dewa went and had a look. Said there was nothing. Maybe being so near the comfort zone while on duty made him feel uncomfortable.'

Comfort zones for Japanese soldiers had been set up in several parts of the island. I had seen the one closest to Chen Mansion in the east. It was along Tanjong Katong Road, where wooden fencing had been erected around some thirty houses.

And I knew there was another in Cairnhill district, where we were now headed.

This section of Cairnhill Road had been an upper-middle-class area. The townhouses here had been vacated by European and Asian families, who had left Singapore or been interned. As in Tanjong Katong, the Japanese had put up wooden fencing around the townhouses so you couldn't see from the road who was coming and going.

As we approached, I saw the barricaded area stretched from Cairnhill Circle to the junction of Cairnhill Road and Scotts Road. A long queue of Japanese soldiers snaked along the fence.

'Only Japanese soldiers are allowed inside,' de Souza said.

'Oh, God. Mimi wasn't ... Was Mimi—'

'She wasn't one of the official *jugun ianfu*.' He used the term for 'military comfort-woman'. 'Most of the women housed here aren't from Singapore or even this region.'

'Where do they get them from?'

It was an amazing sight, or maybe I should say a shocking or ghastly sight. There must have been almost two hundred men waiting their turn. Many looked hardly more than boys. For a moment I felt almost as sorry for them as for the women they were lining up to have sex with.

'I've heard most of them are Japanese, Taiwanese and Korean women, who were shipped in by the army. They look like foreigners or northern Chinese. Very fair-skinned.'

'You said Mimi wasn't working in one of these houses?'

'Ryu Takahashi had an apartment just outside the Japanese Only section. Over there ... Watch your step. We'll walk from here. Out here they are mostly local women. They pick up overflow from the official comfort women.'

Ryu Takahashi rented a three-room apartment in miserable surroundings in Cairnhill. We found two other girls who said they lived there. The taller one had bad skin – she looked worse than I had after my grandmother had rubbed the skin-irritating plant sap on my face – and they both smelt bad.

I was even more impressed that Mimi had managed to keep herself so presentable in these circumstances.

'Can you help us find out where Ryu Takahashi is?'

'He hasn't been around for some time,' the taller girl said. The dullness in her tone matched the emptiness in her eyes. It didn't look like pain or despair, just emptiness.

'You want some company?' the shorter girl asked de Souza. 'I'll give you a special deal. Buy me dinner and I'll make you feel so good you'll dump this lame girl.'

We were speaking English. Despite the Japanese ban on English in offices and stores, broken English was the only language locals and Japanese had in common.

'When was the last time you had food?' de Souza asked.

'She's already too fat.' The taller girl pushed me away and leaned against de Souza. 'I keep telling her she's too fat. Why is she always talking about food? These rooms are paid for. But there's no money for food unless there's work. Ryu's not here. If you don't want company, then get out.'

'We came to get Mimi's things,' de Souza said. 'My friend is a relation of Mimi's. You heard what happened to Mimi, right?'

They looked back at him blankly.

'She's dead,' I said. 'Didn't the police tell you she's dead?'

'A lot of people are dead.'

'My family are all dead.'

'Serves her right. I warned her.'

'Warned her of what?'

'That Ryu would kill her. Mimi went through Ryu's things. He doesn't like us to touch his stuff.'

'She didn't just touch his stuff, she took things. She said, since he hadn't given us money for food, she was going to sell his stuff to buy food. I told her he'd beat her when he got back, but she wouldn't listen.'

'I told her he'd kill her,' the taller girl said. 'That's what must have happened. He must have found out what she did and killed her.' She shrugged.

'Did he say so?'

'He hasn't been back.'

'We think maybe he's watching us. To see if we touch his things. If we do, he'll kill us.'

I felt like giving her a good smack. 'Do you know what Mimi did with Ryu's things? What did she take?' A camera? I wanted to ask.

They looked at each other. 'Didn't see.'

'Look, can you show us where Mimi's things are so we can take them back to her family?'

'We didn't think she had any family.'

'We didn't take any of her things until after she was dead.'

'She shouldn't have touched Ryu's.'

Clearly they had Mimi's things.

'Is there anything at all?' De Souza took out his wallet. Their eyes fixed on it immediately. 'Why don't you two go and get something to eat? Let us stay here and look after the place.'

'Ryu doesn't like us going out without him.'

De Souza handed them a note each. There was no false modesty as they grabbed for underwear and dressed in front of us.

'This dress was Mimi's,' the short girl said, halfway into it.

'That's okay,' said de Souza. 'Did she have any papers or photographs or anything?'

'Notebook,' said the girl. 'Nah—' She dug a small brown book out of an old paraffin tin of rags and papers. I guessed it had been designated for menstrual care.

'Hey, mister,' the taller girl said to de Souza, as she went through the door, 'come back when you're not on duty. No charge for you.'

Sometimes keeping your head down and going with the flow may not be the best way to survive. Because that survival depends on young men dying and old women ending up in whorehouses.

I'd expected to find a lot more photographs, commercial stuff, and the sexy shots that Ryu took to sell to soldiers. Were these girls the models he used? If so, they disproved the saying that 'The camera doesn't lie.'

'There must be more,' I said. 'Where are all his photographs? Where does he keep his camera equipment? Where does he develop his photographs?'

'Probably took his camera with him.' De Souza looked around the miserable room. 'They said Mimi went through his things. He wouldn't dare leave anything expensive with this lot. Why do they stay here?'

'Better than being out on the street,' I said, looking through the notebook. Mimi wrote laboriously, printing with a large, childish hand. 'Especially when it's raining. Look at this.'

It was a note with an address and directions in Japanese, in a precise Katakana script, while the note scrawled above it in Mimi's large, childish handwriting said the directions were to her sister's place. The block-like Katakana script, used for words imported into the Japanese language, was like print versus cursive writing compared to the more commonly used Hiragana script. It revealed less personality. But, still, this looked vaguely familiar.

But the important thing was that I knew this was nowhere near where Mimi's only sister lived.

For some reason Mimi had thought those directions important enough to gum onto the inside cover of her notebook under a false heading.

'Do you know where this is?' I asked.

'This?' De Souza studied it. 'It's an off-trail number, not even a road. Looks like it may be one of the old bunkers.'

The British had prepared for war by building war bunkers. Unfortunately they had not had time to use them.

'They're temporary directions. "Track 377a" shows it's not a proper road marked on the map. Everyone knows those tracks are convoluted and can't be trusted. They all change after the floods anyway.'

It was probably nothing. But we had nothing else.

'I don't have any excuse to follow this up,' de Souza said. 'It was hard enough getting here today.'

'You don't have to,' I said. 'Can you get in touch with Heicho Tsai Chih-wei of East District, Division 221?' That was Formosa Boy's official title since he had been made officer in charge of my grandmother's district. 'Tell him I heard rumours that rebels are hiding there. With bombs. And food. And give him this note. You can trust him. He's not very bright but he's a good fellow.'

I didn't know what was there, but if Mimi had found this scrap of paper worth keeping, the least I could do was follow up on it.

Evening

———◆———

Coming down the servants' staircase, I heard Ima moving around in the big walk-in cupboard in her room, which was on the other side of the thin wall. That was why we had to be extra quiet using this staircase.

It was just one of the things that had changed since Ima and Joben had moved in. In the old days, before the tiny three-foot-square landing of the servants' staircase had been sealed off, the ironing had been done there, where the bed linens, towels and soaps were stored.

Now it was all Ima's territory. It sounded as though she was moving things around. She was probably counting her precious belongings to make sure no one had got in to pinch anything.

No matter how seriously we take ourselves, the presence of nature from sunrise to sunset and sunset to sunrise reminds us that life goes on. We're not the centre of things. We are like chickens scrambling for their feed in the morning and crowding in to shelter at night. That was all there was for them.

Food and death. You eat all you can and don't think about what is to come.

I decided for what was probably the hundredth time that I didn't have the right temperament for working under these circumstances. And there was no way I could change the circumstances. So, the only thing I could do was try to change my temperament.

I tried. For a whole afternoon and evening, I did what I had to do and said nothing I didn't have to say. I bowed, smiled, cleared cups and replenished plates.

No one noticed.

Of course no one noticed. I had become so skilled at not being noticed that it came naturally. It's the best course to take when being noticed usually means getting into trouble.

But being overlooked was my greatest skill. I needed to keep it if I wanted to survive.

'I hear you've been paying visits to the seedier side of town,' Joben Kobata said, that evening. He winked at Ima, who glared at him. She had clearly told him not to mention it in front of her father. 'Taking lessons in case you have to find a real job?' He was talking to me but watching Hideki Tagawa. 'So, did you get hold of Ryu Takahashi? What did that loser have to say for himself?'

'My uncle's wife asked me to collect her sister's things from him,' I said. This was technically true. Formosa Boy had got Shen Shen to sign a form authorising him to pick up Mimi's belongings on behalf of her family. It was stretching that technicality only a little that he'd changed the name on the form to mine and passed it to de Souza for me.

'The dead woman who was found here was your aunt?' Colonel Fujiwara asked.

'My aunt's sister,' I said casually. I was careful not to show too much concern and trigger Colonel Fujiwara's disgust by association. 'May I give you another piece of cake?'

He gestured for me to go ahead. 'And this aunt of yours was living with Ryu Takahashi?'

'That's what we were told. Her sister, my aunt, thought any clothes and shoes she had left might be worth something.'

'Do you need shoes, Su Lin?' Ima missed the point as usual. 'You should try wearing mine. I have so many shoes and I never have anywhere to wear them here.'

'Find him,' Colonel Fujiwara said. 'Find that Takahashi fellow, bring him in and question him. He has no right to disappear like that without warning. How can so many things go missing? Like that photograph from my desk. Where did it go? How can a photograph just disappear?'

'One of the servants probably broke the frame while cleaning,' Ima said. 'They wouldn't dare report it.'

'Question them,' Colonel Fujiwara said to me. 'Tell them, never mind the frame, just get the photograph of my wife and children back here.' He tapped the desk in front of him.

'It's probably gone down the sewage hole,' Ima said.

I asked the servants and searched for it myself. But the photograph that had once held pride of place in Colonel Fujiwara's office had disappeared as completely as Ryu Takahashi.

'Come,' Hideki Tagawa said.

If you went into Hideki Tagawa's office at the Shori headquarters, you would have thought the man did nothing except smoke cigarettes at his desk and nap on the floor mat. I knew that when he was thinking he did press-ups and other exercises on that mat.

I had been into his office before, of course. He was very careful with his official documents and papers, but cared little for his own things. His office was the opposite of Joben's, where artistic prints were arranged very carefully, with scrolls and modern photographs, but official documents were left lying around in stacks, almost though to show the visitor how much important business he had to attend to.

'Don't mess with this,' Hideki Tagawa told me. 'Don't stir up trouble. It will only make more. It's time for this place to show what it can contribute to the Japanese Empire.'

'Maybe you can show it by being willing to arrest a Japanese man for the murder of a local Chinese girl.'

'That's something you would say to the colonel or Major Dewa, not to me. And you have to be careful there too. There are people who think you're saying too much to Colonel Fujiwara.'

It wasn't that there was no news of Ryu Takahashi. On the contrary, it seemed that everyone was coming up with stories about him. For a man whom few had heard of just a month ago, it was as though he had fingers in every business. People whispered about Ryu Takahashi's connections with the INA. Some of those stories tied in with what Prakesh had heard. That he had been photographing prisoners of war, supposedly to document conditions in the prison – and in case they could be ransomed by their families back in England and Australia. The paperwork indicated that the INA were paying him. Joben Kobata's name was on the authorisations, but he said Ryu must have forged them: he didn't know about any such arrangements. And if it was being done for the INA, Joben would have given it to the INA to handle.

There were many hints that Ryu Takahashi had a hold over people in high positions and extorted favours from them, but it was all hearsay. There was no evidence whatsoever.

I tried to ask Hideki Tagawa about Ryu Takahashi having been a spy before the war – he, if anyone, ought to know. But Hideki Tagawa wouldn't talk about it.

'What do you think of him, an artist, using photography as an art form? Do you think that's possible?'

'Why not?'

I knew that Hideki Tagawa was looking for Ryu Takahashi too. He would deal with him in his own way. I trusted that if there was anything to find, he would find it. But it wasn't enough. There was nothing. It was as though the man had vanished off the surface of the earth.

Even if I couldn't prove it, even if he was never brought to justice, I wanted to know if he had killed Mimi, and why.

Because, if not, Hideki Tagawa might be right. Someone had meant to murder me that night, under the tree where I regularly picked flowers.

The waiting was hard. Just when I thought I couldn't stand it any more, de Souza came round with news – of a totally different kind. One good thing had come of Mimi's dying on the premises: the presence of a police officer in the press room didn't seem extraordinary.

'It's not a dream,' de Souza said. 'The Americans are in.'

'What are you talking about?'

'Yesterday. January the thirty-first. Remember the date. The Americans landed in the Marshall Islands. They're calling it Operation Flintlock. They've defeated the Japanese in Majuro and are invading Kwajalein Atoll. Don't you see? It's not over yet. They haven't given up on us. They're not trying to negotiate with the Japanese, they're fighting back. For us. They're coming back for us.'

We were standing just outside the back door of the kitchen, where I could keep an eye on the house as well as the back gate so no one could eavesdrop. 'Are you sure? There's been nothing in the news.'

'Of course not. The Japanese don't want any locals to know. They want to keep us in the dark so that we give up hope and become tame puppets. This is really important. It could be the turning point of the war.'

'Or just one more battle with a lot more men dead.'

I didn't know what to say. But de Souza was right. Hope meant more than anything else.

During the night I heard a bird whistling almost like a song we'd learned in school:

> I'll sing you one, O
> Green grow the rushes, O
> What is your one, O?
> One is one and all alone
> And evermore shall be so.

Except in school we sang:

> I'll sing you one, O
> Orh Bey Soom, O
> What is your one, O?
> One is one and all alone
> And long *chiam* pass will say who.

'Orh Bey Soom' and 'long *chiam* pass' were childhood chants we'd used to select teams and settle disputes. If only everything in life could have been settled so easily! But these weren't strictly games of chance. Like rock-paper-scissors or *roshambo*, the better you knew your opponent, the better your chance of winning.

I forgot about birds whistling tunes ... I wouldn't have done anything to help de Souza with his crazy plan a month ago. But the last two weeks had reminded me of how quickly things could be over. And, in a way, how little we had to lose.

'I have an idea about the flyers,' I said.

Flyers

———◆———

I set up my printing press – a tray of agar-agar jelly. I'd had the idea from Hideki Tagawa telling me about *ukiyo-e*, which were mass-produced with a technique using woodcut prints.

'Why are you doing this, really?'

It was funny seeing de Souza so nervous. 'You're changing your mind now? After I got all this set up?'

'No. I mean I'm committed. But the risk if we get caught – I shouldn't have dragged you into it. You're doing this for me, for old times' sake. It's not fair. I shouldn't have asked you.'

'I'm doing this because I think you're more likely to get caught without my help.'

We were alone in the kitchen. It was a fine afternoon and I'd sent the maids and house-boys out to catch *longkang* fish and clean them for salting.

'I have no right to . . . If anything happens to you I'd better hope the Japanese kill me before Le Froy gets to me!'

'And because maybe this way the news will get to Le Froy.

And because it may compensate for all the false information I'm putting out in the paper.'

De Souza's news was carefully written in block capitals on a piece of paper with a 6B graphite pencil. The paper was then placed on the agar-agar jelly and the words carefully carved into the jelly with a sharpened satay stick. Then I brushed food colouring (a beautiful blue made from butterfly pea flowers) over the jelly and pressed the flyers on top. White letters on a pale blue background. Not striking from a distance but easily read.

That first time, we made about a hundred.

'I'll take care of the flyers. But you'll have to get rid of that before someone sees it.'

'You can help me with it. Make sure they're dry before you stack them.'

Quickly I poured and smoothed a thick layer of coconut icing on top of our agar-agar press. Once it set and the jelly was cut into cubes, we would eat enough of the evidence so that even if they were scraped and arranged together the letters wouldn't make sense, or even words.

I can remember that first post almost word for word. And the one after that, with the news that General Eisenhower had taken command of Allied forces in Europe. And the one after that: the RAF had dropped more than two thousand tons of bombs on Berlin, attacked Magdeburg and was beginning to land on the Italian mainland.

And I understood why it was so important to de Souza to pass on the news. If the Germans were not invincible, it gave us hope that the Japanese, their partners in the East, were not either.

Getting the news out became important to me too.

Luckily, Colonel Fujiwara liked sweets: I needed no excuse to make agar jellies and tapioca cakes for him and his guests.

De Souza left the flyers at tram stops, in the bottom of baskets, and especially around the fencing of the PoW prison yard where they could be reached by a hand that stretched through.

I told myself it was probably my imagination. Maybe things seemed better to me because I was finally doing something. Even if it put me at risk, it was better than doing nothing.

It seemed to me that the mood lifted slightly, that people's faces showed a bit more hope.

There was still no news of Ryu Takahashi. It was speculated that he had left the island. I doubted he was gone for good. Why would he have left when he had set up everything for himself so well? I suspected the *kenpeitai* and the military knew exactly where the man was. They might even be hiding him until people (like me) stopped making a fuss about Mimi's death.

I wouldn't give up. I would outwit them.

Why would they protect him? Well, if Ryu Takahashi was a blackmailer, as I suspected, he might have information on Japanese officials that they didn't want to get out. They protected their reputations as fiercely as they protected their lives.

I wondered about the girls Ryu Takahashi had left abandoned in his apartment. What would happen to them? For them, I didn't even know what to hope for. Was it better to serve men sex in exchange for food or to starve? Was it really worse for them to be left on their own without Ryu Takahashi? Why did they go on sitting in that stinking apartment day after day?

Well, obviously because it was better than being out on the

streets night after night. The look in their eyes told me they had given up hope. It wasn't despair or misery – just that they couldn't summon the energy or spirit to care any more.

Allowing yourself to care in such times was painful, as I'd seen in Mrs Wong and Madam Ngoh. At least Mimi had taken her chance. I had admired her for that. And even though it was too late, I wanted to make up for not helping her.

'It's possible Takahashi was working for the Japanese Secret Intelligence Services because there's a record of them paying him.'

'Paying him?'

De Souza looked pleased with himself. 'They paid all their information gatherers. Even the most patriotic chap needs money for his rice and *sake*. But he wasn't getting much. I'd say he wasn't doing a great deal more than taking photographs of British buildings and officers. He certainly wasn't a big-time secret agent. By the way, there's no record of your Hideki Tagawa getting paid either.'

'He's not my Hideki Tagawa,' I said. 'There wouldn't be. He and his people were probably coming up with the money that paid all these spies.'

But this left me thinking. What if the gossip about Ryu's cover-up operations had been planted by him as a cover-up in itself?

Ryu Takahashi had disappeared soon after Major Dewa arrived and started his clean-up on the island. 'What if your major had learned that Ryu Takahashi wasn't getting special privileges because of the spy work he had done before the war? He might have been getting them in the good old-fashioned way

161

by blackmailing Joben Kobata. And who knew how many other people the man was manipulating? Or what positions they held in the Syonan government?'

De Souza didn't agree. But he didn't contradict me.

'Ryu Takahashi might have run away to avoid Major Dewa's investigations. Or maybe Major Dewa has his own way of cleaning up problems with connections in high places that the local police don't know about. Maybe the *kenpeitai* aren't interested in finding out what had happened to Ryu Takahashi because they already know. In that case, what if the *kenpeitai* killed Mimi too? She had been close to Ryu Takahashi. If he was blackmailing people, Mimi might have known about it.'

'And she might have tried to use it against him.'

'You think Ryu Takahashi killed her for trying to blackmail him? Why at the Shori headquarters? Why not wherever they were staying together or working together or doing whatever they did together?' De Souza shook his head. 'Are you saying Ryu killed her or that they were both killed by the *kenpeitai*?'

'I don't know. I still think it's most likely that it was Ryu who killed her,' I said. 'But it could have been someone who didn't like her living with him, a Japanese man. Or someone else she tried to blackmail with his pictures. Where are all his photographs, all his equipment? He must have a studio somewhere because there's the rental authorisation, and you can't be a photographer without equipment and a darkroom.'

'Have you said any of this to Hideki Tagawa?'

'I haven't seen him.'

In a way, Hideki Tagawa also went missing. He would be gone

for two days, then turn up early in the morning. I almost walked into him when I went out to unlock the servants' quarters. 'Oh, you're back. Where are you—'

He looked and smelt like he hadn't slept, eaten or washed while he was gone. 'Going to wash.'

'I'll heat some water for you. I was just about to start the stove fire.'

'Don't bother. Food. Whatever you can find. In my room.'

I prepared his tray myself. It was just after six, early even for breakfast. But I guessed it had been some time since he'd had real food so I put together a tray that would have done justice to dinner after a heavy day's work. Rice, omelette, tofu, fried fish, slippery vegetables with *natto* and pickles.

He cleaned the plate. And then he slept till late afternoon. Then he was gone again.

I knew Hideki Tagawa had gone to talk to Shen Shen at Chen Mansion – Formosa Boy had said so when he called in at the kitchen for a snack after making his monthly report.

'Did you follow up on the bunker address I got for you?'

'Not yet. Very busy. I will. Can I have another fried banana?'

'If you promise to find out what's at that address.'

Formosa Boy was never very interested in pursuing missions that didn't involve food. 'Can I have the banana now?'

'How about I give you a fried banana now and I'll make you fried banana balls after you follow up on that address?'

'Deal!'

It was very hard to hide anything from Formosa Boy when he caught the scent of something he wanted. He could twist and sneak food and information from anywhere. That was why he was such a help to my grandmother and got along so well with her. He was more like her than either of her sons or grand-daughters, I thought.

If not for the war, Formosa Boy might have turned into a super-entrepreneur. On the other hand, he might have stayed happily on his parents' farm. Content as long as he got enough to eat, he might never have moved beyond his village.

That we would otherwise never have met might have been a 'good' thing that came out of the war. But I wouldn't accept that, not even to myself. What good did knowing Formosa Boy do us? Sure, he had been good at foraging for wild food when we'd first met him a year ago and now, in his new position, he often channelled 'back-door' goods to my grandmother, whom he had adopted as his own. But we would have got by without him. And any favours he did us now might get us into trouble later. To be fair, knowing us didn't do him much good either. Ah Ma and Shen Shen might cook for him but, without the war, his own farm and family would have kept him fed. There might even have been a Mrs Formosa Boy by now, and two, three or more plump brown children. Formosa Boy was always bringing bird's eggs for Little Ling – he always left some in the nest, so there would be more birds. Before I left home he had made her a bamboo dragonfly – a bamboo sheet twisted into a propeller with a hole in the middle. When you stuck a bamboo stick in the hole and twisted it between your palms the 'dragonfly' would fly off. Little Ling couldn't make it fly but she shrieked with laughter when he flew it and demanded he do it again and again.

And I suspected – or I knew – that since Formosa Boy had been promoted to *heicho*, or lieutenant, in charge of our district, my family had been spared the worst treatment. And that was part of what worried me. There was a lot of infighting within the occupation forces. If anything happened to Formosa Boy, my family would pay dearly for the favouritism he was showing us now.

Stick to today's problems, I reminded myself. I had plenty to worry about without imagining what might go wrong in the future.

For a change, the news coming from the outside was good. And I felt I was doing a little bit to help.

Feeling good was dangerous, though, because it might make me careless.

Dead Ryu

———◆———

'I'm sorry. Colonel Fujiwara is busy in a meeting and cannot see anyone without an appointment,' Ima said, barely dipping her forehead in a bow.

It was past ten o'clock, after all, when the horning at the gate and the hammering at the door brought us into the front hall. I bowed low and respectfully though no one was paying attention to me.

'This is important,' the officer who had banged on the door said. 'Very important.' He held open the door for Major Dewa.

'What do you want? Why did you bring so many men with you?'

Ima's voice trembled slightly. I saw she was looking at the group behind Major Dewa, afraid they were staging a coup.

I could see they weren't the right kind of men for that. Not now, at least. The men who had followed Major Dewa up to the house were a mix of soldiers and police. They were whispering among themselves with the excitement of people placing bets at a cock fight.

Major Dewa looked at his entourage as though he had forgotten they were there. He was excited, too, like a man who knows the tiger he's been hunting for days is finally close. 'You lot wait here!'

Major Dewa started towards Colonel Fujiwara's office without waiting for Ima, who ran after him, pushing through the men – they had trailed after him despite his orders.

'Very exciting!' a voice whispered to me in Hokkien. It was Formosa Boy. I hadn't seen him so excited since he'd found a nest of alligator eggs.

'What's happening?' I fell into step beside him. If questioned, I could always say I wanted to offer the visitors drinks and snacks. 'What are you doing here?'

'This is my moment! That address you gave me? They found that man the snake boss was searching for there.'

The snake boss was Hideki Tagawa.

'Ryu Takahashi?'

'I think that's the name. He was dead in there. In a secret place. We had to break down the door. And all his stuff burned up.'

'What stuff?'

'Camera stuff. I can't talk to you now. I have to go and report because my team went in first. I don't think there was anything valuable in that place. It smelt terrible. But maybe they'll give us a reward.'

'What is this? How dare you enter my house without permission?' came from the sitting room.

'Our apologies, sir.'

There was a pause while the men bowed to Colonel Fujiwara

and the Emperor's photograph. Respect took priority over the most urgent news.

'I have to go. Talk to you later,' Formosa Boy said. 'Remember – banana balls.'

I stayed outside as Formosa Boy slipped in to join the other men. Ima was already there, listening. She held a finger to her lips but that wasn't necessary. I knew how to be quiet.

'You told me not to come back until I found Ryu Takahashi? Well, the man has been found.'

'That is no excuse to barge in on me like that! Question him and send me a report.'

'Sir, Ryu Takahashi is dead.'

'Dead?'

'Yes, sir. A patrol found an abandoned bunker – the senior officer is here to report–'

'Forget the report. What do you mean dead? Killed?' Major Dewa lowered his voice and we could no longer make out his words.

We drew back as Formosa Boy slipped out, bowing low as he backed out of the door, like a humble dog.

'I couldn't stand it any more. What is the colonel eating?' Formosa Boy asked. 'I smelt something really good in there. Is it your *otak*? It is, right?'

I didn't know how he could tell. Colonel Fujiwara had finished his rice and spicy fishcake snack long before they'd arrived.

'Yes. I've just made it.'

'Is there any more?'

'Come on,' I said.

We slipped away to the kitchen. Ima remained by the doorway, straining her ears. She had no patience with greedy soldier boys.

'We found Ryu Takahashi dead in that bunker in the middle of nowhere, surrounded by empty buildings. He must have been using it as a photographic studio, because there are painted backdrop screens, props and things.'

'What do you mean "props and things"? Are you sure he's dead? How did he die? Are you sure it's him?'

'Don't know. I didn't know him. Who else would it be? But he smelt terrible. If he wasn't already dead, the smell would have killed him. Two of the men threw up, but I didn't.'

I knew only too well how fast bodies decompose in Singapore's climate. And that's without making allowances for any rats, bats and worms that would be only too happy to take advantage of decaying meat. 'Have some more *otak*.'

'Thanks. This is really good. You put in some lime leaf before grilling, right? Is there any more rice?'

'Of course.'

'They didn't let me go too close. I was only included in the meeting because I put in a missing-person report on him. They wanted to know why I was looking for him. And then they wanted to know how I got hold of the bunker address.'

'Did you get into trouble?'

'Oh, no. I said Aunty Shen Shen, your uncle's wife, asked me to because of her sister, Mimi. They checked with her and she cried so much for her sister that she couldn't talk, and your grandmother gave them yam fritters. Then they didn't ask any more questions.'

Thank goodness for Shen Shen and yam fritters.

'Do you know how long he's been dead?'

Formosa Boy shrugged. His cup was empty and I refilled it. If Ryu Takahashi had been dead for over a week, he couldn't have killed Mimi.

'I think about three weeks.'

'*What?*'

'At least three weeks. Because there were wasp and beetle larvae on him already. And most of his flesh was gone.'

I thought about this. There was something very wrong here. Or very wrong with my deductions. 'Can you take me to see where you found him? Say that I'm a relation of the woman who filed the missing-person report?'

'You mean now?' Formosa Boy looked worried. His senior officers were still in Colonel Fujiwara's office. 'Maybe wait until they take the body out and clean the place. The smell inside there was terrible. It made me sick to my stomach. I was so afraid I was going to vomit all over the place.' Formosa Boy speared a chunk of *otak* with his chopsticks and dumped it on the mashed-up rice and tapioca I had put on his plate. It was already highly spiced but there was plenty of chilli-garlic paste to go with it and he smeared it generously before putting it into his mouth. 'It was disgusting. I thought the *kenpeitai* big boss was going to throw up too. Then he'd have had to shoot us all so that we couldn't tell anybody.'

He laughed. I managed a smile. 'And there was no sign at all of what killed him?'

'All I can say for sure is that he's dead and he's been dead for twenty to thirty days.'

Formosa Boy scraped what was left of the tapioca mash from his plate into his mouth and looked around for more. I took the hint and put the almost empty pot in front of him. 'You might as well finish this off.'

Formosa Boy hesitated. For a moment, I thought I'd offended him. I needn't have worried.

'Are you sure you don't want it? I've had a lot already.' But he reached for the pot as he spoke, unable to resist.

He hadn't changed. Formosa Boy was like a cleaning machine. My grandmother used to joke that after he had finished with the plates they didn't need to be washed.

'The bunker was registered under the INA. That's why we had no record of it. But the INA people say they don't know anything about it.'

I remembered Prakesh trying to track down INA money. Was it possible this had just solved that problem as well?

Maybe I should have been more shocked, but I hadn't known Ryu Takahashi well enough to be sorry he was dead. 'And they're sure it's Ryu Takahashi?'

'If not him, then who?' Formosa Boy said. 'It's his name on the studio lease. It looks like a storage room, but according to the paperwork it's a studio. But even if we'd found him straight away, it would have been hard to say who it was. It's a reinforced bunker. You know what I think happened? I think there was a paraffin lamp and he was working and fell asleep and it caught fire and he couldn't get out. The place there is all cement. Very good for keeping things out, but if you get trapped inside, it's oh-so-very-hard to get yourself out.'

'So it looks like everything was burned by accident?'

'No sign of anything that might have belonged to Mrs Chen's sister.' Formosa Boy misunderstood my question. 'There were no women's things at all. But it looked like there were costumes. Some of them were metal – even with the fire they were not all burned up, just melted in parts.'

'Metal costumes?' I wasn't sure whether Formosa Boy was being fanciful.

'Like old-fashioned armour,' Formosa Boy added. 'They said he was artistic. Maybe he was making artistic photographs.'

I wondered what was going to happen now. A door upstairs opened and slammed shut.

Formosa Boy got to his feet. He rubbed his stomach, satisfied for now. 'Can you bring some tea up? Then I can tell them I came down to ask you to make tea.'

'Of course.' I got up and filled the huge metal pot from the ceramic basin where drinking water was stored. 'Can you take me to the studio somehow?'

He looked startled. 'You don't want to go there. It smells bad. What's more, it must be very bad luck. Because he was just left there with all the – you know – burned things. Places like that, you don't know what kind of spirits get loose and look for people. Better don't go there.'

Formosa Boy was already shaking his head.

'If he died there, I should go to make offerings so he won't come back angry,' I said, 'and for Mimi, so that his ghost doesn't come back to claim her from her family. And so that the spirits don't come after the people who opened the bunker.'

Formosa Boy was very superstitious. I'd seen him praying to Buddha, Guan Yin and Tua Pek Kong, at the family altar at

Chen Mansion and by roadside Taoist and Hakka shrines. But then in war I guess it doesn't hurt to cover every possibility.

'Okay,' he said. 'I will try. But you must be careful. Make sure you don't leave anything there for the ghost to follow you back with if it's still hungry.'

Rethinking

———◆———

I'd thought finding Ryu Takahashi would clear things up. Instead it seemed to make things even worse. To me, if not for anyone else.

Right after the discovery of Takahashi's body, the top brass seemed happy. Major Dewa wanted a statement made with proper documentation – in other words the whole interview recorded by Magnetophon Man on his tapes. 'We must move into the modern age!'

Colonel Fujiwara didn't approve. Neither did Hideki Tagawa.

'Why not?' I asked him. 'You accept photographs. It's the same thing, making sound images.'

'Records can be doctored. Besides, if a man's word of honour is no longer enough, what else is there to stand for, fight for, live for?'

To me, the whole business didn't add up: either Ryu killed Mimi or Mimi killed Ryu but they couldn't have killed each other.

Given the timing of the deaths, the authorities seemed to agree that Mimi had killed Ryu and then ... was killed by a cannonball tree in some kind of karma?

I realised gradually that neither death bothered them. Now that they could officially blame his death on Mimi and record her death as accidental they could move on.

Even Major Dewa seemed pleased to 'start the new year a little late but on a clean slate' with Colonel Fujiwara and Joben. Had he forgotten his aide who had been shot dead and replaced by a Magnetophon?

I felt hugely frustrated. What bothered me most was that, if Ryu had already been dead when Mimi came to see me, could she have killed him? Had I completely misjudged her? I'd thought she was frightened and desperate. But if she'd just killed the man she'd been living with she would have been frightened, wouldn't she?

And why had she come to the Shori headquarters looking for Joben?

Most importantly, who had killed her?

Hideki Tagawa had questions too. 'What do you know about Ryu Takahashi?'

'I know that Mimi was living with him. In that house in town. I know that he was a photographer, that he had been travelling around here as a spy before the war.'

'And you know he was killed some time before her.'

'I know he died – they think – some time before she was killed. I don't know that he was killed.'

'So you think your friend was killed even though she was standing underneath a dangerous tree. But a man found dead in a locked room, who'd clearly been robbed, might have killed himself or died accidentally?'

We weren't exactly arguing with each other. We were just trying to clarify the situation. At least, that was how I felt.

'What do you know about Ryu Takahashi?' I asked him the same question.

'He wasn't a very good spy.'

Aha! I'd known Ryu Takahashi had been a spy. As far as I was concerned, this confirmed Hideki Tagawa had been a spy before the war too.

'He didn't take his work seriously. He didn't take anything seriously.'

'Like Joben Kobata?'

'No. Nothing like Joben Kobata.'

The quickness of his answer surprised me. I'd always had the impression Hideki Tagawa didn't like Ryu Takahashi. Now he sounded almost protective of him.

'No,' he said, reading my mind, 'I didn't like the man but I respected him. He would have treated any other system in which he was forced to work just as he treated us. In his way, he was true to what he believed in. Just because we don't agree with his view of art doesn't mean he wasn't an artist.'

'He took official photographs and pictures of naked girls. Which part of that do you call being an artist?'

I'd raised my voice without intending to. What he was saying was just so crazy.

'You are writing propaganda pieces for the *Syonan Weekly*. Do you still consider yourself a writer?'

'That's not the same thing.' It wasn't something I wanted to talk about with the person who'd got me into doing it. 'Why don't you think Joben was behind it? He insisted we use only Ryu Takahashi's photographs in the paper. And he has access to all the administration papers coming through Shori HQ. It would be just like him to sign off with your official chop. He probably thought it was a joke. And he might even have admitted it if he thought it would make him look clever. But since such a big issue has been made of it, he's not going to admit it now.'

For a moment, neither of us said anything. Hideki Tagawa went on putting away the things on his desk. Major Dewa was waiting for him. Soon he would be gone. And if he was gone, I would be too.

'What do you think being an artist means?' I asked. It hadn't escaped me that he had compared my writing to the dead spy's photography.

I expected him to say something like 'Doing things nobody will pay for' or 'Making decorative objects.'

'It's seeing the world in a way that you have no choice but to share.'

He'd surprised me. 'You think that that's what Ryu Takahashi did?'

'I think that was what he didn't manage to do. Maybe that was why he went a little mad.'

Joben was talking about some new campaign. He made a big deal of not being able to discuss it, though no one was asking him to. I could see things were still strained between him and Colonel Fujiwara, who treated him like a dog that couldn't be trusted not to mess on the carpet, which was true in a way. Even though we'd cleaned away the blood, there was still a bullet mark on the hard wood floor from Joben's gun, and the colonel hated having things disordered around him.

Also, everyone had heard Joben talking about how much you could profit from the conflict if you knew the right people, so he had been a prime suspect for black-market and drug deals though no one dared point a finger at him. I didn't believe it. Anyone familiar with the black-market knows that the last thing you do is talk about it. Now he signed papers saying Ryu Takahashi had tried to involve him in smuggling and profiteering but he had resisted.

And he and Ima were not getting along, which made things uncomfortable for the rest of us. She seemed even shorter with him than before, and he took it out on everyone around. But there were times he seemed so despondent that I almost felt sorry for him.

He barely looked at the second and third drafts of the *Syonan Weekly* editorial I showed him before saying, 'Rewrite it one more time, send it in and stop bothering me.'

'Yes, sir.' I had already sent the first draft to be typeset, just switching some paragraphs around in case Joben compared them but he didn't even bother to open the files.

'Anyway, they'll have to wrap up this song and dance soon. There's a campaign coming up,' Joben said. 'I'll be out of here soon. And you'll be out of a job.'

'I'm sorry about your friend,' I risked saying. 'Mr Takahashi was a good photographer.'

'Shows you know nothing. He was a lousy photographer. But, in his way, Ryu was a true artist. There was something so honest about his dishonesty, you know. Because he made no pretence of telling the truth. According to him, all art is nothing but lies. But then there is no truth greater than the desire that art reveals. Do you understand what true desire is?'

'No, sir.'

'That's why you can't understand art. That's why you'll never understand a true artist. The future will either forget him or revere his art. Ryu always said war was a lousy time for artists to make a living but a great time for art creation because everything is stripped down to the essentials. In his way that man was a child.'

A child who dealt in blackmail and extortion? A child who created graphic pornography? 'He doesn't sound very childlike, sir.'

'Haven't you seen how good children are at blackmail and extortion? They manipulate their siblings and fool their parents. If they get away with it at home they continue doing it out in the world. But at least they're honest about it. Lose that honesty and you lose the art.'

It was the longest I'd heard Joben Kobata talk about anything other than himself. His certainty seemed authentic and grounded in experience. I wondered if he had been the manipulating child or its observer. He leaned back in his chair and closed his eyes. He wasn't looking at all well. I said, 'Thank you, sir,' and had just opened the door to leave when he said, 'Suicide is not heroic at all, you know. Just a waste of rice.'

'Rice?'

'All the rice you've consumed up till that point. You owe it to the people who grew that rice to make something of your life and not just kill yourself.'

'You think Ryu Takahashi killed himself?'

OVIDIA YU

'Of course he did. Nobody could have got to him there. It was his secret place.'

'Don't worry,' Ima told me, when I said her husband didn't look very well. 'There's some top-secret India mission planned. He wants to go with them and then he'll be their problem. I'm sure Hideki Tagawa has told you all about it.'

'He doesn't say anything about his work.'

'I've been telling him he should take the chance to arrange a good marriage for you. You may be small and skinny but you're not that young any more. He should take better care of you than my father did of me. Do you know how I ended up with Joben? My father arranged it in payment for some favour!'

Ima was so unhappy in her marriage. Why did she want to push me into the same state? It was like she didn't learn from experience.

Joben mocked Ima for trying to flirt with Hideki Tagawa: 'You can't even see he prefers a skinny cripple to a fat cow like you! Girl, you were lucky to find a handsome man like me, not a skinny monkey like Tagawa.'

'You can talk! The only good thing about you is your connection to the Fujiwara clan. If you weren't married to me, nobody would look twice at you! Always coughing and sweating and scratching. What woman would want you to touch her?'

'It's this damn climate. Back home I was always healthy. Anyway, don't worry. I'm not going to leave you a war widow.'

'I'm not so lucky that that would happen!'

It was true that Ima had changed. When we'd first met, she had spent all her time worrying about what Joben was doing. Now it was Hideki Tagawa she fussed over. She didn't seem

180

aware of how much it irritated him.

I suspected Ima had seen her own mother fuss over her father and didn't realise it had driven him away.

People will do whatever they have to do to survive. I was seeing this applied as much to the big people at the top as to the rest of us below. The main difference was that their smallest actions influenced our lives but nothing we did made any difference to them. I knew things hadn't turned out as badly for me as they had for many other people. But it was depressing when the best you have to hope for is that things don't get worse. If the British didn't come back to get us out of this, we would have to get used to being part of the Japanese Empire. It was as simple as that.

'I can't believe Ryu Takahashi is dead. He was always doing that, you know. Going off without a word. It was his damned artistic temperament. That was why nobody missed him,' Ima said. 'I'm guessing Mimi found him in the bunker. She must have known he was dead or she wouldn't have dared to help herself to his photographs. Ryu Takahashi was well known for not allowing anyone to come near to his equipment and prints.' Ima nodded. 'If she knew, why didn't she tell somebody?'

'The murder of Ryu Takahashi was a big thing. Mimi would have known that anyone involved with it would be in for serious questioning and interrogations. I don't think she was very keen on being questioned. Did you know that Ryu Takahashi had been extorting money from Joben?'

'That wouldn't surprise me.'

The next morning, de Souza came to talk to me. 'Major Dewa is with Colonel Fujiwara so I said I would come to question you.'

It was a squeeze for him, easing his bulk sideways past crates of paper and ink, but he made it and sat on a stool on the other side of my desk.

"They're saying Takahashi can't have killed Mimi, but he must have had something to do with her death. It can't just be a coincidence they both ended up dead,' I said.

'Not just a coincidence. They think she killed him.'

'What? Why? Why would she?'

My voice went up and de Souza shook his head slightly, warning me. 'You all right?' he mouthed, rather than said.

'Yah,' I said, in the same tone, making myself calm down.

'In fact, they're pretty certain,' de Souza resumed his official speaking voice. 'There's evidence that she was living with him. Apparently she stole things and he threw her out.'

'You got that from those women living in Ryu's rooms?'

'Not me. But I read the reports. The women say Mimi stole Ryu's things and when he found out they had a fight. She killed him and set the fire in the studio.'

'But even if she did, why would she then—'

He held up a finger to indicate he had more information. 'I looked up an earlier report. When questioned about Mimi Hoshi's death, the same two women said pretty much what they told us. That Mimi had stolen his things and *he* killed *her*. Of course, that's before anybody knew he was already dead.'

I remembered Mimi as I'd last seen her. She'd been scared. She had overacted the tough, blackmailing woman role because underneath it she'd been scared and desperate.

Looking back now, it was easy to see it as a cry for help. Because what else could she do? 'She was scared,' I said.

'Doesn't mean she didn't do it. If I'd just killed my pimp I'd be scared too,' de Souza said.

'Pimp?'

'Manager? Call it what you like. Maybe you want to call him her marketing manager.'

'She wouldn't have killed him,' I said. 'She would have been nice to him and done everything he wanted until she found someone else to take his place. That's how Mimi worked. She always had a man. That's why she wanted to see Joben.'

'It might have been self-defence,' de Souza said.

It might. But something else had struck me. 'Mimi was very good at stealing things, even in the old days. Shen Shen said when Mimi visited them, everything seemed fine at the time, but they would find small things missing for weeks after.'

'That just shows she probably did steal his stuff.'

'No. That shows Mimi already knew Ryu was dead. I'm not saying she killed him. But I think she already knew he was dead. That was why she dared to let those women see her going through his stuff. Don't you get it? Mimi was a very good thief. She'd been pinching stuff and picking pockets for years. She didn't care if they knew she was going through Ryu's things because she knew he was already dead and couldn't do anything to her.'

'But you still don't think she killed him.'

I walked myself through Mimi's footsteps. 'I think she found that slip of paper with the bunker-studio address. When Ryu didn't show up for a few days, she went to find out what was there. Knowing Mimi, she was looking for something she could use to hold over him. Instead she found him dead.'

'Knowing it would make her a prime suspect to the Japanese, Mimi didn't report this. She didn't even tell the other women when she went back to the room to collect her things. But she dared to help herself to Ryu's and take anything she could sell because she already knew he was dead.'

'Do you think Joben was a customer of hers?'

'Maybe. I think she came to ask Joben for help. She said she had photographs he would want. Ima said they were *shunga* – sexy art prints. But what if they were photographs of Joben from before the war? Like that one of us she wanted me to pay her for?'

'I can't see Joben Kobata working for the British before the war,' de Souza said. 'Off the record, if you're saying Joben Kobata killed Mimi Hoshi, no, I can't see that happening and I'm not putting that down.'

'Why not? If she was trying to blackmail him? Ima would have told him what she said.'

'You said she didn't see him the first night she came. And when she came back on Chinese New Year, she didn't even get into the house. Whoever killed Ryu must have followed her here and killed her before she could see him.'

'Look, Ryu was always boasting about doing spy work before the war. He might have had photographs of all kinds of people that they would rather not get out. And, look, he was the official photographer for the magazine and for most of our official functions even though he was rude and unreliable. Why?'

'You're saying Ryu Takahashi had something on Joben Kobata?'

'And Mimi found it among his things after he died. And she

came here to try to blackmail Joben. It's obvious. Why can't you see it?'

'Mimi tried to blackmail you too. And me. And Pillay. That's what's going to be obvious to anybody else. And you don't know she was blackmailing Joben. I'd say it could have been someone higher up, and he was going through Joben.'

'You mean like Colonel Fujiwara?'

'Or Tagawa.'

I didn't like the way he was looking at me. As though he expected me to jump to Hideki Tagawa's defence. Hideki Tagawa had said he was afraid Mimi's killer had been after me, but I didn't think that was all. 'I'm surprised he's so interested. And Major Dewa too. If Mimi's death is only of interest to them because she was killed at the Shori headquarters. Ryu's death wouldn't matter much either. Why is Major Dewa himself investigating this?' I wondered.

'I almost believe your Colonel Fujiwara is serious about the new order,' de Souza said, as he stood to edge his way out of my room. 'Such palatial surroundings you're working in here. Remember, no sign of that photo so far.'

I knew what he was saying. Though he'd said it wasn't dangerous, there was no point in bringing it up if they didn't.

'Don't you want more tea?' I didn't want him to leave.

In ten years' time, people wouldn't remember the terrible early years of the Japanese occupation. Children like Little Ling, Uncle Chen's daughter, would think of the Japanese as our designated lords and masters, just as I had grown up thinking of the British. But what alternative did we have?

'The British tried, though. You can see all those pillboxes

and bunkers they built along the coast with supply stations going up to Mount Faber and out to Pulau Blakang Mati. If the Japanese had attacked from the sea, like the British expected them to, they would never have got through.'

'Why are you telling me all this? It's over. The war, the invasion – everything!'

De Souza put on a shocked expression. 'So you're not interested in going to see the bunker?'

'What are you talking about?'

'The war bunker where Ryu Takahashi had his studio. Heicho Tsai Chih-wei submitted a family application for you and I said I would bring you in. This is official. I'm talking to you because you saw Mimi Hoshi a couple of days before she died. I have to ask you if she said anything about Ryu Takahashi. He was probably already dead. But if you're not interested—'

'I'm interested!' At the very least I could do a short piece on wartime art, using Joben's words. He'd like that. At best?

'Come on! Why are you sitting there laughing?'

'I haven't finished my tea.'

'Finish it, then. I'm going to tell the servants what to make for lunch while I'm out – dinner too, just in case.'

The Secret Bunker

———◆———

We went in an army jeep de Souza had got for the day. There were several bunkers built into the hill slopes behind Ayer Gemuroh but we went past them to Loyang.

After the vehicle had brought us as far as it could, we had to get out and walk up a track. It might have been just passable by bicycle. On both sides I could see where Major Dewa's vehicles had ploughed through from the damage done to the trees and undergrowth. Huge clumps of earth had been thrown up and the vehicles had left paint and metal on rock.

Our island has a heart of granite as patiently unyielding as ours.

Chief Inspector Le Froy wouldn't have approved of that. He always said investigators should leave no tracks. Hideki Tagawa wouldn't have approved either.

I shook myself. I had to stop thinking of them as though they were equals. And I had to stop thinking of them in the past tense.

My back and legs were throbbing with pain by the time we

reached the huge bunker, which was overgrown with weeds. There was a semi-ornate gateway with a semi-ornate portcullis, and a paved path connecting the two gun emplacements built and embedded into the coastal cliff-side. The whole thing looked as if it had been designed as a command centre and ammunition store, especially when we got inside and found concrete bunkers linked by underground tunnels.

There was the remains of a burning area outside where a pile of film and negatives had apparently been doused in petrol and set alight. The fire would have destroyed everything there. What little remained suggested that some flamboyant theatre sets and costumes – colourful flags, twisted metal shapes – had also been burned. Streaked on the ground I saw dark stains of what might have been old blood. Added together, it didn't make sense.

But it was definitely where Ryu Takahashi had been working. Inside, I found a deserted darkroom where he must have been developing his own film. I recognised the smell from when Dr Shankar had blacked out his wife's sewing room to develop photos for his customers behind his pharmacy.

What surprised me, given the place had been cleared out, was how little debris we'd found in the burning bins. Even the blackout curtains had been taken down, not burned, before the fire started, because otherwise there would have been ash. From years of emptying prayer bins, I knew what burned cloth and paper leave behind. Had Ryu Takahashi cleared out his stuff? It was almost as though he knew he was going to die and wanted to leave no evidence. That didn't fit with what I knew of Ryu Takahashi the artist, who'd wanted to make an impact.

'It would be just like a woman to try to save all she can before destroying what she thinks is evidence,' de Souza said. 'Looks to me like they're right. That Mimi killed Ryu and started the fire.'

Could Mimi have done that? Could she have found this place, killed him, snatched a few things and a handful of photos before burning everything else?

'Mimi would have taken more,' I said. 'If she had the guts to kill him, she'd probably have moved in here. She'd never have gone back to those rooms in Cairnhill.'

But it wasn't just Mimi I was trying to understand in that bunker. It was Ryu Takahashi.

'If I was an artist with a private workspace, I'd have my stuff all over the place, hoping some of it would be seen by people or posterity or patrons or something. He was a photographer. Why didn't he have more of his work around?'

'Maybe he wasn't ready to show it,' de Souza said. 'I had a great-aunt who wrote poetry but never let anybody see it. She always refused to come to any family events because she was writing. When she died there were tons of notebooks full of her poetry in trunks in her storeroom.'

'Was it any good?'

'Don't know. The silverfish had got to them. Couldn't read a word.'

That was so sad. But I didn't think Ryu Takahashi was the light-hidden-under-a-bushel type. He hadn't been shy about photographing officials at ceremonies and naked people for wish-fulfilment pornography. 'Even if he wasn't ready to show his stuff he must have worked on it somewhere. This was where he worked. So where's his work?'

I looked around. There was what looked like a sunken round bath, about four feet deep, like an *onsen* without water. There was some rubbish in it. That was probably why the soldiers who searched the place hadn't taken a closer look. Some of them had contributed to the stench, but I wasn't going to think about that.

'Watch it. He probably pissed in there. Or worse,' de Souza warned, as I sat on the edge and slid in, feeling for the bottom. There was a raised cushioned seat in the centre. And around me I found four curved wooden work surfaces that slid out on runners, forming a circular 360-degree work surface.

Beneath the table slats, wide slots contained his art folders, and narrower folders were filled with other stuff.

'Look.' I held out a couple to show de Souza.

'I don't get it. It looks like a cesspool,' de Souza said.

'I think that's intentional. He's telling the world it's okay to think his work is junk because it came out of a cesspool.' I could have liked this man, I thought, if we'd met under different circumstances and he hadn't been Japanese.

'The Truth is only true in its own context' was written on one of the work tables. And on the opposite panel, 'Always look at the smallest picture.'

There were drawings as well as photographs of all sizes. Some of the projects were a combination of the two forms. I saw Ryu Takahashi had been a skilled artist as well as technician. He had first printed a photograph, formed a collage with a drawing or another photograph taken on a different scale, photographed that, then painted the resulting print.

That must have been how he produced the photographs with exaggerated genitalia that Ima had shown me.

Even if I didn't like his prints, I was impressed by his work. The coloured photographs were beautiful. They could have been art if you didn't pay attention to the subject matter. Indeed, I found myself wondering why they weren't art. After all, how different were his prints from Western classical art that showed the naked Venus de Milo or saints being tortured?

'This shows Mimi knew about this place.' I held up one of the half-coloured prints. 'He photographed her here. This looks like it was taken outside at the front. The burned stuff we found could have been the backdrop.'

Bare-breasted and smiling in a snake headdress, Mimi's lower half had been cropped off. No doubt Ryu had been planning to graft her on to some other creature.

'If Ryu went missing, Mimi would have waited only so long with the other girls before coming here to look for him.'

'She should have reported it,'

'She probably wanted to get away before he was found. But then nothing happened. The body wasn't discovered. Everyone thought he was off on a photographic jaunt. That suited her. She wasn't going to stick her neck out. Since she knew he wasn't coming back, she dared to go through his stuff and started selling off his photographs and equipment. She must have opened his mail to find out who had tried to contact him, which was probably how she got to Joben Kobata.'

I had seen Joben Kobata kill a man in cold blood. So why didn't I think he had killed Ryu Takahashi?

Everywhere he went, Joben left messes for other people to clear up. He wouldn't have cleared up after himself here. He would have tried to burn everything where it was, not carried stuff outside where fresh air would feed the fire.

'If Joben knew Ryu was dead, he wouldn't have been so angry with him for not coming to take the official photographs. I don't think he's that good an actor.'

But I wasn't so sure.

'I'm going to pass this stuff up to you. See if you can figure out how to get it all back.'

The folders contained not just photos of war scenes but of documents: records of transactions and requisitions. A brief glance was enough to tell me that the plan for the India mission was to use the INA as a shield for the Japanese Army. They were not to be given ammunition because they could not be trusted with it. My heart twisted for Prakesh and his fellow soldiers.

This alone showed that Ryu had had access to top-secret papers.

'You're going to tell them?' De Souza looked worried.

'No. You are. Or, better still, your boss.'

I could see this was way too big for me to follow up. Someone like Major Dewa would get results.

'I'll just say, "I don't know what I found. There were sex pictures so I didn't look." Then they won't have to kill me for seeing their top-secret stuff. You'll say I fell into this great stinking hole and couldn't get out. So you climbed down to get me and saw all these papers in Japanese that you can't read so you brought them straight to Major Dewa.

'And if you get the chance, tell Prakesh he was right about funds being siphoned away from the INA. Or maybe don't tell him. If they follow up on this he'll know, and if they don't follow up, he'll be so angry he'll just get into more trouble.'

*

Once Major Dewa's men started digging, it turned out even worse than we'd thought. The deep pit we'd examined had been Ryu's current work area. Apparently he'd turned his previous work areas into rubbish pits. When they dug up those pits they didn't just find rubbish. They found the bodies of the PoWs who'd probably been forced to dig the pits before they were killed in Ryu's photographic enactments.

That explained the heavy odour of death in the place.

Problems at the Top

◆

The discovery of Ryu Takahashi's papers sparked a huge furore. The bodies found buried within and outside his bunker were no more than a footnote. And, as I'd hoped, Major Dewa glossed over how they'd been found: 'A local girl fell into the pit where Takahashi had buried them. The officer who rescued her couldn't read Japanese but brought them to me because they looked important.'

'I hear Ryu Takahashi was a spy in the region for years. Many people wanted him dead,' Colonel Fujiwara said. 'He was in a dangerous line and he must have been aware of the risks. I don't know why you're making such a fuss over this. Many thousands of our men have died. Takahashi knew what he was getting into when he signed up.'

'This is no longer just about who killed Ryu Takahashi,' Major Dewa said. 'Photographs we found clearly show he had access to top-secret information and clearance from someone at the Shori headquarters.'

*

Even down in the kitchen we knew Colonel Fujiwara could be in big trouble. That copies of top-secret documents had been leaked was treason and betrayal of the Emperor.

Ima was in the corridor outside the room when I brought up fresh tea. She had clearly been there, listening, for quite a while.

'I'll take that in.' She lifted the hot-water pot off my tray and pushed open the door. I followed slowly, stopping to bow and take in the rest of the room.

'Ryu Takahashi had a small office in the Cathay Building, which he hardly ever used. What we found interesting is that the funding for this, like his bunker studio, his salary and equipment, came from the INA.' Major Dewa was so pleased by his discoveries he didn't make me sample his tea to check for poison.

With its sixteen storeys – seventeen, if you counted its misshapen basement, which compensated for the steep slope it was built on – the 230-foot Cathay Building at the foot of Mount Sophia in the Dhoby Ghaut area had been the pride and joy of Singapore when it opened in 1939. Not only had it housed Singapore's first air-conditioned cinema, it was the tallest building not just on Singapore island but in all of South East Asia.

Now the Cathay Building housed the offices of the Japanese Propaganda Department and ran Japanese movies and propaganda films. This was where issues of the *Syonan Weekly* were vetted and printed. It was also where the Japanese displayed the freshly severed heads of 'traitors'.

The Japanese were harsh on criminals. Anyone who

challenged their authority was a criminal. On the day they took over the Cathay Building, five 'looters' – employees who had been living in their offices after losing their homes – were publicly executed as a lesson.

Their heads were stuck on spiked poles and displayed in a row in front of the Cathay Building. They remained there till replaced by fresh heads. When the Cathay restaurant became a dining room for Japanese military officers, the rotting heads were moved to either side of the building, out of sight of the restaurant windows, to continue deterring local foot traffic without affecting Japanese appetites.

Not surprisingly, locals avoided the area.

Magnetophon Man was seated as usual in the corner with his huge machine. I bowed to him as I put a cup and a dish of mango cubes by him. He nodded an acknowledgement without lifting his eyes from his notepad.

Major Dewa said, 'The Indian National Army was unaware of this. Or that they had Takahashi on their payroll. The security is set up so that no one there seems to know who authorised this. But confirmations for several of the authorisations were issued by Hideki Tagawa's office.'

This was clearly the point Major Dewa had been working up to. You could almost hear the drumroll when he turned on Hideki Tagawa.

'Issued?' Hideki Tagawa seemed unperturbed. 'With my signature? Or was it an office chop?'

'What difference does that make?'

Major Dewa was clearly struggling not to arrest him immediately. Or at least to tell him to stand to attention and show some respect. 'All the authorisation chops have individual codes. It's the same thing.'

'Well? Which is it?' said Colonel Fujiwara.

Major Dewa fumbled through his papers till he found an authorisation form. 'Tagawa's official chop. And, as you can see, the Shori headquarters chop is there too. So you must have been in the office here when you signed it. I mean, chopped it. Signed it with your chop. See? It's messy. Only half inked and partly off the paper but it's undeniably yours.'

He handed it to Colonel Fujiwara, who passed it to Hideki Tagawa.

Half inked? But Hideki Tagawa was fanatically particular when it came to official matters. People who looked only at his drab clothes, the dents and scratches on his nondescript car, might think him careless and unconcerned. But I knew there was order in his chaos. There were mountains of documents in his room and he always knew if anyone moved something. A maid had been called in for brushing a pellet of lizard dung off a stack of papers and straightening it. She hadn't been scolded, she assured me, somewhat confused. Mr Tagawa had only wanted her to tell him what she had done and why.

For some reason I found myself thinking of the gold hairpin he had given me, then taken back, and spoke without thinking: 'May I see one of the authorisations?'

They all turned to look at me, almost as shocked as if the potted plant in the corner had suddenly asked a question, but no one objected. Major Dewa's eyes bulged with interest.

Hideki Tagawa handed me the form he was holding,

'Hideki Tagawa did not write such a messy requisition,' I said. 'Have you compared this to his papers? His language is precise and correct, both in English and Japanese. And the writing is different. He didn't fill in this form.'

'Maybe the messiness was deliberate.' Major Dewa took the form from me. 'Maybe he deliberately wrote badly to set someone up. Joben Kobata, perhaps?'

'If Hideki Tagawa had wanted to set up Joben Kobata, he would have used his name and you would already have arrested Joben Kobata,' I said, barely conscious of how reckless I was being.

But I saw they were looking at Hideki Tagawa.

'The documents were chop-signed in my name, you say,' Hideki Tagawa said. 'In the Cathay office? Here in this office?'

'Found in the Cathay office. Signed in this office ... here in the Shori headquarters.' Major Dewa looked confused. 'They were authorised at the highest level—'

'Probably you signed it without reading. All you men sign so many papers all the time. If you just used your seal to chop-chop-chop, you wouldn't remember,' Ima said.

She was talking to her father. Colonel Fujiwara was notorious for chop-chop-chopping his documents without reading them. He claimed that by the time anything got to him it had already been through so many levels of discussion and approval that a monkey could handle it.

I realised Ima was trying to persuade her father to take the blame for this. But why? She was always complaining her father preferred Hideki Tagawa to her husband. Why would she try to get her father to admit to trying to frame her husband?

'What's the date?' I asked.

'The date on the application?' Hideki Tagawa repeated my question to Major Dewa.

'The date is not relevant. I have come here as a courtesy but if you think you can—'

'The date,' Colonel Fujiwara said. He still hadn't touched the hot green tea Ima had put on his desk. She hadn't filled Joben Kobata's cup.

Colonel Dewa studied the paper in his hand, 'The date is smudged.'

'Have you an approximation?'

'What does it matter?' He turned on me. 'What difference does it make when something was ordered?'

Hideki Tagawa looked at me and raised one eyebrow.

'Respectfully, sir,' I said, 'I had just started working on the *Syonan Weekly* when Ryu Takahashi was appointed the official photographer. That was three months ago, when you were away on a mission to the Philippines.'

'I am aware of that.' Hideki Tagawa had been following the delivery of certain 'donated' treasures to the Prince's Japanese Army Fund.

'Any arrangements made for Ryu Takahashi would have been made during that time.'

'Stop wasting our time!' Joben Kobata flared up suddenly. 'Sneaking around, spying for the rebels! You'd better get out of here before we have you beaten and arrested!'

'You say she is here to spy on people?' Hideki Tagawa said lazily. 'Who do you think my cousin is spying for?'

Joben's jaw sagged. He looked at his wife, then at his

father-in-law. Neither of them met his eyes. I shouldn't have enjoyed it, but it felt good.

Major Dewa collected his wits. 'Whether it was you or a member of your family who used the authorisation chop, if it is your official seal you have to take responsibility.'

In trying to excuse Hideki Tagawa on the grounds that he had not been on the island at the time, I had opened myself to take the blame. I saw it would be pointless to deny it. They needed a scapegoat because Joben Kobata was Colonel Fujiwara's son-in-law and bringing him down would make the colonel look bad. The intention might have been to sacrifice Hideki Tagawa. Even his connection with the Emperor's brother wouldn't save him if they decided to throw him under the train to save Colonel Fujiwara. But it would be easier all round to settle for his cousin.

Joben Kobata was grinning. But he grinned too soon.

'All this will have to be fully investigated.' Major Dewa said, 'Thank you for your help, Miss Chen, Mrs Kobata.'

Major Dewa dismissed me from the room and as a suspect. He left Hideki Tagawa alone once the Prince had confirmed his travel missions, but Joben Kobata spent hours in Colonel Fujiwara's office being questioned.

Unfortunately, from my busybody point of view, there was a constant murmur of voices that didn't sound very happy but I couldn't make out more than that.

I saw Ima in the corridor several times carrying cold tea, an empty mopping bucket, a clothes basket, but I doubt she heard anything more interesting than I did. 'Don't worry,' I said.

'Worry? Why should I be worried?'

'About Joben. You're worried, aren't you? I'm sure he'll be all right. At the very worst, he can say that Ryu Takahashi lied to him or something. In any case, he's not responsible for what that man did. Major Dewa has to make a fuss to show the INA they're taking it seriously.'

Ima looked at me blankly for a moment. 'Oh, yes. Yes, of course. Joben means well, but he's really got no experience or training. They don't care about the INA. I heard Major Dewa say that if they hadn't missed the money before they don't need it now. And good luck to them going through all their accounts to find out where the money was coming from.'

'What?' I thought of what Prakesh had said. 'But the INA is very short on funds. They've been trying to find out what's been wrong for some time.'

'Well, serves them right for keeping their accounts in such a mess.'

But though Ima might have been worried about her husband, the two were barely civil to each other when they were together.

'You're so lucky you don't have a husband!' Ima said to me, more than once, in front of him. Or 'You're lucky not to be married to a husband like mine.'

I didn't like Joben Kobata, but he seemed to me no worse than any of the other Japanese officers Ima might have married. But I knew I was lucky. Especially after Major Dewa had got me off the hook I'd practically hung myself on. Every additional day I survived I reminded myself of how lucky I was. And never to count on it lasting.

Maybe that was why I decided to do something while I could.

There was actually less work for the kitchen because the

official visits had been suspended and Colonel Fujiwara took most meals off a tray in his office. The maids and house-boys were playing fivestones on the kitchen floor. They had finished their duties for the day but had stayed in case someone upstairs called for anything.

'You can leave,' I said. 'I'll watch the kitchen. Why don't you go outside for a while? I'll come and lock the doors later.'

'Thank you!'

I knew they'd go to the edge of the wilderness to see what fruit they could scavenge through the fence. They got enough to eat, but they were hardly more than children and a little time outdoors had to be good for them. 'Don't go too far, and don't disturb the guards.'

I'd have to check they were all in their rooms before I locked them later. But, first, I had something to do.

Message to Prakesh

———◆———

It didn't look like Major Dewa was going to do anything about the dead PoWs and the money that had been channelled to Ryu Takahashi. But I knew someone who would be very interested. I hadn't been guilty of leaking Shori headquarters information when Major Dewa had accused me of it. Now I felt he had driven me to it by not doing his job. Maybe that's what every 'traitor' feels. Doing what I did best, I wrote up a recipe for Prakesh Pillay.

I put down in my basic Malay the information I'd seen in Ryu Takahashi's papers about funds siphoned from the INA being routed to and through the Propaganda Department without it being aware of it. Most importantly, I noted where records of those accounts could be found. And I pointed him to the unit that had uncovered the PoWs' bodies. As far as I knew, the bodies were still there.

I knew some Japanese officials understood English. But few, apart from Hideki Tagawa, had any knowledge of Malay. Prakesh, who, like me, had grown up in Singapore, should have enough *pasar* or market Malay to understand it. I wrote the details in lines of four or five words each, hoping that if someone didn't understand the language, it would pass as a recipe. And I hoped that any locals who saw it would have the sense to keep quiet.

At the top of the paper, I wrote in English that this was the recipe for *ulam*, made from edible wild plants, which Prakesh had demanded. I thought it was believable because, these days, everyone was looking for sources of food. To make it more credible, I added line drawings showing some of the wild leaves, shoots, nuts and flowers that could be eaten raw or lightly blanched: kaffir lime leaves, lemongrass and mint. And, of course, *ulam raja* and *remayong* or *saan choy*, which were once seen as weeds because of how fast they grew, now valued for the same reason.

At the bottom, I scribbled the quote about the INA being used as a shield for the Japanese Army and added a chirpy *Itadakimasu!* after it.

It was the best I could do.

Finally, I printed *Ryo⁻ri⁻ho⁻* – 'recipe' in Japanese – at the top and on the official dispatch envelope I sealed it into. I addressed it to Prakesh at the INA and added it to the outgoing mail generated by Colonel Fujiwara and the other officials. The dispatch riders came to deliver and collect mail every two hours. It made me realise how easily someone in the Shori headquarters could have added 'official' instructions. They didn't seem to have increased security checks. But why would they? Major Dewa seemed to think the threat was over and the perpetrators dead or in custody.

Of course I hadn't signed my name but Prakesh would know it was from me. I could only hope that if the Japanese intercepted and translated it, Prakesh wouldn't get into too much trouble for receiving a piece of anonymous mail.

I didn't mention Joben Kobata by name. But I was more and more certain he'd had something to do with the missing funds. Not only with arranging for money to be sent to Ryu Takahashi. I was sure he had planted the evidence to make Hideki Tagawa look guilty.

I was even more sure when Joben Kobata came into the press room after lunch. I was eating at my desk, as was usual when no official lunch had to be supervised. The maids and house-boys had distributed bento boxes to the various offices and would collect them later.

By now Colonel Fujiwara would be asleep on the daybed in his office with both doors locked.

'The food here is not as good as when your lord and master is here,' Joben said. 'It's barely edible. Too salty. Were you crying salt tears into it while you were cooking?'

I stood up and bowed. 'Would you like me to make you something else, sir?'

'Nah. What are you doing anyway?'

He looked around the small crammed room. So close to the kitchen, it smelt of the lunch that had just been prepared there, and because of the stacks of box files, which contained records of previous issues, instructions for future issues, there was barely enough room for him to come fully in unless he sat on the stool I stood on to reach the high shelves.

I had been working on translating points sent from Japan to be included in the editorial piece for the next issue of the *Syonan Weekly* – his job as editor, really. I had to do it because Joben's English was nowhere near as good as he wanted people to think. It wasn't my job any more than supervising meals because

Colonel Fujiwara didn't trust Japanese cooks ('Assassins all train as cooks!') and didn't like the food local cooks gave him.

'Your editorial, sir. It should be ready for you to go through by this afternoon.'

Maybe I overstressed 'your' before 'editorial'. But I don't think it made any difference. Joben had come down looking for someone to bully.

He leaned forward, laughing as I instinctively flinched from him. He was sweating and looked more than a bit crazy as he picked up my lunch tray and flung it at me. I ducked and cried out as it slammed just over my head into the wall shelving.

Rice, soup and beans, chopsticks and broken crockery splattered all over me. The papers, files, photographs and the layout of the personal advertisements page that I had spent hours putting together that morning and carefully spread out to dry were smeared.

'It's for your own good. You must learn better taste when it comes to food. If you go on eating rubbish, you'll go on cooking rubbish.'

I saw two of the house-boys in the doorway behind him. Ah Peng had a knife in one hand and the knife-sharpening stick in the other. Tanis was carrying the heavy stone pestle with both hands. They looked terrified but determined to save me from whatever had made me cry out. I was touched but frightened for them. I shook my head sharply and mouthed, 'Go. Go away!' and gestured for them to leave fast. There was nothing they could do and no point in them getting into trouble too.

Joben saw them backing away and, for a moment, I thought he was going to turn on them. 'You shouldn't waste food,' I said, to draw his attention back to me.

It worked.

'You've no right to tell anybody to do anything. You're finished here, don't you understand? That pig Tagawa is finished. Make up your mind to it. He's not coming back. You'd better start being nice to me if you want to go on staying here in luxury.'

'We'll find out what's really happening when they let us know,' I said. My voice was steady even if my fingers trembled as I wiped food from my face, 'unless you want me to leave now. If not, I must get back to work or next week's paper will be late.' I bowed respectfully. 'Unless you would like to take over, sir.'

'Your fancy words won't do you any good. You think anybody even reads that? You still think Tagawa can help you? He's probably dead already. You don't understand how these things work. People don't matter. It's who they're connected to that makes all the difference. Hideki Tagawa is nobody. His whole family is in the graveyard. No matter how much incense he offers them, they won't come and save him now.'

Once he was gone, two of the maids came back with the house-boys to help me clean up. I could have done it myself, but I was grateful for their help.

'If we rinse the food, maybe still can eat,' Ah Peng said, as I saw them collecting the grains of rice. Food was scarce and their families would be hungry.

'Give it to the chickens,' I said. Chickens ate grit and small stones, so any dirt on the the rice wouldn't hurt them. 'Next time you mustn't be so stupid. You must never ever hold any kind of weapon when a Japanese is near. He could have had you both killed for attacking him.'

I only hoped Joben had enjoyed bullying me enough to forget them.

'We thought he was attacking you,' Tanis said. 'We were only trying to help you.'

'I know that. Thank you.' I loved them for it. 'Thank you very much. But you mustn't. I don't want any of you to get hurt.'

'I didn't stop them attacking my mother and sisters,' Tanis said. 'My mother made me hide inside the charcoal bin, and when I came out, my sisters were all gone. They never came back. I don't know what to do now. I don't want to—'

'I want you to live to grow up,' I said. 'That's the most important thing you can do right now. All of you. I'm not telling you to give up. For your families and for yourselves, you must all do everything you can to stay alive.'

I told myself I had something to live for too. At the very least I was trying to keep these children alive. But what kind of future were they growing up into?

Nobody would touch Joben Kobata because he was the son-in-law of Colonel Fujiwara. To attach any suggestion to him of wrongdoing would be to insult the colonel. And that was treason.

Making *Onigiri*

———◆———

Hideki Tagawa did not return that night, or the next day. I couldn't get any information on where he was or what was happening, which shouldn't have surprised me. Indeed, Colonel Fujiwara asked me twice in an hour if I had heard anything from Hideki Tagawa, which showed he was equally in the dark.

Could Hideki Tagawa be shipped back to Japan? Would Major Dewa arrange an accident to get rid of him? Had the whole mis-appropriation-of-funds investigation been part of a plan for Major Dewa to take his place as Colonel Fujiwara's primary adviser?

To make things worse, I hadn't seen or heard from de Souza for several days. I could only hope and pray he hadn't got himself into trouble with his wireless or the flyers. Right now it seemed so pointless. The Japanese had already won the war here. Why had we thought we were being so clever distributing news of the war in Europe? We might as well have been signing our own death warrants!

And, though I knew it was far too soon to expect to hear from Prakesh, it worried me that I didn't know whether my 'recipe' had got to him. Had he read and understood it? Or had he assumed it was an anonymous tip from an informer and thrown it away unopened?

Every jeep load of soldiers at the gate made me jump because they might be coming for me: de Souza had been forced to tell them about my part in producing the flyers or a Malay translator had exposed my note to Prakesh.

But underlying it all was the anxiety of not knowing what was happening to Hideki Tagawa. Why was I worrying about him? As far as I was concerned, he was still the enemy. But whatever happened to him affected me, as I had already seen from Joben's behaviour.

The only good thing about all this going on inside my head was that it distracted me from the tangle of worry that throbbed deep inside me all the time. It wasn't just Ferdie de Souza and Prakesh Pillay. There was Le Froy in prison with a foot amputated. My grandmother, Uncle Chen and Shen Shen depending on the black-market to keep a houseful of relatives and former tenants fed. My best friend Parshanti somewhere up-country with the rebels – was she still alive? – and her parents in prison. I tried to focus on work so my thoughts couldn't drive me mad. But if I stopped to take a deep breath, the ache of worry tried to surface.

So, I was glad when Ima appeared. 'Joben was boasting about how he'd taught you a lesson,' she said.

I saw her looking at what was left of Joben's bullying. We had cleared up the food and the broken soup bowl – luckily the tin rice plate was indestructible – but there were still damp stains on the papers I had tried to sponge clean.

She looked at me too – my hair was still damp. I had gone out to the rainwater barrel to rinse my face and hair. My clothes were still damp too. I had only two work dresses, which meant not washing one till the other was dry.

'I came to make sure you're all right. He's under pressure right now, that's all. Don't worry about him. My father won't let him send you away even if Hideki Tagawa isn't here.'

'Did Kobata-san say why he wants to send me away?'

'He said you're doing a bad job on the paper because your Japanese is as bad as your English, and he wants to replace you with someone more skilled. Also that you're lazy, you work too slowly, your office is filthy and you waste all your time sitting in the kitchen eating our food.'

The press room was certainly a mess right then.

'I am a bit behind schedule now.' I couldn't help adding, 'But I wasn't before he came down.'

'Don't worry. My father saw right through him. He told Joben that if he sacks you, he can't replace you with some slut. He'll have to do all the work himself. That was when my father sent me to find out if you know how to make *onigiri*. He has a meeting at four o'clock and he thought tea and a light snack would be good. I told him I would show you how to make *onigiri* like my mother used to make for him.'

Onigiri is to the Japanese what sandwiches are to the British or *bak zhang*, glutinous rice dumplings, are to us Singapore locals. No one asks if you know how to make a sandwich. Of course there are fancy versions but, chances are, if you've eaten or seen one, you pretty much know how to put them together.

'Of course,' I said. 'I'll wash the rice.'

I should have called one of the maids to do it, but Xiao Xi and Xiao Yu had bowed to Ima and scuttled away. Joben's earlier visit had spooked them. They were more used to Ima in the kitchens, but she also threw things when she lost her temper.

I didn't mind. I liked the feel of rice grains shifting under my fingers in cool water. I couldn't remember a time when I didn't know how to cook rice. One of my earliest memories was of squatting over the rice pot, picking out bits of grit and weevils before rinsing it with water I emptied over the kitchen garden. Rice grains I missed that were washed out of the pot were found and eaten by the chickens. If any escaped, the chickens ate them later when they sprouted. And, of course, we ate the chickens.

I had grown up thinking this was the pattern of life, would always be the pattern of life. In a way it still was. Only now we were the chickens, scratching for any grains we could find, until our Japanese masters decided to slaughter us.

Although Ima had said she would show me how to make her mother's *onigiri* recipe, she sat on the high stool by the window and ate slices of pickled mango while I worked. I didn't mind. It was nice to have company that prevented me from thinking too much. Because this rice would be shaped, I cooked it in less water than I would have for rice that would be fluffed. This way the cooked rice would be slightly stiff instead of sticky.

There is an old saying:

> *Boiling first,*
> *Steaming next,*
> *Do not touch the lid*
> *Though your baby's desperately crying.*

The point is, the rice pot should not be touched until the steaming process is complete as this cannot be rushed.

Because there were so many similarities between Chinese and Japanese food, the differences had become even more important. The competition between siblings is always fiercer than it is against strangers, because the need to prove yourself different is much greater. You can never hate a stranger with as much informed detail as you can hate a brother. That's how it is between the Chinese and Japanese.

Luckily for me, I'd learned about *washoku* or Japanese food from Mrs Maki, my first Japanese teacher. Mrs Maki was Hideki Tagawa's cousin. Like him, she was the cousin of my dead mother. I had not seen her since she returned to Japan.

As she'd taught me, I tossed the rice with a flat scoop to bring air into the cooked grains and release excess moisture. Handmade *onigiri* with salt was the most popular comfort food in Japan; Mrs Maki told me every time she made it that she remembered hungrily watching her own mother making it.

Which made me realise why I was worried about Hideki Tagawa. He was my last link with my mother. He had told me he and Ryoko had grown up together till he was sent away to school. But I was sure he had other stories to tell. If he didn't come back, my last connection with my mother would be gone for ever, and after I had come so close to finding out more about her.

'What's wrong?' Ima cut into my thoughts.

Caught in my reverie, I had stopped stirring the rice. 'What? Oh, nothing. Just seeing if it's ready.' I went to the pantry cupboard for the earthenware jar of salt.

'Not too much,' Ima warned, 'but it must have enough.'

How much is enough but not too much? I dampened my fingertips and dabbed them in the salt I had poured into a dish, then picked up a ball of rice. 'Hold it like you would hold your baby's hand,' Mrs Maki had said. 'Gentle but firm. If you press too hard, the *onigiri* will stiffen to a hard shell when it cools. You must allow a little air to remain between the rice grains so they remain moist and soft. When the salt spreads from your fingertips to your palms you have worked it enough.'

I was unlikely to have a baby of my own, I thought. I was practising on rice balls for nothing.

As though reading my mind, Ima said, 'Hideki Tagawa should be making plans for you to go to Japan where he can arrange a good marriage for you.'

The way she looked at me told me she was fishing. She had been working around to this because she wanted to know whether Hideki Tagawa had discussed his ideas with me. Did her father really want *onigiri* or was that part of her strategy too?

'He shouldn't wait too long. You're what – twenty-five, twenty-six years old?'

'Twenty-four. I was born in 1920, the year of the metal monkey.'

'Not good. Women age faster than men. Hideki Tagawa isn't anti-marriage, is he?'

'Not that I know of. He's never talked about it to me.'

'It doesn't matter so much for men. They can marry at fifty, at sixty even, as long as they have money, connections and parts that still work. But a woman should have daughters so she has someone to look after her in her old age. My mother always told me that. She even told me she was glad I was not a boy because

my father would have taken me with him. Do you know if Hideki
Tagawa knows someone who can fix up engagements?'

Cooking is like making clothes out of cloth scraps. I was
putting different fillings inside the *onigiri* rice casings, salted
fish, salted cod roe, mushrooms, pickled plums, and turning
these leftovers into novelties in rice casing. And as my fingers
worked, my mind picked out information from what Ima had
said, even if she had not put it into words..

This married woman with a very important father was in
love with Hideki Tagawa. I could see it even if she couldn't.

'What?' Ima demanded again. She looked suspicious. I must
have let some of my thoughts show on my face. I couldn't afford
to offend her. 'I was just wondering if Hideki Tagawa will be back
in time for the *onigiri*,' I said. If you're going to lie, it's always best
to distract at the same time.

It worked.

'Maybe he will,' Ima said. 'Let me help you. I'm going to make
some special ones for him. Are there any eggs?'

Of course there were. This was the Shori headquarters: if there
were eggs anywhere on the island, there would be eggs here.

'How many do you want?'

Ima hesitated. 'Just one. Maybe I should make one for my
father too. And that greedy fool Joben. But perhaps I should
practise first.'

'What do you have in mind? If you want to fry it first, one
each should be enough.'

'The *onigiri* my mother made for him had a whole soft egg
inside ...'

'That sounds good.'

'I don't know. Soon after that, he left us. And she never made it again. She hardly ever cooked after that. That was why I never had a chance to learn properly. Though she was a very good cook, you know.'

Ima had lost her mother as well as her father. That was what she was trying to recapture. At least her father was still alive.

'You'll need *ajitsuke tamago* for that,' I said. The eggs are poached briefly, then left to firm and gain flavour in a marinade of stock, soy sauce, mirin and *sake* for up to two days. After that time the whites are set like silk and the yolks deliciously oozing.

'Make me one, then.' Ima clearly didn't have any idea how long it took. Even if her mother hadn't taught her to cook she should have known something so basic. 'Make an extra. I also want one. Or better make two extra. Joben is such a pig.'

As it happened, I already had a batch of eggs marinating. I'd learned that an egg and a slab of salted pork in ramen was the quickest solution if Colonel Fujiwara demanded a meal in the middle of the night. And leftovers could be halved and served with any meal.

I scooped five eggs out of the marinade. They would be tasty – I had added sugar cane, dried shiitake mushrooms and dried anchovies.

'Whole egg or half egg in each *onigiri*?'

'Whole, of course. I remember his face when he took a huge greedy bite and the yolk spilled on his uniform!'

Ima laughed, but her face sobered immediately. I wondered what had happened.

'You'd better warn your father this time, then.'

Ima nodded, her face grim. She made no further attempt to

help, but watched as I squeezed a damp towel, then dabbed my fingertips in the dish of salt and scooped up a ball of rice. Not too much, just enough to give the already bulky egg the thinnest coating of sticky rice.

Ima said something, but—

'Sorry, what's that?' I asked. It had been a long time since I made *onigiri* and I'd never made them with ramen eggs before.

'You don't have to worry about making them all perfect. He probably won't eat more than a bite. Once he's messed up his shirt!'

'You're going to warn him,' I said again. 'I'll do my best. But I'm sure he'll like them if you say you made them specially for him.'

'Can I say that?'

'It was your idea. And you told me how to make them. So of course you can. It's not the egg *onigiri* that matters. A child writing "I love you" in the worst brush strokes means more to a parent than the most beautiful calligraphy of a stranger.'

'Not my father.' But Ima looked more cheerful.

I found my mood had improved too. Working with food always makes me feel better. I think it's a primal animal thing: if you have a meal to look forward to, things can't be totally hopeless.

'Do you think it's true nobody can touch Joben?'

I thought about it as I went on wrapping eggs in rice. Major Dewa had been right about me the first time we'd met. I would have been very happy to poison Joben Kobata if I could have got away with it – which was important to me. The murder of Joben Kobata wasn't worth dying for. At least, as far as I was concerned.

'Who would want to?'

'My husband seems to think everyone's against him. But he says he can bring down too many people with him.'

I thought Ima suspected Joben too. But how do you ask a woman if she believes her husband is a murderer? Or if she has any evidence to support it? And whether, if the worst happened and Hideki Tagawa was charged, Ima would sit back and say nothing while her husband sent an innocent man – well, not totally innocent, just more innocent than him – to die in his place?

'Why are you making that face?'

'When you say "my husband" your face looks like you're thinking "my problem". And you tell me to get married?'

'I'm not thinking "my problem", I'm thinking "that bag of shit". The kind of husband makes a lot of difference.'

'You think Hideki Tagawa would do better?'

'How dare you say that?' Ima slapped me before I could react. I dropped the *onigiri* I was holding. 'How dare you? Get out of here!'

'Hey, you're the one who said he should find me a husband.'

It took a moment for my words to filter through her rage. Then she turned and left the kitchen. I cleared up the mess of rice and egg on the floor. The other mess would be harder to deal with, but I had a new thought. Was Joben Kobata framing Hideki Tagawa because he suspected his wife was in love with him?

Rotten Winter Melon

———◆———

The egg *onigiri* were a success. I brought them into the dining room before the main meal and warned Colonel Fujiwara, 'Be careful. The egg inside is still soft.'

Colonel Fujiwara laughed and smashed his *onigiri* in his bowl, then scooped it up with a soup spoon. 'Good!'

'Your daughter made these *onigiri* specially for you.'

'What?'

'Don't you remember my mother making this for you?' Ima asked him.

'A lot of places make *onsen tamago*,' Joben said. 'What's the big deal?' But I noticed he ate two with gusto. I was glad, because I'd made sure to hand him the one made with rice I'd scraped off the floor.

I left them once the maids had finished serving the meal. I didn't eat with the family unless Hideki Tagawa was present, which meant I might never eat with them again. I wouldn't miss it at all.

If you'd seen them eating together, you wouldn't have thought there was a war on.

Around them, I had to act as if nothing was threatening our lives and nothing was missing, because what was the point of saying something everyone knew?

It was like everyone pretended we seasoned everything we ate with salt, *belacan*, shrimp paste, and chilli because we liked it, not because there were no shallots, onions or garlic to be had. They didn't grow well here and were no longer imported. It was such a small thing, but at times I felt I would have killed to taste the sweet, sharp crunch of raw red onion.

And while I thanked tapioca and coconuts – both fast-growing and readily available – for keeping us alive, right then I would have been happy never to taste either of them again.

Given the mood I was in, I thought it best to get away from everyone else. If only I'd had somewhere to go! I wanted to walk away from everything there and never come back.

Instead, I went back to the kitchen. And it was lucky I did.

'Miss, somebody want to see you. About vegetables,' Ah Peng said.

'What vegetables?'

'Don't know. Back gate. She don't want come in.'

It was Mrs Wong, Corporal Wong Kan Seng's mother. She had a small wooden handcart with her, the kind farmers use to trundle vegetables to market and charcoal and oil back home.

'Su Lin, sorry to come here like this—'

'Is it Kan Seng? Have you heard something?' A wild hope leaped inside me.

'No, no. It's Sergeant Pillay. He has been locked up.'

I felt dizzy with horror. I was sure it was because of the note I'd sent him. Why had I been so stupid? Of course the Japanese would have Malay translators! Why had I risked Prakesh's life?

It took me a moment to realise Mrs Wong was still talking, 'I'm sure it's because he arranged for us to sell vegetables to the PoW prison. He got us a travel pass, you know. And he signed it. He was only trying to help us. Now he cannot leave the camp. Cannot even come out and talk to me. Oh, I'm so worried. *Sekali* he also *habis*. How?'

'*Habis*' was a good word. It might mean gone or finished or – but not necessarily – dead. I knew she was thinking of her son as well as Prakesh Pillay. As for '*sekali*', it meant 'What if?' in a way that could be either bad or good ... '*Sekali* you win the lottery tomorrow?' or '*Sekali* tomorrow we all die?'.

'He couldn't talk to you? How do you know all this, then?' I asked.

'The guard said I must leave the *brinjal* and tapioca outside. Usually I go inside and if Prakesh is there he gives me water to drink. But today the guard said I cannot go in. Nobody can go in and nobody can come out.'

It wasn't just Prakesh in detention, then. The horror bubble in my chest eased a little. 'So you didn't talk to Prakesh?'

'I did. I unloaded everything outside, like they said. But then before I left, Prakesh ran out and threw a winter melon at me. He shouted that it was rotten and I must take it back to the Chen bitch I got it from – sorry, that's what he said – and make sure you look inside it and see for yourself.'

'He threw a *dong gua* at you?'

'Yes. This one.' Mrs Wong handed me a paper-wrapped bundle. I could tell whatever was inside was rotten. It was soft and smelt bad. 'I never ever sold them any winter melons. But when I tried to say so, he shouted at me to shut up and leave, and bring it back to you right away.'

'Did the guard say anything?'

'The guard was laughing because Prakesh was so angry with me.'

'I'm sure he was acting,' I said. It could hardly have made a difference to her, but looking at the worry lines that pain had carved into her face, I didn't want to add to them. 'Thank you for bringing it here.'

Mrs Wong nodded. 'Our Kan Seng likes him very much. And Kan Seng likes you also. Tell them I scolded you, even though I got no more strength to scold.'

She was acting too. She mightn't have had the strength to smile or glare at me, but she squeezed my fingers hard before leaving, like she was trying to pass on what little energy she had left to me.

I brought the *dong gua* with me into the toilet and hooked the latch into place.

The winter melon had been cut in half and tied back together. Its insides had been scooped out and the hard half shells of a cannonball fruit stuffed in. Still lined with pulp, this was what was causing the stink of rot and decay.

But what was written on the papers folded into the cigarette tin inside stank even more.

Prakesh wrote that he'd followed my recipe and found evidence that the disappearance of the PoWs had been sanctioned by someone high up in the INA hierarchy. Their transfer had been authorised by someone in the Shori headquarters.

I assumed Prakesh had been detained because his investigations had triggered something. But it seemed more that the information I had sent him had made him decide to trust me with his.

Very Important. Send to Wooden House.
INA confined to training barracks. Sending us to
India with no ammo in weapons. See invasion
plans re: Jap planned attacks on civilians in
Kohima and Imphal via Burma.

The plans were a scribbled series of numbers – coordinates, times and troops.

At least Prakesh was alive for now, but what was I supposed to do with this? What did he expect me to do? I felt a wild desire to stuff the notes back into the melon and dump the whole thing into the WC hole. I would forget all about it, pretend I knew nothing. No one could blame me for doing that. How dare Prakesh drag me into this? It was a hundred thousand times more dangerous than de Souza's sharing news he'd heard on the wireless.

'Su Lin?'

I jumped when Ima banged on the door.

'Why are you inside there so long? What are you doing?'

What did she think anyone did in the WC?

Quickly, I tucked Prakesh's notes into my underwear as I noisily used the dipper to scoop water into the WC hole. I kicked the hollow winter melon and cannonball shells behind the pile of leaves and rags that served as toilet paper.

Ima pushed open the door and barged in as soon as she heard me lift the latch hook. She sniffed, and I was grateful the odour of cannonball pulp still hung in the air, making the always foetid WC stink even worse. 'What's wrong with you?'

Had the servants told her about Mrs Wong coming to see

223

me? I was too upset to act naturally so I didn't try. I crossed my hands over my lower belly, making sure the papers didn't slip, and said, 'Nothing. I'm fine.'

'Well, come on, then. Didn't you hear me calling for you?'

'No. Is something wrong with the food?'

'What? No. Why are you always thinking about food? Nothing like that. Joben's saying that you or one of the servants went into his office and planted papers in his safe. Did you?'

'No! Of course not!'

'Then come and tell my father and Major Dewa that.'

'Major Dewa is here?'

'I told you he was. About the papers in Joben's office! Come on!'

Ima grabbed my arm and tugged me towards the house. I felt the papers slipping. Loose knickers are comfortable, but not much good for hiding things. I clutched at my belly again.

'I got to go to the WC again – and I need to go back to my room. I'll come as soon as I finish–'

'Well … at least you're not pregnant.' Ima looked disgusted. 'If you were healthier your moon periods wouldn't bother you so much. But hurry up, and bring tea for Major Dewa and my father when you come. I want sour-plum water. Don't bother to get anything for Joben.'

I fled back into the WC.

Once I was sure she was gone, I hurried to my room and looked for somewhere to hide what was left of Prakesh's note. I'd shredded his message and put it down the WC, but kept the list of numbers and coordinates. My memory was good, but without knowing what they stood for, it would be too easy to make a mistake. What did Prakesh expect me to do with them?

More importantly, where could I hide the list? If Major Dewa was with Colonel Fujiwara, they could decide to search my space at any time, and I had to get myself to Colonel Fujiwara's office before Ima came to look for me again.

In the end, I decided not to try to hide it. I fixed it with a casual paper clip to the inside cover of the *Syonan Weekly*'s operating-expenses log.

The recurring payment for the 'Mokuzō jūtaku' or wooden-house advertisement caught my eye. Was that what Prakesh meant? Did he know something about the advertisement that I didn't?

I put the kettle on to boil and set out four cups. For Major Dewa and her father, Ima had said. If Major Dewa was there, Magnetophon Man would be too. And whatever Ima said, I would bring a cup for Joben Kobata. He was Colonel Fujiwara's son-in-law, not just her husband.

Ribbons for Noriko

———◆———

The loud voices in Colonel Fujiwara's office stopped as soon as I knocked, but no one told me to enter. I waited until Ima came to unlock and open the door. She looked tense and excited, like a child who has told tales on others and is waiting to see them get into trouble.

The men in the room looked grim. Colonel Fujiwara was sitting behind his enormous desk and Major Dewa was standing with his back to the bookshelf. Both were glaring at Joben Kobata, who was slumped in a chair in the corner.

And I had been right about Major Dewa's shadow, Magnetophon Man. He was standing against the wall by the door, his huge recording machine on the table where I'd meant to place the tea tray.

Magnetophon Man bowed an apology but his tape reels were turning and he made no attempt to move. I bowed my acknowledgement of his immobility - wasn't that what I spent most of my life doing? - and found another table.

'We don't need her any more,' Major Dewa said. 'Girl, get out of here.'

'Sir?' Was he ordering me out of this room, this job or this life?

'You think she had nothing to do with it just because Ima says so? Why should you believe anything my wife says? Don't you know women are all liars? Beat the truth out of her and see what she says!'

They couldn't possibly know Prakesh had sent word to me, could they? But if not that, what was this 'truth' they were after?

'The worst day of my life was the day I married you,' Ima said. 'All you do is sweat and cry.'

I felt almost sorry for Joben.

'You brought tea?' Colonel Fujiwara said.

'Yes, sir.'

I served them all tea. Joben petulantly knocked over the cup I put beside him and said, 'Bring me some English rum.'

'Not now,' Colonel Fujiwara said. 'Miss Chen, Kobata-san accused you of planting photographs and papers among his personal belongings—'

'I never accused your precious Ebisu-chan of anything. All I said is, anyone in this house could have sneaked into my room and hidden stuff there. Like her and those servants. They're probably all spies for the rebels. You should question them! Let me question them!'

The thought of him torturing lies out of the servants lit anger in me. 'Is something missing from your room, sir?'

'You'd know, wouldn't you? Anyway, all I said is those photos and papers aren't mine.'

'The photograph from your desk?' I looked at the spot on Colonel Fujiwara's desk where the photograph of him with his wife and children used to stand. Ima had accused the servants of stealing it for its gold frame, but a search of their quarters had revealed nothing.

'You found the photograph of your wife and children? Even if the frame is broken, I can try to fix it for you. You should have it close to you.'

'Photograph of his wife?' To my surprise, the soft exclamation came from Magnetophon Man.

'No,' said Major Dewa, 'these photographs. Come here, girl.'

Major Dewa spread the photographs over Colonel Fujiwara's desk. They were the standard 3½- x 5½-inch prints, and showed soldiers in Japanese armour and masks fighting naked, unarmed Indian and European men and women. They were more like Mimi's photographs than the ones Ima had shown me.

I stared. Major Dewa watched me. I didn't have to pretend to be shocked but what I was thinking was *They haven't been pissed on.* If these were the photographs Mimi had been carrying under her dress, whoever had killed her had taken them before Joben emptied his bladder on her body.

'And there are some papers that suggest he's been selling information to the rebels via Ryu Takahashi.'

'Rubbish. Lies. Ima, say something! Can't you see they're trying to attack me to get to your father?'

'We have to talk.' Colonel Fujiwara said. 'In private. Go away.' This was to me. 'You too.' This was to Magnetophon Man. 'Stop that machine and get out.'

'No,' said Major Dewa. 'This investigation must be recorded.'

'Get rid of him and that damned machine. Or both of you can get out. For good.'

Major Dewa looked between Colonel Fujiwara and Joben. Then he jerked his head at Magnetophon Man. 'Go.'

I waited as Magnetophon Man put his machine onto its folding trolley and we left the room together.

'Would you like something to eat or drink, sir?'

'I don't want to be any trouble. I can wait for the major outside.'

'There are mosquitoes outside. Come and sit in the front room. The windows are screened,' I suggested.

'Thank you. I would like to sit down for a while. With my spectacles and magnifying glasses I can see what I want to see, and for me that is perfect eyesight. But it gets tiring sometimes. I will close my eyes, if you don't mind.'

He was older than I'd realised. 'It can't be easy for you, following Major Dewa around with that machine. Do you transcribe the recordings?'

'Only if there is something the major wants to recall. There isn't time to transcribe it all. Are you interested in recording machines too?'

'Too?'

He smiled. 'An ambiguous question. You are interested in cameras, I believe. I thought you might be interested in this machine that records sound as your camera records images. And, second, I am interested in modern technology, especially German technology like this. I was hoping you shared the interest.'

'Is that why you're here?'

'You mean, is that why an old man like me is doing a job like this?' He laughed at my confusion. 'Yes. It's partly because I have a passion for modern technology. But only partly. My name is Akio Yamamoto. I am the uncle of Colonel Fujiwara's wife.'

'You are Ima's uncle?'

'The colonel's third wife, I should have said. Colonel Fujiwara's first wife was Ima's mother. Colonel Fujiwara's second wife died with their young son several years before Colonel Fujiwara married his third wife, my niece.'

Ah, the wife whose photograph had been in the gold frame on Colonel Fujiwara's desk. The photo that had disappeared. 'Why didn't she come here with him?'

'Why indeed?' Akio Yamamoto said placidly. 'I advised her to stay in Japan because of her ill health. Ima already said she would come out to care for her father and it is good not to have too many women in one house.'

His face was tanned dark, with fine deep lines, like cloth that has been wrung tight and left to dry. But his eyes were sharp behind his spectacles. He reminded me of my grandmother assessing a new business contact.

'Do you need anything, sir?'

'At the moment, only patience.'

'You have a greater supply than I do.'

He smiled as I bowed and left him.

Leaving Akio Yamamoto in the front room, I went back upstairs quietly to see if I could make out anything through the door. The only person I could make out clearly was Joben, alternately raging and whining. The other men muttered and growled, and

Ima murmured or was silent. I heard 'Tagawa' several times, but couldn't tell what they said about him.

I locked the servants into their quarters as usual. I knew better than to try to sleep while my fate was being decided. If it came down to a choice between putting the blame on Hideki Tagawa or Joben Kobata, the answer was clear. The image of Colonel Fujiwara as supreme authority of Syonan had to be preserved, so his son-in-law had to be preserved.

I was only there because of Hideki Tagawa. If he was charged with treason, I would be finished too.

An hour later, I went out and quietly unlocked the doors of the servants' quarters. If anything happened in the night, they deserved a chance to run for their lives.

All I could do was wait. I sat in the press room, because from there I could hear the kitchen bell ring if Colonel Fujiwara wanted anything.

The next issue of the *Syonan Weekly* was ready to go to the printer. I would miss even this. It might be propaganda hack work, but at least I was still working with words and translations.

I looked again at the prominent advertisement that had run since Miss Briggs's time: 'Take two steps forward from each new beginning and if you ever need HELP, just give Noriko ribbons.'

I must have seen it a hundred times, but now, to my tired brain, it read like a cryptic-crossword-puzzle clue.

Miss Briggs had loved the cryptic crosswords in the *Observer.* That was why she ordered the paper shipped out east. It took a month to arrive, so its news was always outdated compared to what was reported on the wireless. But Miss Briggs didn't care.

What mattered to her was the cryptic crossword, which she took pride in completing in ink, never pencil.

If I needed HELP I should 'just give Noriko ribbons' after I'd obeyed the 'take two steps forward from each new beginning'? There was something: I felt it.

But I didn't know what to do with Noriko and her stupid ribbons, so I started with 'help'.

It felt stupid to be playing with acrostics, but what else could I do? If playing word puzzles took my mind off what was going on upstairs for a while, that could only be good.

H-E-L-P

If I moved each of these letters two steps down the alphabet, H became J and E became G . . . I got J-G-N-R.

As in Just Give Noriko Ribbons.

Could it be as simple as that?

'Come on,' I said out loud. 'That's it?'

Took you long enough, didn't it? I heard Miss Briggs say in my mind. It was the same dry voice she'd used when I'd asked for extra time on an exercise because I was almost there. She'd given me the extra time though. 'I like your determination,' she'd said. 'Always remember determination will do you more good than money or connections.'

I suspect she deliberately set impossible times to challenge us. Some girls, those who only attended the Mission Centre school because their parents wanted them to marry English-educated boys – who could get jobs with British-run companies – called Miss Briggs unfair and over-demanding. Since I'd never expected life to be fair, I enjoyed her challenges.

Now I only hoped I would have a chance one day to tell her

I'd worked out the advertisement puzzle she'd planted in the *Syonan Weekly*.

I prepared a message to 木造住宅 Mokuzō jūtaku or Wooden House. I left Prakesh's numbers and coordinates exactly as they were, in the centre of the advertisement. But I used the code to explain where they had come from. Having to use words starting with certain alphabets made for awkward sentences, but all Japanese–English translations were slightly awkward. I created a soppy romantic message about how many cherry-blossom seasons had passed since we were children studying arithmetic side by side in our schooldays. That should be enough to explain what appeared to be a sequence of nonsensical numbers.

And then I pulled apart the personal column and reset it. I'd finished the typesetting earlier in the day, but inserting this meant changing the layout and resetting everything.

In the end I worked through the night, only realising it was morning when the sleepy-eyed maids and house-boys came out of their quarters to wash. Seeing me, they assumed I'd unlocked their door early, which spared me having to explain my possible disappearance and other consequences I'd been imagining as the result of last night's meeting.

I had even forgotten about that meeting.

Now Colonel Fujiwara's office was empty and Magnetophon Man gone from the front room. They had all gone and I had no idea what our fate was to be. But the new layout was typeset and I had it sent on to the printer.

Of course, there was no guarantee anyone would receive the message, even if I'd got the code right. I could only hope someone in the Allied forces or the Resistance was still following the personal advertisements in the *Syonan Weekly*. And that the wrong people wouldn't notice it.

Even if they got the message, would it be in time? The Japanese soldiers were already moving into position.

I've always hated waiting.

I tried to think of it as practice.

Waiting Games

———◆———

The waiting continued through the day. I knew Hideki Tagawa was back because he asked the house-boy to bring him food, but he had not come to see me.

To be honest, I couldn't have coped with anything more. I was proud of myself for managing to reset a whole page layout before the morning pick-up, but I was dazed from lack of sleep. Was this what being drunk felt like? It wasn't totally unpleasant. I felt detached, as if I was watching myself move like a puppet through the routine actions of the day.

The *Syonan Weekly* was published. The first proofs were delivered before 10 a.m., as usual, for editorial approval. As usual, Joben glanced at and approved them without paying much attention.

And then – nothing. Now all I could do was hope someone (but who?) aware of Miss Briggs's code was still following the personal column in the *Syonan Weekly*. Though surely everyone connected with the Allied forces in the region was either dead or in hiding.

My greatest dread was that the Japanese would notice. Wooden House's vague sentimental message had been running for as long as I could remember, but till now I'd never seen a reply posted. Surely someone would find that suspicious.

Luckily, I wasn't the only one out of sorts that day. The whole household was tense with not knowing what would be the result of the Hideki Tagawa/Joben Kobata investigation, because it was also a power struggle between Major Dewa and Colonel Fujiwara. Major Dewa wanted to shake things up and make sure every cent and every action was documented and approved. Colonel Fujiwara wanted to go on administering things in the way he always had. He had run several businesses in civilian life and, as far as he was concerned, running a country was not so different. He put people he liked in power and they remembered what they owed to him.

Their disagreements had grown petty. Colonel Fujiwara had objected to Magnetophon Man sitting in on all their meetings. I didn't know if he was aware of the part he'd played in keeping the colonel's third wife in Japan.

'I don't like that old man in here. He gives me the creeps.' Colonel Fujiwara had used the word 'ima-imashii', which translates to something doomed to damnation but worse, though Akio Yamamoto had been standing right there behind his machine. I couldn't tell if the colonel was just being bad-tempered or whether he was deliberately attacking him. 'My Ebisu-chan can record meetings.'

Of course, and to my relief, Major Dewa had objected to my being in the room if his Magnetophon Man wasn't. They had compromised by sending for a second recording machine, to be operated by an official chosen by Colonel Fujiwara. Until it arrived, the interviews were suspended. As far as Colonel Fujiwara was concerned, it was business as usual. But Joben was sulking in his room and refused to put his chop of approval on the *Syonan Weekly* so it could go into the archive. 'You sly, sneaking bitch! How dare you barge in here? "Yes, sir. Can you approval chop this so I can file it?" You don't mind ruining people's lives, do you?'

He sounded so pitiful I felt a sudden urge to laugh. Then I really would have sounded like the crazy vengeful witch he saw me as.

'You're finished here, you know that, don't you? You're dead. Your whole family is dead. Just do your job and leave me alone!'

'Yes, sir.'

I backed politely out of his bedroom and closed the door gently behind me. In his office I paused and listened for footsteps. They didn't come to the door but went to the locked cabinet. I guessed he was fortifying himself with a drink.

'Sir, this issue?' I said, through the door.

'Approve and file it,' he snarled. I heard the key turn in the lock, then the sound of an animal in pain – something between a roar and a groan – through the locked door.

I authorised the magazine with Joben's official chop and sent it to the archive. I didn't know where the message would be picked up and couldn't afford to miss any steps.

Copies were being printed and distributed across the island. I didn't know anyone who used it for anything other than lavatory paper, so could it really do any good? But I had done all I could.

That's true, is it? I heard Miss Briggs's wry, dry voice in my mind's ear again. *As long as you're still alive, you haven't yet done all you can.*

'I've done all I can for now,' I said out loud. And I was going to have a short nap. At my desk, of course, in case anything came in for Joben that I had to take care of.

'No, please, cannot.'

'We are scared to go outside at night.'

'There's funny sounds out there.'

I was woken by the maids' and house-boys' voices in the kitchen outside the press room. It was evening, I realised. I had fallen asleep after lunch had been cleared away. I could only hope there would be no unexpected guests for dinner.

'Don't be ridiculous. It's completely safe. You're just being lazy!'

Ima was there. I rubbed my eyes, smoothed my hair and went to find out what she wanted.

'Please, ma'am, can we wait until tomorrow?'

'If you don't want to work here, you don't have to.'

'I'll deal with it.' I limped out, my good leg stiff from sleeping twisted in a chair. 'What do you want from the outside? More flowers for the house?'

'That's not it. But while you're out there, you might as well get some from the cannonball tree. Especially for Joben's room. He's always complaining about mosquitoes, and the smell is supposed to keep them away.'

'He says he doesn't like it,' I said. Joben had smashed one floral arrangement I'd set up in the corridor outside his room. 'He thinks flowers attract insects into the house at night.'

'It doesn't matter what he thinks. Nobody cares what he thinks. But it'll be good for him, good for his health,' Ima said. 'Are you afraid of going outside at night because of that tree, like these fools?'

The maids and the house-boys shook their heads at me. I couldn't tell if they meant they weren't scared or didn't want me going outside.

'What are you afraid of?' I asked them.

'Nothing.'

'It's late. We have to cook,' Xiao Yu pleaded. Xiao Xi nodded vigorously.

Dinner was to be *zosui*, or Japanese rice soup, made from what was left of yesterday's hot pot. I had only to add the leftover rice and vegetables to the heated soup. It would be a tasty dish, thanks to the dried fish, mushrooms and seaweed that had gone into the stock. But it didn't take much work.

'Is everything all right?' I tried to look as though I'd been distracted from a tough work session.

'I was just teasing them. They're so superstitious. They think that that woman dying so near the shrine summoned a Mononoke demon, who's outside looking for revenge.'

In other words, that was what Ima had told them. On their own, locals would have lit a joss stick to show respect and assumed the dead had enough business of their own to worry about.

'The Mononoke is a monster that comes from a human soul that's died carrying a grudge,' Ima said. 'It is full of anger and misery and wants to take it out on living people. Some can look very human. By the time you're close enough to see it's not, it's too late. This Mononoke has successfully killed one person so it will be hunting for the next.'

I saw the girls, pretending not to listen, glance fearfully out of the window. One of the house-boys who'd started to go out with the kitchen scraps hesitated and came back to drag the other with him. Ima nudged me and rolled her eyes at them.

It made me angry. Yes, they were silly. But they were also very young. If not for the war, they would still have been at school or at least with their families, and they must already have lived through horrors that were unimagined when they were born.

'We have stories about spirits here too,' I said. 'A lot of the time, anything we can't explain is blamed on the spirits. Better to blame the spirits than your neighbours' children for stealing your *jambu*.'

This made the girls giggle. *Jambu*, or rose apples, were mostly ignored by adults unless they had mouth ulcers or throat problems, but children often challenged each other to climb the tall *jambu bol* trees for the brightly coloured but tasteless or sour fruit.

They had probably grown up with *jambu* as well as cannonball trees. But the stone shrine was evidence of how locals acknowledged the superstitions and moved on. Once you made your offering, you and the spirits were at peace. That gave me an idea. 'Why don't we make an offering to the dead woman at the stone shrine? Then she'll leave us in peace.'

The little stone shrine looked like the ones set up along trails for fallen travellers. Those outside grand buildings were often for any injured in the construction process. They weren't so much supernatural as a reminder of those who had gone before.

I was more concerned about live Japanese than ghosts of dead locals. 'Tomorrow we can put some flowers and tapioca in the stone shrine for anybody who died around there.'

The maids liked the idea. Sometimes it's what we do that sets us at peace, not the spirits we do it for.

'Really, the most dangerous thing about cannonball trees is that wild pigs love the fruit,' I added. 'But with the fencing in place, that shouldn't be a problem. There's nothing to be scared of.'

'We heard funny sounds coming from the cannonball tree,' Xiao Yu said.

Ima snorted.

'Ghosts!' Xiao Xi whispered, more scared of the supernatural than of Ima.

'I heard them too,' I said. 'It may not be ghosts. It's probably a bird or an insect or a Japanese burglar.'

'What?'

'In Japan they believe whistling at night will attract burglars or snakes into your home. If a snake comes we can make snake soup.'

'Don't talk rubbish about snakes,' Ima snapped. 'Why wait till tomorrow? You're as scared as they are, aren't you?'

Ima was scared, I realised. She was trying to frighten the girls and me so that she could laugh at her own fear in us. If I'd had any sense of self-preservation I would have acted scared and let her feel superior and happy.

'Fine. No problem. Want to come with me?' Actually it would feel good to get out of the house for a bit. It was evening, not even completely dark yet.

'It's not just any old offering. You have to burn a photograph,' Ima said. 'A special photograph.'

'I already saw those photographs.' I wasn't acting when I winced at the memory. I knew Ima only mentioned the pictures because she knew they made me uncomfortable. 'Look, you want flowers? I'll go and get them.'

I would have to climb up to get the flowers, which grew in large bunches off the trunk above the smallest fruit. With my leg, walking wasn't easy. But, surprisingly, climbing was. On an uneven surface, legs of different lengths don't count as a disadvantage.

'You have to burn one so that the spirits won't come into the house. Take this one. Look at it. When you burn it at the snake shrine, apologise to the spirits in the photo for what they had to go through in life.'

I glanced at the photograph she was holding out. It was different from the ones I'd seen in Colonel Fujiwara's office. How many were there? Then I looked more closely.

Horror and disbelief competed in me as I realised why something about the masked figure standing over the naked prone body was familiar. Suddenly I knew who the pissing soldier in the photograph was.

'What's wrong?' Ima looked pleased. She had found my weak spot and was going to make the most of it.

I shook my head. It was easiest to let her think I was still upset over the photographs. Joben wasn't the only one who was a bully. His wife was too.

'Do you see anything familiar?'

Till then I'd been acting scared. Now I tried to act casual. 'Ha!

You recognise his birthmark! Don't lie to me! I can see you do! My husband has been playing with you with his pants down! Oh, Miss Pure and Virtuous, what is Hideki Tagawa going to say when he finds out you've been sleeping with my husband? What do you think my father will do to you? You can't look at photos of naked men but you have no problem looking at naked men, ha?'

I ran out into the garden to get away from her. There was too much going on in my head to worry about ghosts. Too many thoughts were fighting for attention in my head. I couldn't figure out which chain to follow first.

I thought I heard strange whistling sounds coming from beyond the fence. It was too dark and the undergrowth too thick, and I couldn't see anything. The tune was familiar. If some spirit was trying to lure me to my doom it had picked the wrong time. I was too fixated on figuring out the evil in live humans to have any brain space for spirits.

I had no time for ghosts. I had to talk to Hideki Tagawa.

Bum Evidence

———◆———

'Joben Kobata has something called dermal melanocytosis on his behind,' I told Hideki Tagawa. 'I recognised it because Dr Shankar told us what it was when my uncle's daughter was born with what looked like bruises on her lower back, as if someone had beaten her. Her mother was afraid that spirits had tried to hurt her, but Dr Shankar said it was a birthmark and would probably disappear by the time she went to school. He said in the West people call them Mongolian spots, but he didn't like telling Chinese and Korean people their babies had Mongolian spots—'

'So?' Hideki Tagawa looked at me and waited. I had interrupted his exercise session when I'd barged into his room without asking permission.

He had once told me I didn't talk as much nonsense as most women. He might be changing his mind now, but I had too much information to give him to keep it all in the right order.

Much better to dump it all out first. We could sort the rice from the grit and weevils later.

'That was why when I saw that photograph I knew it was him. The birthmark that's shaped like Australia on his buttocks. It's the same one that's in the photograph.'

'You recognised Joben Kobata's buttocks.'

'Yes, but it's not what Ima thinks. That's not Ima's fault – everybody here knows what Joben is like. That's the real reason I told Colonel Fujiwara I would lock the servants in at night, more to protect them from him than to protect the colonel from them.'

'Did Joben Kobata try to have sex with you?'

Why was he asking irrelevant questions instead of letting me get on with the facts?

'Once. But never again. The thing is, this shows Joben not only knew about Ryu's photographs and studio, he was acting in the photographs. And maybe they weren't all acting. Maybe some were really getting–'

But Hideki Tagawa still wasn't paying attention, 'What do you mean he tried? What did he try? What happened?'

'What?'

'Where is that man?' Hideki Tagawa got to his feet and started for the door.

I'd gone to his room because I wanted to talk to him before Ima or someone else got everything confused. But it looked like he was confusing himself without Ima's help.

'Wait.' I grabbed his arm and winced when he spun round, tight with fury, and barely stopped himself reflexively elbowing me in the face. 'Listen to me first. I've got to tell you everything before you talk to him!'

'Then tell me what Joben Kobata did to you.'

'I'm telling you he didn't do anything. He tried when they first came to Singapore. He tried to charm me and then he tried to frighten me. He said he would get you into trouble unless I did what he wanted.'

'And?'

'And I said he could do what he wanted but I would tell you. I think he's scared of you.'

Hideki Tagawa shook his head. 'All right. Tell me everything.'

'That day when I came back and found the dead body, Joben came and sent me into the house. But I looked back and saw him pull down his pants and pee on her. That's when I saw the birthmark on his bottom. And that's why I know the masked soldier urinating on the dead man in the photograph Ima showed me is him. You can see only part of the birthmark, but it's there.'

'Why didn't you say something before? Where is this photograph? Where did Ima get it?'

'I don't know. It was so weird, and nobody said anything about there being urine on the corpse. I didn't know if it was some weird Japanese custom ...'

'What?'

'And he's Colonel Fujiwara's son-in-law.'

'So he can't do anything wrong? Be careful. You're starting to think like a Japanese bureaucrat.' He paced rapidly. Five steps left, five steps right, five steps left ... it was a small room but he needed to work off the energy generated by his mental processes.

'Are you going to tell Major Dewa?'

'I need to talk to Joben first. And Colonel Fujiwara. You said Ima has this photograph. Where did she get it?'

'I don't know. She said she wanted me to burn it, to set free the spirits of the dead in the photo.' Looking back, though, I suspect Ima had wanted to gauge my reaction on seeing it.

He snorted. 'You're sure it's him?'

'A hundred per cent.'

'I have to check on a few things. Don't say anything to anybody until I get back. Don't do anything.'

'I have to make dinner.'

'Just make dinner.'

The confrontation took place that evening in Colonel Fujiwara's office. Major Dewa was not there, but Hideki Tagawa asked Ima to come and bring the photograph with her.

Far from minding that Hideki Tagawa knew about it, Ima seemed girlishly pleased. 'I should have known your little cripple was faithful to you!'

Both Hideki Tagawa and I recoiled, which made her laugh. 'I'm sorry I suspected you of sleeping with my husband. But you don't know what it's like, being married to a man like him. Everywhere we go, all the young girls start having babies!'

'Except you!' Joben snarled. He had stayed in his room until then, claiming he wasn't well. And he did look sick. 'If your precious family line dies out, don't blame me. I'm not the one cursing the family with infertility.' He used a much more offensive term than 'infertility' that I won't translate here.

Ima ignored him. 'Anyway, I'm sorry.'

'Why say sorry to that bastard?' Joben riposted. 'Tagawa's the one who killed Ryu. And he killed that slut in the garden. If you're not careful he'll kill you next. All of you!'

'You can't blame this on Hideki Tagawa,' I found myself saying, 'You are the one Ryu photographed in the bunker killing unarmed men. You're pissing on that dead man just like I saw you piss on Mimi. The authorisations must have come from you. Look, all I want is to clear Hideki Tagawa's name and for you to promise to be good to Ima. None of this will go public unless you mistreat Ima.'

'I'll piss on you too,' Joben sneered. 'I'm not listening to any more of your talk-talk-talk. What can you do to me? Nothing. I'm not wasting any more of my time here. And show some respect when you talk to me, or I'll have you shot.' He got up and started for the door. Ima pulled at his arm and he slapped her away. It was a weak blow and I don't think she was hurt, but she screamed and Colonel Fujiwara roared, making them both shut up.

'The authorisations had to have come from you,' Hideki Tagawa said. He spoke quietly, but Joben winced as though he'd jabbed at him with a hot grill stick. 'This afternoon I went through all the transaction records Major Dewa collected. In less than two hours I was able to determine with a high degree of probability that you were involved in at least two information leaks around the same time as funds were given to Ryu Takahashi. I was also able to identify five similar coincidences since your arrival on the island that I believe you were also connected with. Now that we know Ryu Takahashi was part of it, things are easier. He didn't bother to hide his tracks as well as you did.'

'Liar! You've been making up stories and faking records to frame me. Everybody knows you're a nobody who can't be trusted. Anyway, so what? The man's dead. What are you going to do? Arrest me based on evidence from a dead man? Will you

tell Major Dewa to dig him out of the ground and question him?'
Joben tried to look as if he didn't care, but he just looked sicker.

'I will inform Major Dewa,' Hideki Tagawa said. 'I will provide
him with what I've found so far. It should keep him occupied for
a while.'

'No,' Colonel Fujiwara said faintly. 'That won't be necessary.
Just tell him everything is resolved. There will be no more leaks,
no more money disappearing.'

'It must be put down on official record. Officially but
confidentially. We must give Major Dewa a reason to stop the
investigation.'

'Impossible. People will talk,' Ima said. 'Besides, what's to stop
the major using it to force my father to step down?'

'Make him confess into that Magnetophon,' I said, 'and keep
the tape. Then you'll have proof in his own words. Mr Akio is
related to Colonel Fujiwara. He will keep it confidential.'

Hideki Tagawa shook his head. 'Major Dewa will keep it
quiet. It's his job to maintain authority and that includes your
father's image and position. But he must be satisfied or he'll go
on digging.'

'Can't you just order Major Dewa to stop? Say you're satisfied?'
Ima asked her father. 'Order him to go back to Japan. Or to make
trouble somewhere else. Tell him Hideki Tagawa will help you
handle things here.'

This triggered Joben: 'I'm the one who's supposed to help
him handle things. Isn't that why you dragged us out here? Look,
I didn't want to come to this bloody hot island in the middle of
nowhere, but I did. You want me to take your family name? I'll
do it. You adopt me formally and I'll get your daughter pregnant

with your grandson. Major Dewa will have to bow to me and won't dare pull any of his tricks. Hey, once you adopt me and give me a proper inheritance, any child I have will carry your name. You won't need her any more.'

'How dare you?' I was shocked and angry, and expected Ima to be even more so. But I saw she looked satisfied.

'Now everyone sees you for what you are,' she said. 'No more pretending.'

She smiled at Joben, which seemed to unnerve him more than any threat.

'I don't want to hurt you or your family,' he said. 'We can work out something that will make us all happy.'

'Very well,' Hideki Tagawa said. Then, turning to me, 'Leave us.'

I was glad to go. The session had gone better than I'd dared hope. I could still feel the rapid heartbeats in my throat, and my head ached from the effort of looking calm and agreeable. But Joben Kobata had all but confessed that Ryu Takahashi had extorted money from him and that he had killed the man for it.

I just wanted to know why he had killed Mimi. Or, rather, I wanted to know that I couldn't have done anything to prevent her death.

Long after I'd left, I heard Colonel Fujiwara and Joben shouting in the office. Now and then there would be a shrill tirade from Ima. I knew Hideki Tagawa was still there too, though I didn't hear his voice.

I don't think the big bosses realised how sound carried in that old colonial building because everyone but them whispered. I couldn't make out everything, but they started with photographs and damage control, then veered into how badly Colonel Fujiwara treated women in general, his wives in particular, and how he had turned Ima into the monster she was, so he had no right to judge his son-in-law's behaviour.

I really wished I had Magnetophon Man's recording machine running.

I was certain this wouldn't be the end of Joben Kobata's career. He was the son-in-law of Colonel Fujiwara. And as soon as the name-changing ceremony took place, he would be considered his son. As Joben Fujiwara, he would have his pick of positions to choose from in the new Japanese Empire.

But at least Major Dewa would stop persecuting Hideki Tagawa.

Things had to get better now.

I had left a single cannonball blossom in my little room and its fragrance greeted me when I opened the door. I lay on my bed in my day clothes, thinking I would rest my eyes for a moment but it was no use trying to go to sleep.

The next thing I knew, there was shouting in the kitchen and someone was banging loudly on my door.

'Miss Chen! Miss Chen! Please get up! Kobata-san is dead!'

Dead Joben

◆

'Looks like a wasp sting,' the Japanese medical officer said. 'He must have been stung before – it could have been up to a year or two ago. Yes, even before coming out here. That must have sensitised his body to wasp venom so when he got stung this time he developed a huge allergic reaction. The first sting would only have caused some pain and itching. But the allergic reaction made the linings of his air passages swell up and that killed him.'

Joben had died all swollen. Even his face was red and bloated.

Once the medical team had left with what remained of his son-in-law, Colonel Fujiwara told me to have the room cleaned. 'Quickly. It's disgusting. No point leaving it in that state for people to see.'

As though someone might have thought of preserving it as some kind of shrine for pilgrims to visit.

It made me wonder about the shrines to people in places where they had died. How long after the death were they set up? Joben's bladder and bowels had released and the whole room stank. It would be some time before anyone would want to use that room.

'You mean they sent the wasp to sting him?'

'I mean, who's to say it was a wasp sting? Maybe he was injected with a poison made from wasp venom.'

Like Colonel Fujiwara, Joben had got ahead by knowing whom he could bully and whom he couldn't. They knew how to get subordinates to do all their work while buttering up their superiors. He had left me alone because he was afraid of Hideki Tagawa. But now he was gone the women were free to talk.

I could tell the authorities were satisfied it had been wrapped up because they had other things on their minds. I had to pretend I didn't know. So why did I feel something was wrong here?

Even if Joben had confessed to killing Mimi, what good could it have done?

'You might as well know,' Ima said to Hideki Tagawa, 'Ryu was blackmailing Joben with photographs taken years ago. When they were young men, long before he was married. Joben was worried about the damage to my image and to my father's. He said it was no more than active young men sowing wild oats. That was why he took the money from the propaganda funds. To protect my father's reputation.'

'Whether he killed himself or was killed by the gods, what difference does it make?'

That seemed to cement the fact that Joben was guilty after all, that he was selling secrets to Ryu. But it was not in Joben's character either to keep secrets or to kill himself. And other people there were much better at keeping secrets and wouldn't balk at killing him.

Whistling Ghosts

———◆———

The next evening a new personal advertisement came in from Wooden House: 'Thank you. When birds sing of the past, we'll be together.'

I didn't know what it meant. It sounded as though someone had got my message. I only hoped it was the right someone and they'd understood it better than I did theirs.

'What's all this?' Ima took the form from my fingers and looked at the English words suspiciously.

'Personal advertisement.'

She'd already flipped through my notebooks and asked about the scribbles I'd made trying to work out anagrams and codes – 'Trying to improve my handwriting,' I'd said. I don't know if she believed me.

'What is the meaning in Japanese?'

'It says to think of him whenever she hears a bird sing.'

'Birds!' Ima snorted. 'The birds here never shut up!'

Ima Kobata was the new editor of the *Syonan Weekly*. Of

course I would continue to do all the work. Ima might be more responsible than Joben but her English was even worse.

I knew what she meant about the birds. Nowadays, it wasn't just the usual jungle fowl in the morning and the starlings in the evening. Even before Joben's death I'd been hearing the night birds whistling what sounded like snatches of familiar tunes. Now it was as though some madness had infected the wildlife around us and they were mocking us ...

I wasn't superstitious. I certainly didn't believe Joben Kobata – or Mimi – were returning as walking ghosts. Certainly they wouldn't return as whistling ghosts. But surely the jungle around here had never been so noisy at night. I could have sworn that right then something out there was whistling the chorus to 'Auld Lang Syne'. What was happening?

'Whether Joben killed himself or was killed by the gods, we have to move on.'

Ima's words cut into my thoughts. She hadn't heard anything. But, then, an unfamiliar song is just a collection of notes, and maybe I was imagining patterns in random birdsong.

'Joben was not at his best here. But that's because the climate wasn't good for him. He was a different person back home. Much more efficient and dedicated. Much more respected too.'

I had the feeling that Ima was trying to create memories of a different Joben. Well, why not? It made no difference to the dead man if misremembering him as wonderful helped his widow get on with her life.

So many women shaped their lives around men. Mimi had had relationships with different men and, like Ima, she saw improving her life as improving the men she was attached to.

And Ryoko, my mother, had run away from the family who had tried to force her to live in that way. The three had lived very differently. But although she had died and remained forgotten for years, I thought Ryoko had ended up the best of the three.

Ryoko had married a man she loved and who loved her till the end. As far as I knew, when she and my father died, they were still in love with each other. And they had left a daughter who hoped some day to find out more about them.

I admired Mimi's guts and attitude even though I hadn't liked her. I wondered about her life even though I wouldn't have liked to live it. How had she ended up in a life so different from her sister Shen Shen's or mine? Where had our paths diverged? Had she made the choice to step into the unknown, or had we chosen to stay?

At least Ima was alive and free of her husband.

'We should burn his things,' Ima said.

I remembered the photograph that had triggered Joben's exposure. 'You mean that picture?'

'I mean all his things. It's a ritual. That's what the bin outside is for, yes? You are Chinese, you should know all about it.'

I knew about burning joss sticks on altars and paper money in bins during the Seventh Month. 'Maybe they do that in China. But people here try to save and reuse things. Like the zips and buttons, even the cloth – if it's good cloth that's hardly worn through it can be cut up and used for something else.'

Ima wavered. Her scavenger nature won. 'Yes, maybe you should cut the buttons off first. And—'

We both heard the night bird whistling ... Surely it was whistling 'Auld Lang Syne'.

'What's that?'

'Probably a nightingale,' I said. Another bird I knew something of, thanks to Mr Meganck. 'They are shy and stay hidden but they can sing all night. And they can imitate cats, hawks, insects, frogs, even music. That's why people like to put them in cages to sing.'

'I'd like to put it in a pot for soup! Anyway, when you finish, take everything else out to the shrine bin. And hurry up. Father will want his evening drink soon.'

There wasn't much left of Joben's old clothes after the maids and I had unpicked them for all the scrap cloth and fastenings we could salvage. There was enough to make each of the house-boys and maids a pair of drawstring trousers, and I left them happily negotiating for strips and scraps as I carried out the bags to the shrine.

Without thinking, I sang softly what I'd heard the bird whistling –

> 'Should auld acquaintance be forgot
> And never brought to mind?
> Should auld acquaintance be forgot
> And days of auld lang syne?'

– then stopped, startled, as the bird whistle came back and joined in. Because it wasn't mimicking what I'd sung. It was carrying on:

> 'For auld lang syne, my dear,
> For auld lang syne,
> We'll take a cup o' kindness yet
> For auld lang syne.'

'Why are you taking so long?' Ima shouted from the kitchen. 'Feeding the mosquitoes, are you? I'm taking my father his nightcap. You'd better finish burning everything. I'll check tomorrow.'

I stayed where I was. Taoists believe trees are spiritual beings, connecting earth and sky and cleansing both. Shintoism holds that forests, trees and other objects all contain spirits or gods, not all friendly to humans. My Mission Centre upbringing had drummed into me that anything supernatural from anywhere other than their Bible was rubbish.

But what did I have to lose?

I sang the first line of 'Auld Lang Syne' again.

Sure enough, something unseen whistled the second line back:

> *'Should auld acquaintance be forgot*
> *And days of auld lang syne?'*

Then a whistling ghost appeared on the jungle side of the fence. And another figure followed. Two men dressed like coolies. They were filthy, their faces and hands black with dirt. Their heads were shaded beneath huge tattered straw hats. Large wicker baskets were strapped to their backs and secured by bands across their foreheads.

'Hello there. Remember me?'

'Harry? Harry Palin?'

If I was the kind of girl to swoon or faint I would have done so. Instead my legs gave way under me and I landed awkwardly on my bottom on the damp grass.

They came through the barrier swiftly and silently. I saw a section of fencing had been cut away and held in place with metal twists.

'Sorry. We shouldn't have sprung it on you like that,' the other figure said.

'It's not you, it's me. I have this effect on women. Watch and learn, Meganck.'

'Mr Meganck? What are you doing here? I thought you two were up north in Pahang! How did you get here?'

'Most of the way we travelled as Indian women tea-pickers. The Japanese are as snooty as the Chinese about darker skin colours and they place great importance on the tea crop so they left us alone.'

'Then we swam across the strait. That was challenging. You don't know how many illegal fishermen are out there.'

They looked lean and brown, like wild jungle men. They smelt like wild boar and monkey droppings. They were the most beautiful things I had seen in years. I hugged them both, holding on hard to make sure they were really there. Not wanting to let go even if they were walking ghosts. I don't know if they were crying or whether it was just me. For a while none of us could say anything.

Then: 'Got your news. The information has gone to the Pacific Allied command. You don't have to know how. But thanks.'

'We suspected something like you told us. But there were so many other possibilities. Your information helped verify they've already started moving equipment and supplies into place. For the invasion of India via Burma. Very secret.'

'But how – and so quickly?'

'You know your paper goes to the Cathay Building for vetting?'

'The old Cathay Building, yes.' That was where the Japanese Propaganda Department and the Military Information Bureau were located.

'You know what was in there just before the war? Thirteen floors of the British Malaya Broadcasting Corporation, two floors of the Ministry of Economic Warfare and two tiny rooms occupied by the Royal Air Force,' Harry Palin tapped his chest, 'which is how I learned you can get into the building through the basement on the Mount Sophia side. We don't wait for *Syonan Weekly* to be delivered. We get it when their censors see it. Joan Briggs set everything up. Her price is far beyond rubies. She saw before anyone else that we would need a communication network that would stick even after the government went down. She linked us up with the Secret Intelligence Service. Wodehouse in Hong Kong, in India–'

Meganck stopped him with a shake of the head. 'Anyway, it's jolly good of you. We've had no news since our last contact went down.'

'Your last contact?' I thought incredulously of Mimi. Surely not.

They looked at each other.

'Can't hurt now he's dead. A photographer named Ryu Takahashi. He got us some very secret information from some very high places.'

'Ryu Takahashi was working for you? How?'

'After Miss Briggs was arrested we needed a new conduit. Our friend Ryu sent his information via codes in his photographs.'

'Easy for him and his camera. He worked them into his *Syonan Weekly* pics. Magnify the old photos and check the flower arrangements, the wallpaper patterns ...'

'But why ... I thought he was a spy.'

'Maybe he was. He was a pacifist. He hated war. So he attacked war people. He did what he did to mess up the people who were fighting. And he was a crazy artist. He liked cocking a snook at the government. He liked being clever.'

'Do you know where he got his information from?'

'Wherever he could buy it. He was given money to pay for it and probably took a fat share for himself.'

'I thought he murdered someone,' I said though I no longer believed it. 'Right here, under the cannonball tree.'

'It's a good tree,' said Meganck. 'I'll take a couple of cannonballs if you can spare them. The insides are good for disinfecting wounds and a great insect repellent.'

'Oh, no. I'm not rubbing anything else on myself,' said Harry Palin. 'But Ryu as a killer? Not likely. The guy was a *kansha* nut – wouldn't even eat meat.'

I had so much information to process, but I could do that later. Now I just couldn't get enough of looking at them. 'It's so good to see you both. But you shouldn't have risked coming here just to tell me—'

'Oh, the timing worked out but you're just a side trip. We really came down because of Dr Shankar.'

'Dr Shankar? What's wrong with him? Is it Parshanti? What's happened to her?'

'Nothing's wrong. At least, I hope he doesn't think it's wrong.' Harry rolled his eyes.

'Tell me, what is it?'

'Don't be an idiot, Palin,' Mr Meganck said. 'We came to sneak him the good news. To get his blessing. Or maybe his permission. I'm not sure how these things work. We came to tell him his daughter and Leask are engaged.'

'Dr Leask? Parshanti? Parshanti and Dr Leask? But she never told me! When – how – and now?'

Harry Palin gave a low laugh. 'When there's time I'll sit you down and explain about the birds and the bees,' he said. As he talked, his eyes shifted and darted in the direction of the house, making sure no one was coming.

Mr Meganck, standing with his back to me, was doing the same in the opposite direction. He was watching the perimeter of the fence and the jungle beyond it. 'Don't be an ass, Palin. I don't think there was anything to tell when we went up-country. Parshanti didn't have an easy time, but she stuck to it. Don't know how we'd have lasted without her.'

'I'm so glad. I wish—' I stopped.

'I expect you know it's not all fun and games up-country,' Meganck said quietly. 'We found an old rice farmer crying over handfuls of crushed rice seedlings because soldiers had walked through his padi fields in boots and destroyed his crop. He didn't know how he was going to tell his family there would be no harvest, no food. We went on to his house and found the bodies of his wife and daughters. The soldiers had torn them them apart too. It would have been kinder to kill him.'

'Do you want to get out of here? Can't promise much in the Jungle Ritz but you'll meet like-minded company,' Harry said. 'The thing is, we could really use you right here, if you'd stay.'

I thought of Mimi, Ima and Ryoko, whose lives had been ruled, run and ruined by men. I didn't want to be another female dragged down by my family.

I wanted to be like Miss Briggs.

'I'll do what I can,' I said.

Miss Joan Briggs had made a difference. Parshanti was making her own way. They had moved on from the lives they would have lived had it not been for the war.

Careless Flyers

———◆———

To my surprise, I slept dreamlessly after the late-night visit. And the next morning I woke and stretched, feeling better than I had in a long time. I hadn't noticed the constant worry about my friends up-country until it was relieved – temporarily at least.

But as I got up to face the day, other thoughts came in. The biggest issue of all: if Ryu Takahashi had been selling secrets to the Allies, secrets he'd got from Joben, Joben would have had no reason to kill him.

But Hideki Tagawa would.

Would he have killed Mimi too?

If she had got in his way, he would.

But I didn't want to believe it.

I had to find out what had happened so that I could clear Hideki Tagawa in my mind.

Now I was seeing Ryu as an eccentric, playful artist creature. Kind of like the cannonball tree in human form. Part of him stinky, part of him strangely beautiful, forming a package that did not fit comfortably into human social strata. But he had his place in nature and probably got along better with other life forms than people. Yet he had taken those savage photographs. It must have been a huge strain on him, maybe even driving him mad. Was the explanation as simple as that? The artistic photographer had cracked under pressure?

But Ryu Takahashi couldn't have killed Joben Kobata.

The neatest explanation I could come up with was 'What if Joben found out Ryu was selling the secrets he extorted from him to the Allies? So he killed Ryu. And then he killed Mimi, because he was afraid she could expose him. And then, when the game was up anyway, he killed himself. It's the samurai way, isn't it?'

'Kobata's not samurai,' de Souza said. I had already told him about the visit from Harry Palin and Mr Meganck and ploughed on with my deductions. 'Anyway, he died of a wasp sting. It ends there.'

'Hey. You two. Stop. What have you got there?'

We had been careless – I had been careless, high and excited, so that when de Souza had appeared with news that Allied soldiers had landed on the beaches of Normandy and were pushing inland through northern France we had rushed out another set of flyers.

I'd quickly made a *kueh bengka*. This sticky, dense golden cake tastes much richer than you'd expect of something made with tapioca, coconut milk, palm sugar and water. Half baked, its warmth was already releasing fragrance from the banana leaves I'd wrapped it in when I took it out to press lines of type into its half-baked dough.

We'd advanced from gouging letters in jelly to setting rows of type in a basic letterpress frame using dark caramelised palm sugar. And, because paper was scarce and strictly rationed, our flyers were now carefully cut rectangles of dried banana leaves. The palm sugar dried a darker brown on the green leaves, easy to read if you knew to look for it, easy to overlook if you didn't. Even better, they were dismissed as food wrappers and the 'ink' dissolved in water.

I had been talking so much while we were walking that we hadn't distributed them all. Several of the banana-leaf flyers were still on us. And now I saw it wasn't just the normal guards at the gate. Major Dewa was there, with his own security men. Had he been watching out for us? Had they found evidence I'd carelessly left in the kitchen?

Major Dewa was watching me. Even if Hideki Tagawa got me off somehow, de Souza would be in for it. Caught red-handed with the flyers on him.

'What have you got there?' One of the security men was pointing at de Souza's bag, with the leftover flyers.

'Nothing,' de Souza said. I could see him thinking, *So this is how it ends.*

Well, it hadn't ended yet.

'That's not fair!' I said, grabbing de Souza's bag and pulling out the flyers. 'Even if you're the one carrying them, I was the one who saw them first. It was my idea to bring them in to get the reward for collecting the seditious papers! You can't say they're all yours. I should get at least half the reward.'

Luckily de Souza caught on fast. 'What do you mean half? I'm the one who climbed into the *long kang* to get them.' He handed them to the security man. 'These are the flyers you're after. Don't we get a reward for collecting them?'

The man looked uncertain. 'I don't know about a reward.' He looked at Major Dewa for direction.

'Hey, I know you're calculating what you'll get if you claim that you collected the flyers yourself. But Major Dewa saw you take them from him. You saw that, didn't you, Major Dewa, sir?'

'Let me see.' Major Dewa took one of the flyers and studied it. De Souza's *long kang* story worked because they were damp. I saw him raise it to his nose and sniff. Then he stuck out his tongue and touched it. The soldiers stared. This was going to be a good story back in the camp. Especially as they thought it had come out of the storm drain.

But I was afraid I knew what the major was thinking. And I thought we were sunk.

Of all the stupid, reckless, careless ways to lose it all!

I wouldn't even get to congratulate Parshanti on her engagement. And I'd been looking forward to teasing her for settling on shy, earnest Dr Leask of all people.

'Definitely seditious. There should be a report made and a reward given. If you make up the report you can keep half the reward. Give the other half to these two.'

That pleased the security men, who went off with the flyers.

'A stupid thing to do,' Major Dewa said, when they were gone. 'How did you learn of this false news?' He was looking at de Souza.

'Found a flyer, sir.' De Souza was still standing at attention.

'So I heard. In the drain, right?'

'Yes, sir.'

'You should stay out of drains. For your own safety.'

'Yes, sir.'

'Dismissed, man.'

De Souza gave me one last, despairing look and went.

'Come,' Major Dewa said to me.

We went back to the kitchen, as I'd expected. Xiao Xi and Xiao Yu watched, looking curious but not really frightened. Major Dewa did not shout at them, like Joben had and Colonel Fujiwara did, and they probably didn't realise he was just as dangerous.

'Cake?'

'Yes, sir.'

I wasn't worried about the cake I had used as a stencil for the flyers. Before leaving I had coated it with a mixture of hot coconut milk, cornflour and *gula melaka* that had started setting immediately. Colonel Fujiwara's sweet tooth was excuse enough for making all the cakes I could. He was particularly fond of my mango coconut jelly squares and coconut *pandan*-layered jelly cake. Now no one questioned the trays perpetually standing and cooling on the kitchen tables. That was why I'd thought using them as stencils was a good idea.

Ima would come to me in the press room and say, 'Father's in a bad mood. Can you make something to sweeten him up?'

'This is wrong,' Major Dewa said, looking at it. So maybe I should have worried about the cake.

'Sir?'

'This should have rice cake underneath, not tapioca cake, right?'

'Yes, sir. But there's so much tapioca, I didn't want it to go to waste. I thought if I made a topping it wouldn't be so plain. And Colonel Fujiwara likes it.'

'Does he?'

Major Dewa was looking in the basin where the alphabets and strip frames I'd used were soaking in soapy water. My bright idea didn't seem so bright now.

'The ink sticks to them,' I said. 'Unless you clean it off regularly, it makes blobs. It gets worse and worse. When I can soak them in really hot water it cleans them up much more easily.'

'Only cleaning some of the keys?' He lifted a handful and fingered them as though looking to form words. And, yes, he could have fingered every word on the flyers we had just surrendered.

Again I cursed myself for being stupidly careless. Next time – if there was a next time – I would soak the whole set of type, no matter which keys I used.

'Just the most stained ones.'

'Where do you get the sugar to make all this? There is a shortage of sweeteners, yes?'

'I use *gula melaka* or Malacca sugar that I make myself.'

'I thought Malacca sugar comes from factories in Malacca.'

Was he joking? I couldn't tell. I didn't want to take another risk.

'There are enough coconut palms around here that I can send the house-boys to collect sweet sap by cutting flowers and immature fruits. They have to cut them anyway, or the remaining fruits won't grow to full size. Then I boil it down and reduce it. Most of the *gula melaka* sold in the market comes in discs cut from tubes shaped in rattan, but here I set it in coconut half shells. It's the way I saw it made at home when I was young.'

'You sound passionate about it.'

I passionately hoped the thick sweet dark brown layer obliterated any typescript marks on the surface of my cake stencil.

'You are a very resourceful young woman. I wish you could believe that I'm not the enemy,' Major Dewa said. 'You've saved us a great embarrassment and I appreciate that.'

'Thank you, sir.'

'You continue helping us and we'll make sure you and your family remain safe.'

'I can't help you, sir. I don't know anything.'

'You can start by telling me everything you know about Hideki Tagawa. I don't want to get him into trouble but I intend to find out what he's done.'

Investigators Investigated

———◆———

Of course I told Hideki Tagawa what Major Dewa had said. All right, maybe there was no 'of course' about it, but I wanted to see his reaction. 'Major Dewa still thinks you're behind the security leak, not Joben. I thought they were satisfied it was him.'

Hideki Tagawa didn't seem surprised. 'It's officially settled. But Major Dewa takes his job seriously. If he suspects I killed Kobata, he would see it as his duty to get me out of the colonel's household.'

'Even though you saved Colonel Fujiwara's life last year? And even though everyone agrees Joben was killed by a wasp?'

'Are you pretending to be stupid?'

'I thought that was what everyone agreed to believe.'

Hideki Tagawa started walking around the tiny office. Any other man would have been smoking or drinking or at least grinding his teeth but he looked as if he was doing a walking meditation. 'He really wants to find out?' he asked the floor mat.

'Are you in trouble?' I asked him.

He looked at me like he'd forgotten who I was. 'Is that why you spoke up to the major? Because you thought I was in trouble?'

'If they're using me as an excuse to make trouble for you, should I leave here?'

He was looking at me with the strange expression that meant he was thinking of my dead mother. He had looked up to her as a cross between a mother and a big sister and– 'First thing you think of is leaving. You're as bad as your mother.'

Ha! So I had been right. 'Did you make the arrangements for Ryu Takahashi?'

'No one would believe for a moment that I did. If someone wants to get me into trouble, the question is who. And why?'

'For Ryu. To get him money and a place to work?'

'There are a hundred ways to squeeze funds out of the official and unofficial budgets. But using my name and my official chop shows someone is deliberately mocking me.'

'You think this is serious, then.'

'It's not something for you to worry about. But if Major Dewa was not behind it, then who?'

I had got it wrong. Hideki Tagawa hadn't worried so long as he thought Major Dewa was trying to frame him. That would just have been part of the police bulldog's job. But if Major Dewa wasn't, then someone else was. Someone who had not hesitated to kill Joben, Ryu and Mimi.

'I can understand what your mother did. Or, rather, I have always understood why she did it. Now I can say that maybe she did the right thing.'

'What?'

'She found love with your father. It might not have lasted but they died young and still in love. There are worse ways to live and die. If she had stayed, she would likely have been placed with a useful alliance. As a mistress, not a wife, for as long as she remained useful to her relatives.'

Hideki Tagawa had loved my mother too. I saw that now.

'You're right,' he said. 'You should leave here.'

'What?' I said. 'I mean – where would I go?' I had a sudden vision of the filthy room where Mimi had been staying.

'You can go home to your grandmother's house. That would be safer for now.'

Was my grandmother's house still my home? I missed the Chen Mansion and the blessedly long, dull days of my childhood so much it hurt. Now it was full of relatives and tenants displaced by the war. I didn't know if I could ever live there again. I didn't know if I wanted to. I had changed so much.

'Yes. That's the best plan for now.' As far as Hideki Tagawa was concerned, the matter seemed settled.

'For now until . . .'

'Until I make arrangements to send you back to Japan.'

'What do you mean "back" to Japan. I've never been to Japan. There's no "back" for me.'

'There are some old family retainers in Hiroshima you can stay with. Their family has worked for ours for generations. Or, better, you can go to my old teacher in Nagasaki. He is old, but you will learn from him and your time won't be wasted. Unfortunately we have no other living relatives. I will book your passage on a supply ship.'

'Mrs Maki?' I said, though I had no intention of going to stay with her or anyone else in Japan.

'She is in the Philippines. You won't be any better off there than here.'

'No,' I said.

'You still don't trust me.'

'I can look after myself. I always have.'

'Chief Inspector Le Froy would have made sure you were safe.'

He hadn't mentioned Le Froy in some time. I'd allowed myself to think he'd forgotten his fixation with the man who'd hunted him so obsessively before the war. 'He was my boss. He watched out for everyone in the department.'

'Is he the reason you won't let me send you somewhere safe? With that leg of yours, you can't even run to save yourself if the house catches fire!'

'What's happening?' Ima came into Hideki Tagawa's office without knocking. 'You two are fighting like an old married couple. I could hear you all the way down the corridor. Tell me what's wrong and let Ima make it better for you.'

She looked between us, her face hungry – greedy, even – for information. 'Now that I'm an old widow, all I can do is make other people's lives better.'

'What did you do with the hair ornament?'

It wasn't immediately clear which of us he was talking to. But I'd not seen the heirloom hairpin since the night I'd rejected it. Had he given it to Ima after I'd shown myself – in his eyes – unworthy? 'Did you find the poem on it?'

'Are you afraid she sold it on the black market?' Ima asked. She reached out and punched me playfully on the arm. 'You can't blame her if she did, you know. She has a big family to feed.

Your sentimental family jewellery isn't worth anything when people are starving.'

Hideki Tagawa turned away from her and left the room without answering. Ima hurried after him. Her concerned expression had slipped and she looked satisfied.

I wasn't worried about my family starving. When Formosa Boy came to the Shori headquarters to submit his reports, he always visited me in the kitchen for a snack while he told me how everyone at Chen Mansion was doing. I could tell Formosa Boy was helping Ah Ma re-establish her black-market network. He had an animal's instinct for food and danger, and a naive pragmatism worthy of any local. Sometimes I felt he fitted better in Chen Mansion than I did. As long as he was there, my grandmother would be well looked after.

I had helped get some flyers out. But that was just bravado. What good did spreading information do even if it was true? If the British tried to free us, the Japanese would kill every man, woman and child on our island rather than surrender.

Looking at the big picture could drive a person crazy because there were so many possibilities. Was that why Ryu Takahashi had written, 'Always look at the smallest picture'?

Then it struck me that he, like Miss Briggs, might have included another meaning.

I had no trouble in finding the photograph I was looking for in Colonel Fujiwara's office. Major Dewa had been right about security being slack in the Shori headquarters.

It had been left where Colonel Fujiwara had dropped it, since the case against Joben was officially closed. But I wanted to study that strangely shaped birthmark on his buttocks more closely.

But first I held the magnifying glass over the back of Joben's headband. The words that almost said *Divine Wind* instead read *Deadly Fart*, thanks to creases and shadows.

I was on the right track. For a moment I could hear Ryu Takahashi cackling with laughter. *You get it? You finally get it?*

I hadn't known the man but I wanted to avenge him too.

Magnifying Things

———◆———

I tackled Hideki Tagawa in his room at seven the next morning. 'I have to go to Major Dewa's office,' I said. 'Can you get me in there?'

'Major Dewa won't see you,' Hideki Tagawa said. 'Even if he does, he won't listen to anything you say. He's got his own agenda.'

'I don't want to see Major Dewa,' I said. 'I want to borrow Magnetophon Man's magnifying glasses.'

'Yes. I have magnifying glasses. What do you want examined?'

Akio Yamamoto didn't seem surprised to see us. The thick glass of his spectacles made his eyes look unnaturally large and shiny, like those of a housefly.

'This photograph. Right here on his bottom. That mark is made up of lists and numbers. I can see them but I can't make them out. I know you have some very powerful magnifying glasses. Could you help us?'

I had tried through the night using my tiny sewing-stitch magnifier and had a good idea of what was there, but recording it was taking me far too long.

'This is one of Ryu Takahashi's photographs?'

I'd been looking at the large adjustable table-top magnifier on his desk, but the old man squinted at the paper, then reached and exchanged his spectacles for magnifying glasses.

'Numbers ... dates ... accounts ...'

'If you could read them out to me while I record them?'

'If only I had my equipment with me, I could make a print for you.'

'Can you do that?'

'I would have to photograph it again. Make a new negative and develop it by bringing out the latent image on the film and fixing it in place to get a translucent film bearing a negative image. Then I would use an enlarger, a light projector that shines light on the negative and passes it through a magnifying lens onto your paper. But this must be done in a darkroom or the least light will affect your photo paper, fogging your image. Generally the more you enlarge, the worse your results are. Going from a one-inch negative to an eight-by-ten-inch print is an enlargement of about seventy-two times, so you can imagine.'

I thought of Dr Shankar's pharmacy. In the old days, he had developed photographs for customers in the back room. Even though the building was now deserted, it was possible that no one had considered his photographic chemicals worth taking. 'If you had the right chemicals and a darkroom, could you do it?'

'I would have to photograph it first. With a good camera and shot through a magnifying lens, obviously.'

'I'll get you the camera,' Hideki Tagawa said. One of the best things about the man was that he was happy to follow someone else's lead, even when it wasn't yet clear where it was going. 'What else?'

A gleam appeared in Akio Yamamoto's eyes. I had been right: the man was fascinated by technology.

'Same as for any film. But you cannot unroll it until you're in the darkroom. Immerse it first in a water bath or it will be too stiff to handle ...'

I didn't know where this was going either. But I had to find out. 'We need developing fluid and acid, to stop the process. And fixer. So that if we succeed, we won't be the only ones to see what's on these film reels.'

Before we left, Magnetophon Man sent word to Major Dewa that he was occupied with personal matters. 'No point worrying him until we know what we've got here. When you're over seventy, people don't ask questions when you take time off. It's a reward for growing old.'

He seemed in a remarkably good mood for someone who might be uncovering treason to his country at the highest level.

Hideki Tagawa got us the keys to the Shankars' pharmacy shophouse since Dr and Mrs Shankar were in prison and no one knew where their children were. Well, I did but I wasn't telling. If we all survived, I'd make it up to the Shankars for breaking into their home – I hoped what I was doing would contribute to our survival. If we didn't survive, this wouldn't matter anyway so I was going to give it all I'd got.

'Not German,' Magnetophon Man said, of the equipment we found in Dr Shankar's darkroom, 'not modern German technology,' but he was pleased to find a red light in the darkroom. 'This is orthochromatic film, sensitive to all visible light except red. We can handle it here.'

The old man ordered us around like technicians, changing lighting, backgrounds and camera lenses as he photographed the picture of Joben pissing on dead soldiers. I'd hated the photo at first. But now I came to see it as a collection of clever components. Labelling Joben a deadly fart was just one of Ryu Takahashi's sly digs. Akio Yamamoto found a Bashō death poem in the dripping blood and crushed grass around the dead bodies:

> *falling sick on a journey*
> *my dream goes wandering*
> *over a field of dried grass*

When he was ready to develop his film, the shades were pulled down and the room transformed into a red chamber. First he unrolled the strip from its protective canister and, holding the ends in both hands, immersed it in a water bath, 'to soften out the stiffness'.

Then, holding the strip of film, he coaxed it into a tray of developer fluid from one end to the other and back again, so every section was soaked. We could see the images starting to develop. When he was satisfied that everything was complete, he moved the film to the next tray for a bath of diluted vinegar to stop the process. The final tray was fixer.

It felt like a long time, but when he lifted the fixed film from the final tray and demanded the clean water, which I had ready, less than twenty minutes had passed. We could already see images on the film. Magnetophon Man was pretty pleased by what was appearing: 'There's something called the Callier effect. That means any dirt, scratches and the grain of the paper appear on the image as defects. He seems to have deliberately inserted defects into the print. Like here, where a superficial glance might make you think he was trying to erase an identifying feature' – the birthmark across Joben's backside – 'actually he has added dates, times and other information.'

'Let me see that.'

Ryu Takahashi had recorded them for a reason. Someone like Miss Briggs would probably already have found his key or code and scored top marks or won the prize or the war but I was still trying to work out what I was looking at without touching the damp strip hung up to dry.

'Not yet. They must dry before they can be handled. I will print them on paper and you can handle the paper.'

Hideki Tagawa had slipped away without explanation a while ago. I didn't know if he found the dim red room claustrophobic or had decided to go ahead with booking my passage to Japan in the cargo hold of one of his prince's loot-transporting ships.

When he returned he was carrying several folders of Ryu Takahashi's printed photographs and a stack of *Syonan Weekly* back issues. 'I couldn't find the photo negatives Takahashi submitted to the paper,' he said. 'Can you photograph and magnify these and see what you get? I've indicated the sections I'd like you to enlarge.'

Hideki Tagawa had marked out a framed painting on the wall, a row of floral decorations, a window and the mishmash of tree branches beyond ...

'From a newspaper, it won't be so clear.'

'Just see what you can do.'

*

When Akio Yamamoto finally gave me the prints, I took myself upstairs to Parshanti's old bedroom to study them, leaving Hideki Tagawa to play assistant to the old man. I didn't know what he was looking for any more than he knew what I was trying to work out.

Come to think of it, I didn't know either. I just knew there had to be something there.

Akio Yamamoto had said the more you enlarge, the worse your results – generally. But Ryu Takahashi had put together patterns that only emerged when distorted by being enlarged. What I was seeing had not come about by accident. But I still didn't know how they fitted together to make sense.

'What are you doing?' Hideki Tagawa appeared, startling me. I hadn't heard him come up the stairs.

'Has he finished?'

'He's still at it. I tried to get him to take a break to rest and I thought he was going to hit me.' He looked at the papers I had spread out on the floor around me. 'Found anything?'

'Almost. Ryu Takahashi was an artist, wasn't he? He seems to have liked using modern machinery.'

'Like Mr Yamamoto,' Hideki Tagawa said wryly. 'That doesn't mean he wasn't an artist. Your Westerners celebrate Leonardo da Vinci, who was a scientist as well as an artist.'

'Ryu Takahashi would have done everything he could to protect his work from the chaos going on. More than he did to protect himself.'

'That chaos might have fed his work.' He lowered himself to the floor, carefully avoiding my papers.

He looked stiff: hours of filling, moving and holding trays

steady for a demanding old man takes its toll. 'I thought you didn't like him.'

'I didn't know him. Ryu Takahashi was like a ghost. He had contacts in high places and the ear of important men. But you couldn't pin down who he was. Like a ghost that doesn't exist outside its effect on you.'

That could have described Hideki Tagawa pretty well.

'Ryu was a travelling photographer before the war. You cannot photograph people without looking at them. And if you look at people and really see them, you cannot help but get to know them. Every time you capture an image on paper, a piece of that image is imprinted on your soul.'

Again, he might have been talking about himself. But it was something else I had to put off thinking about until later.

'We may just have made things much worse,' Hideki Tagawa said, after a pause. 'The scraps of film plainly incriminate someone at the Shori headquarters because it's already clear from the fragments I've seen that that was where Ryu photographed the papers. And that means there'll be more of a mess to clear up.'

I still had no proof. But I had an idea where I could find it. 'Don't book my passage to Japan just yet,' I said. 'I'm going to ask Akio Yamamoto for his help again. This time I'll need his Magnetophon machine too.'

Out of the Closet

———◆———

Colonel Fujiwara and Major Dewa were discussing whether transcriptions from the Magnetophon machine would be acceptable as testimony when they heard voices shouting nearby.

'It can't be, but it sounds like Joben,' Colonel Fujiwara said, 'and some woman.'

The woman's voice was chanting, 'I know who you are! I saw what you did!' in crudely accented Japanese.

'Where's it coming from?'

'Upstairs, it sounds like.'

Major Dewa was already striding swiftly out of the room and up the stairs, his guards, caught by surprise, running to catch up with him.

Colonel Fujiwara followed with his own security man, who was radioing for back-up. The maids and house-boys, trailing them from a safe distance, were joined by Magnetophon Man.

'In here.' Major Dewa paused for half a second, listening, before pushing open the door to Ima's room.

Ima stood by the door, petrified with terror.

'Wake up, you fool!' There was no mistaking Joben's voice shouting. 'I'll get you for that!'

Along with the unearthly growling, snarling and slobbering sounds, it seemed to be coming from the large walk-in cupboard at the far side of the room.

Ima covered her face when Major Dewa strode past her, pistol in hand, and tried to pull open the cupboard door. 'It's locked. Where's the key?'

A crash and moaning came from inside the cupboard.

'Who has the key?'

'I do. But—'

More sounds.

Ima shook her head. 'No. You can't. Please don't.'

'Give him the key.' Colonel Fujiwara stood by his daughter and stared at the cupboard door through which they could now hear his dead son-in-law laughing.

'No,' Ima said.

'Isn't there another entrance to that cupboard?' Major Dewa demanded.

'Sealed,' one of the security guards said, 'sealed and plastered. Mrs Kobata said it was a security risk.'

A long slobbering groan came from inside the cupboard.

'Break the door down!' Major Dewa ordered.

'No!' Ima screamed. 'No, you can't. You have no right. This is my room.' She tried to claw at the men battering the door, but Colonel Fujiwara's security man grabbed her and held on to her.

'Ima, why did you kill me?' the woman's bad accent shouted from inside the cupboard.

'Don't listen to her! She deserved it! She's got no business coming back! You all just get away from there! Get out of my room! I'll have you all shot! Just go away and get me a temple medium or exorcist or something!'

The door was shattered. They didn't find any ghosts inside, but they did find all the things Ima had hidden there. A superficial glance showed a surprising amount – camera equipment, American canned meat and American chocolate.

It was enough to make them investigate further, even with Colonel Fujiwara's daughter shouting imprecations at them and trying to shoot them with their own pistols.

'Take her to the station,' Major Dewa said, after his security aide had retrieved his gun and pinned Ima's flailing arms behind her. 'Tell Akio Yamamoto to bring the Magnetophon. I want every item in here documented.'

'Wait,' Colonel Fujiwara said. 'I must talk to my daughter first.'

'Sir.' Major Dewa's other aide held up two objects the size of cricket balls, with pale yellow square-gridded surfaces and metal stick caps. The missing pineapple grenades.

Major Dewa flinched. 'Be careful, man!' he hissed, then answered Colonel Fujiwara: 'It's out of my hands.'

'And in mine,' said Colonel Fujiwara. 'Give me an hour to sort through what is in my house. One hour. Then I'll hand everything over to you. Please.'

'And all this?' Major Dewa looked at the contents of Ima's walk-in cupboard. 'And her?'

'Everything here goes down to my office now. And then give me one hour. Please.'

The security guards searched the cupboard but there was no sign of what had caused the ghostly voices that had led them there.

'The spirits did their job so they left,' one of the men said. The others didn't disagree. There was plenty for them to haul downstairs, so they got to work.

Colonel Fujiwara, dragging Ima by the arm, pushed past Yamamoto Akio in the corridor. 'Get out of my way. And get your damned machine out of my office.'

'Yes, sir.'

Akio Yamamoto went to the back of the house where tomorrow's washing was soaking in collected rainwater. 'Well done,' he said.

'All I did was press the buttons you told me to press.' I returned the black zippered bag with the tape recorder. It was much smaller than his Magnetophon machine, but weighed at least as much as a bag of granite chips. It had taken me all my strength to get it quietly up to and down from the tiny landing on the other side of Ima's cupboard.

Crouching by the thin wall, I could hear them start breaking through the cupboard door, which was when I'd turned off the machine.

'What happened? What did they find in that cupboard? What did Ima say to them?'

'That can wait. Colonel Fujiwara and Hideki Tagawa are in Colonel Fujiwara's office now asking her questions ...'

I gave Akio Yamamoto a cursory bow – I was hugely grateful to him but in a hurry – and ran as fast as I could. At times like this I really cursed my crippled leg for slowing me down. I had to hear what Ima said. More importantly, Colonel Fujiwara and Hideki Tagawa had to hear what I said *before* they believed whatever Ima came up with.

But it was all right. When I got to Colonel Fujiwara's office the security personnel were still carrying things in from upstairs and the three principals had isolated themselves in silence. Colonel Fujiwara sat at his desk staring at a photograph in a cracked frame. Hideki Tagawa poked through a decorated jewellery case that contained pens, signature chops and vials of powder as well as jewellery.

The photograph of me, de Souza and the others in front of the Detective Shack was there too. I could tell by the creases that it was the one from Mimi's underwear. But it hadn't been pissed on, meaning it had been removed from her body before I had found her.

There were things that might have been taken from Ryu's studio. Among them, two reel carriers with rolls of film inside them. The edge of one was caught and the film ripped. Like the strip of film I had found hooked on the heel of Mimi's shoe.

Ima, one wrist shackled to the heavy teak chair she sat on, glared at me. But she was glaring at everyone who came through the door so I didn't take it personally.

'Come in and lock the door, Su Lin,' Hideki Tagawa told me. 'But first make sure no one is in the corridor.'

I did. I was glad they all seemed to accept I had a place there. I had gone to a lot of trouble to put this together. I could never tell Hideki Tagawa what I had done and I sensed he suspected enough that he would never ask.

'Yours, I believe.' Hideki Tagawa picked up something from the table and handed it to me. It was the hairpin he had given me.

'You have no right to give it to some *ainoko*—' Ima had started up from her chair but was jerked back down by her bond.

'Ainoko' was a contemptuous term used to describe children born of mixed marriages.

'That's not a decent word to use.'

'You shame your family. That *ainoko* has no right to it.'

That was when I knew I'd been wrong. Ima hadn't been trying to protect her dead husband's reputation. She was the one who'd framed him. And killed him.

'You killed Mimi in the garden,' I said.

Ima's Way

'Why would Ima kill that woman?' Colonel Fujiwara said. I noticed he didn't say Ima couldn't have killed that woman. Maybe this wasn't coming as such a surprise after all.

I turned to Ima. 'You killed Mimi because she was using the pass you had made for Ryu Takahashi. That was how she got into the Shori headquarters. You were afraid that if Major Dewa found it they would realise Ryu Takahashi was getting information from you, not from Joben. But that's not the only reason, is it? I think Mimi Hoshi saw you with Ryu at the studio bunker before he died. The day you went there and killed him.'

'Did her ghost come back and tell you that?' Ima asked. 'I don't even know where that place is. How could I? Why would I?'

'That's why you had the address written down,' I said. 'You must have known Joben was meeting Ryu there. It was Joben who had the directions to Ryu's studio bunker. I don't know if he gave them to you or if you found them among his things and copied them down. But the note with the address and directions we found in Mimi's notebook was in your handwriting.'

Ima snorted and rolled her eyes.

'Why?' Colonel Fujiwara was shaking his head slowly. I didn't know whether he was talking to me or to Ima. Ima didn't answer him so I went on.

'Mimi didn't need directions to Ryu's bunker studio. Ryu had taken her there many times. He used her regularly to model in his photographs. She saved the note because you must have dropped it at the studio the day you went to confront Ryu there and killed him. I think Mimi was there, too, hiding, and saw the whole thing. She didn't know who you were until she came to Joben for help and found out you were his wife.'

'That slut didn't come to Joben for help,' Ima said. 'She came to try to blackmail him!'

'I remember Mimi wanted me to arrange for her to see Joben alone. But once she learned you were Joben's wife, she pounced on you instead. I thought she was just bad at blackmail. I didn't know that you were the one she was blackmailing. Mimi knew it was you who had killed Ryu Takahashi.'

Colonel Fujiwara closed his eyes and moaned softly.

'I remember Mimi met you in the kitchen the first time she came here, on New Year's Eve. She must have assumed Joben was involved, that he had sent his wife to seduce Ryu. Actually Ima went on her own and Joben didn't know anything about it.'

How could Mimi have been so stupid? After seeing what Ima was capable of, how could she have had so little sense of danger? It showed how little imagination she had. But a lot of us are like that. We go on what we've experienced in the past and expect the future to follow the same pattern. Never having been killed before, it didn't occur to Mimi that she could be in any danger from Ima. It was a naive, childlike side to her that was quite touching.

Ima looked contemptuous. 'When I talked to her outside she dared to threaten me, told me that if I didn't treat her with respect and give her what she wanted, she would ruin my husband. That worthless husband! To think I'd be driven to protect him in such a way!'

'But you had to protect yourself,' Hideki Tagawa said.

'Of course. I couldn't have her making a scene there with all the dignitaries present. Those spiteful old cats would have jumped on any chance to make more trouble for my father. So I told her to come back. I gave her a card and a delivery time. She was supposed to come and collect cushions for cleaning and restuffing. But I told her to wait outside under the cannonball tree. I wasn't going to let her inside the house. I didn't want anybody to see her.

'What was more, she found two of the photographs Ryu took of Joben in one of his play sessions. The little fool thought Ryu was using them to blackmail him. She didn't know how much Joben was paying Ryu for those sessions! It was Joben who was making Ryu do those things, just to keep his job as official photographer!'

'Ima, stop!' Colonel Fujiwara said.

'Because you don't want to know what kind of a pervert you married me to? Well, open your eyes for once in your life. This is your fault, you know. You picked him as a husband for me.

'Do you know why those grenades disappeared from your office? Joben took them. He wanted Ryu to photograph the real-time effects of a grenade explosion. He wanted Ryu to film men

and women being blown up. That's how sick he was. I overheard
them planning it. And, yes, I killed Ryu but not really. He killed
himself but I burned the evidence linking him to Joben because
I was afraid people would blame you. I wanted to put the
grenades back but once you'd told Major Dewa you'd taken them
yourself I didn't have to.'

'Why didn't you just tell me what Joben was doing?'

'She's still lying,' Hideki Tagawa said. 'The real reason she
killed Ryu Takahashi is that he threatened to reveal she was
giving him access to top-secret papers.'

'How would you know? You'll never prove it.'

'Takahashi photographed the papers. Not with his big
camera. With this No. 2 Folding Autographic Brownie.' Hideki
Tagawa picked the little camera off the table.

'All right. So I shouldn't have kept it.' Ima turned to her father.
'Joben shamed me. As long as he was alive he would have gone
on shaming me. But now that fool is dead we can put it right.
This will all be covered up. The security guards who were on
duty tonight will have to be killed, of course.'

I was staring at Ima. So was her father. Hideki Tagawa had
turned his back on us and was facing the window, but I could
tell he was alert to everything that was going on.

'Can you believe that woman thought she could blackmail
me? Or that Joben thought I would be afraid to expose him?
Why would an eagle be scared of worms in the mud?'

'You killed them all,' I said. 'Joben, Mimi, Ryu…'

'What if I did? What difference does it make to anybody? Ryu
Takahashi was a useless piece of human waste. Going around
corrupting and perverting people. He called himself a camera

artist? He was a monster. And that woman? You don't fool me – I saw the way you looked at her. You would have given anything to kill her yourself. Well, I got rid of her for you. I did you a favour. You can't even call her a worthless thing. She was worse than worthless.'

It was true that I had wished Mimi gone, 'never to darken my door again', as Benjamin Franklin once wrote, but I wouldn't have killed her. 'I didn't like her. But I would have helped her if I could.' Mimi hadn't trusted me enough to ask for help. What reason did she have for trusting me? The stories people told about me were probably just as bad as the ones I'd heard about her.

'Oh, really?' Ima sneered. 'You would have paid her off like any other useless parasite. You're as hopeless as Joben.' Ima turned on Colonel Fujiwara. 'If you had picked a better man to be my husband, none of this would have happened. You couldn't even be bothered to choose a good husband for your daughter. Of course it was that fool Joben who took the money for Ryu. He thought it was a great joke putting it all in the name of the great Hideki Tagawa. He said nobody would ever doubt or question Hideki Tagawa because nobody knew what he was doing anyway.

'But when Hideki Tagawa started investigating, I knew he was in trouble.' Ima turned to Hideki Tagawa, who now faced her. 'I never meant to get you into real trouble, you know. If it got too serious I would have done something to get you off. But it was my only chance to stop you investigating Joben's links to the missing money.'

'If you did all that to protect Joben, why did you kill him?' I asked.

'You don't understand, Su Lin.' Hideki Tagawa's voice was quiet and cold. 'You think she was protecting him out of love?'

Ima sneered at him. 'You think you're so clever? You think you've got something to hold against me now? Against my father? You still don't get it, do you? You still think that because you have the ear of Prince Yasuhito Chichibu nobody can touch you. Well, your precious prince is far away and he can't help you here. Wake up, man! Nobody is going to believe a story that makes the great Colonel Fujiwara look bad. Because it makes them all look bad. It doesn't matter what you think you know now. You'll never prove anything. You're even more of a fool than I thought. You know what's going to happen now? Nothing.'

'And it wasn't just Joben she was protecting,' Hideki Tagawa said. 'This is all part of your cover-up, isn't it, Ima? What Joben took was all on the surface. I knew what he was doing. Petty theft, petty graft. No more than petty cash expenses. You were afraid we would look deeper. Joben could not have set up the requisitions and transfers that took Miss Chen over three hours to untangle.'

'Impossible! It took me at least a hundred hours to set up!' Ima sneered. 'You're bluffing. And you can't prove it.'

'I took the figures off Joben's buttocks,' I said. I showed her the much magnified print that Akio Yamamoto had made. The original birthmark had been replaced by a mass of instructions, dates and transaction data, typed in the same shape then shrunk and copied over his bottom.

She smiled at me. 'You're too clever for your own good. I could have helped you, you know. I would have found you a good husband and got him a good position. Help me talk some sense into your precious Tagawa now and I'll still help you.'

'And Joben couldn't have had anything to do with the deaths that occurred in the Fujiwara family before he married into it,' Hideki Tagawa continued, as though Ima hadn't spoken. 'You suspected something, didn't you, sir? That was why you insisted your wife and children remain in Japan once you heard Ima and Joben were coming out here to join you.'

Colonel Fujiwara's eyes went to the cracked photograph of his wife and children on his desk. 'She took their photograph, but she couldn't touch them.' And finally he looked at his daughter. 'Fumiko? And little Toru?'

Colonel Fujiwara's Wives

———◆———

I knew Fumiko and Toru were Colonel Fujiwara's second wife and infant son. They had both died when Ima was twelve years old.

'It was a matter of honour. It was that cheap husband-stealing slut's fault that you dishonoured my mother.'

Colonel Fujiwara's mouth opened and closed without any sound coming out. But we could all see the words he was trying to form: *You killed them?*

I was stunned too. All my life I'd been told I was responsible for my parents' death because of the bad luck I had brought into the family by being born a daughter instead of a son. I'd assumed Ima meant the same thing when she'd said she'd brought death into Colonel Fujiwara's family.

'I used rat poison,' Ima said. She looked proud and smug, like a schoolgirl who knows she has cheated in a test and got away with it. 'I put it in that woman's confinement soup and on that baby's sucky toy. You should have learned your lesson then. But even after Fumiko died, you didn't come back to my mother.

You should have. You owed it to her. Her father got you your first official position. You would never have had your start if not for his help. If you had come back to us then, my mother needn't have died. And she would have made sure you found me a better husband than Joben Kobata.'

'What happened to your mother?' Hideki Tagawa asked gently, as Colonel Fujiwara seemed beyond talking.

'My mother!' Ima snorted. 'She wasn't living, she was wallowing in pain and self-pity. But as long as she was alive, he could ignore me, writing me off as my mother's responsibility. He should have known she wasn't capable of providing for me as she should have.'

'You did not kill your mother.' Colonel Fujiwara's tone suggested he believed the opposite.

'Her life was useless. I set her free. She knew you would be forced to take me in as long as she died before I married. She should have seen it was the only way she could do her duty by me.'

Hideki Tagawa seemed to be fighting to keep down a laugh that was trying to burst out of him. I recognised his expression because I was feeling the same crazy disbelief trying to burst out of me.

Everything Ima said, in that calm, practical voice, seemed impossible. Either she was mad or we were going mad and imagining things.

'Look. You can't deny I did everyone a favour by getting rid of Ryu Takahashi. I did Japan a favour. You don't want men like him representing our nation and empire. If you knew anything at all about what he's done, you'd be forced to agree with me.

'Anyway, so many people have died. And many of them – most

or all of them – probably deserved it less than Ryu Takahashi. You want to talk about justice? He probably caused more deaths than all of you put together. And not heroic deaths. And that stupid woman, trying to profit from something she didn't understand, she deserved to die too. And, anyway, I owed Su Lin a favour. I did that for you,' she said to me. 'We're even now.'

'Thanks,' I said automatically. Hideki Tagawa was shaking his head. A snort of laughter came out of him.

But suddenly I didn't find it funny any more. A cold lump was forming inside my chest, making it difficult for me to breathe.

'And Joben chose to die. He chose it when he treated me as if I was no better than a shopkeeper's daughter. He should have known better.'

'That's not all, is it?' I said. 'Joben realised it had to have been you, didn't he? He must have put two and two together and realised you were the only person who could have found his photos. It wasn't a heroic act at all. You were just trying to save yourself! As for Mimi, you weren't doing it for me. You didn't want to face the humiliation of letting everyone know that your husband was taking part in these dress-up killings. And you were afraid Mimi might know you were the one who was selling top-secret documents to Ryu.'

'How did you kill Joben?' Hideki Tagawa asked. He might have been asking for a recipe. *How do you cook oden?*

'It was easy. I injected him with rat poison. Joben was always fussing about his bites and rashes. Especially because there are so many insects here. I knew nobody would find the mark.'

There were always insects inside the house because of the cannonball flowers Ima insisted on having indoors. How long had she been planning this?

'So what are you going to do now?'

'I'm going to marry you, Hideki Tagawa,' Ima said. 'I will marry the great Hideki Tagawa, even if he looks like a monkey. When you think about it, you will see it's the only solution.'

She had finally succeeded in shocking him. I felt an irrational urge to laugh at the mix of disgust, bafflement and fear on his face, and I so wished I had my Brownie camera at hand to capture his expression.

In that instant I understood Ryu Takahashi's love of photography. It was being able to capture and share such a moment for ever.

'It doesn't matter that you don't like me. Marriage is a business contract. I can make something of you. My father and I will help you keep your position if you're reasonable,' Ima said. 'But you know nobody will believe your word against Colonel Fujiwara's. And Su Lin's life is on the line too, not just your own. So. What are we going to do?'

Though Ima said 'we', it wasn't our answer she was waiting for but her father's. This was all up to Colonel Fujiwara.

It wasn't fair. Not to me or to Mimi or any of Ima's other victims, including Joben. But right or wrong didn't count as much as who was in a position to make the decision.

'Fumiko,' Colonel Fujiwara whispered, like a man in pain.

'Sir, consider what your wife would want you to do,' I said.

'Which wife?' Ima laughed. 'My mother was the first. If he's going to consider a wife's wishes, my mother has priority. She was there first. Well, I can tell you my mother wouldn't want him to turn his back on me the way he turned his back on her!'

'Think of the woman who loved you, sir,' I said. 'The woman

who was killed along with your child. What would she want for you?'

'He only wanted that bitch to give him a son.' Ima looked like she wanted to spit something bad-tasting out of her mouth. 'That was all he ever wanted. A son. A precious son who would inherit his family name. That was all that mattered to him. If I had been a boy he would have stayed with my mother. All my life, my mother told me it was my fault my father left her. She was a good wife. She came from a good family and was worthy of him. Her only failing was that she had a daughter. He could have given her a second chance, but of course he didn't.'

The photograph of Colonel Fujiwara with his third wife and two young children was back on his desk now. The little girl was clearly older than the boy.

Colonel Fujiwara's eyes followed mine to the photograph. 'That wasn't the only reason. Having a son is good but it's not the only thing. Sometimes people just don't get along ...'

The colonel looked at me. I read fear and indecision in his expression. He reminded me of Formosa Boy saying, 'They want to make me district commanding officer. In charge of East District, Division 221. But I can't. I don't know what to do. You know me – all I like to do is eat!'

'Then why not do your best to make sure everyone in the district gets enough to eat?' I'd said.

And he had. Not only was Formosa Boy still commanding officer of the district where my family lived, he had turned down several promotions because he wanted to stay there. He made sure the families in his district got good rations and they all fed him well. He was a model commanding officer because there were so few problems in his district.

'I was not a good father,' Colonel Fujiwara said.

'That's in the past,' I said. 'Do your best to be a good father now.' I glanced at the photograph of Colonel Fujiwara in all his military honours. 'And to protect your family. Especially from those who want to harm them because of who they are.'

'I must stand up for my children,' Colonel Fujiwara agreed, looking at the children in the picture.

'For all your children.'

'Yes. For all my children.'

Ima looked pleased. She smiled at him, like a loving daughter. Either she didn't notice him wince or she didn't care.

Colonel Fujiwara looked at his daughter as if she was a vengeful ghost come to pull his spirit out of him through his nostrils. 'I've always depended on others to point me to the honourable thing,' he said. 'Or to apply the gold coating after.'

'I will see to that,' Hideki Tagawa said.

'What's that? What are you going to do?' Ima asked. 'What have you decided?'

Colonel Fujiwara ignored her. He had opened one of his desk drawers and was fumbling around inside it.

'I'm going to take my cousin home. Come, Su Lin.'

I got to my feet.

'About all this! What are you going to do about all this?' Ima demanded, her voice suddenly harsh and shrill. She slammed her free hand on the other arm of the chair – I could tell she would have liked it to be my face she was slapping. 'You don't just walk out of here until I say you can go, damn you!'

'I'm going to take my cousin home and see whether she's learned to brew a good cup of tea yet. There are things that should be stirred up and things that should be given time to settle.'

'Thank you for not bearing a grudge,' Colonel Fujiwara said. He tipped his head to Hideki Tagawa, then to me. Colonel Fujiwara bowed to me! 'This is my family matter and my responsibility. I will deal with it.'

Hideki Tagawa bowed low to him and I followed suit.

'Wait,' Colonel Fujiwara said. He came after us and handed me the hair ornament, with the photograph of his third wife and children.

This made Ima uneasy but the colonel was calm and powerful for once.

Ima looked at me. 'You can't trust them, you know. You can't trust men to watch out for you. The more they tell you that you can count on them, that they'll be there for you, the faster they drop you once it suits them. It's the old story about how men take advantage of us women.'

I thought it was rather more a story about women attempting to use men. Both Mimi and Ima had tried. But it hadn't turned out well for them, had it? So maybe Ima was right after all.

A Final Explosion

$\blacklozenge$

'It's not fair! She killed Joben. She killed Mimi and Ryu. And you're just going to let her get away with it?' I hissed at Hideki Tagawa, as he dragged me through the house to the front door.

'Get out,' he said, to one of the house-boys in the hall, 'you and all the other servants. Get out of the house. Go and catch fish or something.'

Tanis nodded and ran off, having given me a shy smile. He probably thought some secret visitor they weren't supposed to know about was coming.

Once we were outside, Hideki Tagawa wouldn't say another word. He took my arm and hurried me to his car, dragging me painfully fast. I was panting by the time he slammed the door on me in the passenger seat and ran around to get in, start the car and race to the gate where he jammed on the brake and pounded the horn till it was opened for us by the guards.

I sat and kept my mouth shut. I've practised enough to know I'm good at that.

It was only when we got to the police security station at the end of the road that Hideki Tagawa slowed down. In fact, he stopped the car and got out to make small talk with the men on duty.

After all that crazy rush, there was suddenly no hurry.

I stayed in the car but opened the door on my side.

The men were smoking cigarettes, probably provided by Hideki Tagawa. I saw him looking back at the Shori headquarters. Did he expect Colonel Fujiwara to send someone after us? If he did, why weren't we getting more of a head start while we could?

Suddenly there was a loud explosion and shouts of alarm – I saw smoke rising. The checkpoint soldiers started running towards the Shori headquarters, one shouting into his radio as he went: 'Fire at the Shori headquarters. Possible bombing attack. Send reinforcements!'

I struggled out of the car to go to Hideki Tagawa where he stood in the middle of the road, watching the flames that were now starting to show through the smoke.

'You planted a bomb in the Shori headquarters?' I asked, aghast. Never mind his gracious patron and connections. Even being the illegitimate son of the Emperor himself wouldn't get him off something like this.

'He took his time about it. I almost thought he was going to back away from his duty. Again. But he has redeemed himself.'

I realised he was talking about Colonel Fujiwara. 'You knew Colonel Fujiwara was going to do this? Why didn't you say something? Or do something to stop him?'

'Colonel Fujiwara did what he had to do. He has judged himself as well as his daughter. And he has rendered justice.'

'But . . .'

I stared at him. I hadn't realised how much tension he had been carrying until now. Now that it was suddenly gone.

'It wasn't just a matter of justice, you know. He was protecting those who will have to live without him now. But at least he knows they will be able to live. You helped make up his mind. Even if you didn't realise what you were doing.'

'I never thought he would kill himself.'

Colonel Fujiwara had had many faults, but he had enjoyed and respected my cooking and I had respected and appreciated his honest appetite. I'm sure many lasting relationships have been based on less. Tears filled my eyes. Suddenly I felt sorry for the man. If he had been born to run a grilled-fish stand or *sake* bar, he would have lived a much happier life.

'Blowing up himself and his daughter was not the act of the coward,' Hideki Tagawa said softly. He looked sad, too, but more than anything he seemed relieved and refreshed. 'It may have been the bravest thing he's ever done.'

'What if Major Dewa decides that you're responsible for blowing up Colonel Fujiwara and Ima?'

Hideki Tagawa shrugged to show he didn't care. 'The poison has been neutralised. That is what matters.'

'You mean Ima.'

He and Major Dewa were on the same side, after all. They were protecting the offices of the Japanese Empire, even if that meant destroying the individuals occupying them. Major Dewa had said he thought I could work very well as one of them, but I wasn't so sure. I wasn't sure if that was what I wanted.

'I think it's time for me to take you home,' Hideki Tagawa said.

'Home?' I gestured at the black smoke wafting out of the Shori headquarters compound.

'Home to Chen Mansion.'

'Oh. I don't know . . .'

'They'll be glad to see you,' Hideki Tagawa said.

I wasn't sure if I was ready to see my family. I hadn't thought to wonder if they wanted to see me.

'I have your papers and your security pass in the car. You can come back to collect anything else you need after the smoke has cleared.'

'I should check on the servants. They'll be so scared.'

'They'll be all right. They're not your responsibility any more.'

But my family was my responsibility? All right, I wanted to defend them and keep them safe. I just didn't want to see them.

'I'm not sure I belong there any more. I thought they were my family – my only family – but now I don't know.'

I was cross with myself for whining like a spoiled child, but it had been a heavy day and I had just seen my job, boss and temporary home go up in flames. What's your identity once your family, job and home are taken away from you?

'They rejected my mother,' I said. 'If I look like her, as you say, I'm sure they see her every time they look at me.'

'I would say they see your father too. I do. I believe your father loved your mother very much. I respect him for that. I will do all I can to help you in honour of his memory. Not just hers.'

He drove me back to Chen Mansion.

There, I wrapped the *kanzashi* hairpin in a clean towel and put it away carefully in my underwear basket. The photograph of my mother I put in my top drawer.

And he was right. My family was happy to see me. Even happier that I was back to stay.

Epilogue

———◆———

According to the official report, Colonel Fujiwara and his daughter were innocent victims of a bomb attack by rebel forces, aided by Communists and Australians.

A separate report noted the range and efficacy of two American-manufactured yellow pineapple grenades had been enough to blow out all the ground-floor windows of a standard-size house.

The colonel was loaded with posthumous medals and Ima was credited as an ideal role model of Japanese womanhood, nobly sacrificing her husband, her father and her own life in service to the Greater Japanese Empire.

The official unofficial version was that Ima Kobata, driven mad with grief by her husband's death, had committed suicide, killing herself and her father.

Not surprisingly, the bodies of the PoWs in the jungle were not mentioned.

Prakesh Pillay was released from detention and offered a promotion within the INA.

'They know I was right about the missing PoWs all along. They just can't say it.'

Photographs of Mimi Hoshi with her Japanese officials were of great interest to the war-crimes tribunal so she became famous, though not in the way she'd expected.

Ryu Takahashi's art photography enjoyed a small revival after his light-streaked photographs were compared to Picasso's *Guernica*. The pain and terror of his bound victims and the blank stares of their masked killers were described as a statement of the horror of people caught up in the nightmare of war.

Japanese defeats at Kohima and Imphal were their largest so far. The Allied forces suffered sixteen thousand casualties, the Japanese more than sixty thousand. It was almost as though the British and Indian forces had been warned of their plans.

I learned a Japanese proverb – 'Fall seven times, rise eight' (*Nana korobi ya oki* 七転び八起き) – that I found very useful in surviving the Japanese occupation. Maybe there is something larger than us in this universe that allows us to shape our best selves from our worst experiences.